SPIDER-MAN®

AND

IRON MAN®

SABOTAGE

AND

SABOTAGE

DOOM'S DAY BOOK 2

PIERCE ASKEGREN & DANNY FINGEROTH

Illustrations by Steven Butler

BYRON PREISS MULTIMEDIA COMPANY, INC.
NEW YORK

BOULEVARD BOOKS
NEW YORK

SPIDER-MAN and IRON MAN: SABOTAGE

A Berkley Boulevard Book
A Byron Preiss Multimedia Company, Inc. Book

Special thanks to Ginjer Buchanan, Steve Roman, Lara Stein, Stacy Gittelman, Mike Thomas, John Conroy, and Steve Behling.

PRINTING HISTORY
Berkley Boulevard paperback edition / March 1997

The Penguin Putnam Inc. World Wide Web site address is
http://www.penguinputnam.com

Make sure to check out *PB Plug*, the science fiction/fantasy newsletter, at
http://www.pbplug.com

Check out the Byron Preiss Multimedia Co., Inc. site on the World Wide Web:
http://www.byronpreiss.com

ISBN: 0-425-16907-3

BERKLEY BOULEVARD
Berkley Boulevard Books are published by The Berkley Publishing Group, 375 Hudson Street, New York, New York 10014.
BERKLEY BOULEVARD and its logo are trademarks belonging to Berkley Publishing Corporation.

PRINTED IN THE UNITED STATES OF AMERICA

10 9 8 7 6 5 4

For Archie Goodwin, whose run on *Iron Man* in the 1960s gave me so much pleasure.

—PA

For my family. One small step for a Fingeroth, a giant leap for Fingerothkind.

—DF

The authors would like to extend
special thanks to Eric Fein
for his invaluable contributions to this work.

— CHAPTER 1 —

The invitation said "proper dress required," which meant a tuxedo, and that meant trouble, because Peter Parker didn't own one. Since the invitation also served as press credentials, trouble in this case meant finessing expenses out of the *Daily Bugle*, and finding a decent rental for the price that J. Jonah Jameson's accounting clerks were willing to pay. Neither task was particularly easy. The *Bugle*'s publisher instructed his accountants to treat each penny as their own, and apparently most of them had formed their impressions of reasonable costs sometime during the 1950s. They were especially reluctant to part with expense advances for freelance press people, even those with assignments and authorization.

Now Peter had to wonder if it had been worth the trouble. He was resplendent but uncomfortable. Worse, the suit he wore fit too snugly to allow him to wear his Spider-Man costume beneath it. He tended to wear his costume under his street clothes in case he needed to adopt his super heroic persona in a hurry, and not being able to do so bothered him.

"Having a good time, Peter?" His wife Mary Jane Watson-Parker, also resplendent, but totally at ease in a shimmering lavender evening gown from her own wardrobe, asked the question in an amused, almost sardonic tone of voice. He had come to know that tone all too well.

"Is it that obvious?"

She laughed and nodded, making her scarlet tresses shimmer and flow like a waterfall. She was wearing her hair down tonight, and the red mane splashed against her creamy shoulders as she replied. "Oh, yes. You keep fooling with the collar like that, and you'll embarrass yourself before the evening is over."

With a rueful grin, Peter took his hand away from his neck. "Can't help it," he said. "It itches." At times like this, he envied his wife; her background in show business and modeling had made her at home in any kind of wardrobe and at any kind of social gathering. Deep inside the adult Peter Parker, however, there still lingered traces of the gawky, lonely boy he had been during his teenage years, and every once in a while, those traces chose to make their presence known. He hated gatherings like this and had been delighted when MJ decided to tag along.

She wasn't out of place, either. She looked utterly appropriate in the crowded reception area at Stark Enterprises's Long Island facility. Ballroom-sized, it was a cavernous space tastefully finished in an updated art nouveau motif. Thick carpeting, marble columns, and vaulted ceilings contrasted pleasantly with high-tech lighting and displays. Automated serving trays drifted lazily though the crowd, hovering at about elbow level without means of visible support. The trays paused just long enough to allow patrons to accept drinks and hors d'oeuvres. Peter wondered how the gadgets worked. *There must be some kind of proximity sensor and feedback loop tied to the antigravity generators*, he thought. From what he knew of Tony Stark, it seemed utterly in character for the millionaire industrialist and futurist to use advanced technology for such a mundane purpose.

Just now, an unusually motley throng filled the room, many members of it far more out of place than MJ could ever be, anywhere. Peter easily recognized political dignitaries and top-ranking city officials, the civic representatives he would expect to see at the unveiling of a major new industrial project. More surprising, however, was the presence of members of the scientific community, men and women who spent most of their lives clutching calculators and reviewing test reports. At least half of the physics faculty from Empire State University was in attendance. He could recognize a dozen or more bespectacled visages that he had seen before only in the pages of scientific journals. For a moment, he considered snapping a few quick photographs, but decided against it. Jameson wanted pictures of bona fide celebrities. These distinguished men and women wouldn't fit his definition. It was a shame, really; some of the minds in the room had done more to reshape the world than any number of politicians.

We're here to see something big, Peter realized. *Whatever Stark's unveiling, it must be important to take these people away from their work.* He suspected that much of their work was done on Stark's payroll, and might be the subject of tonight's exhibit. He wondered what it would be.

"Earth to Peter," MJ said, still amused. "Earth to Peter, come in, Peter."

The words cut through his thoughts. He smiled, shrugged, and looked at his wife. "Sorry," he said. "Woolgathering."

She looked at him reproachfully. "Nothing to be sorry for, silly," she said, her voice like light silver bells. "Just try to relax and have some fun."

"Hey, you know how JJJ feels about 'fun' on the clock," he said. He tapped the Nikon that hung from a strap around his neck. It was a nonfashion accessory that made him feel even more out of place. "And on the clock I am."

"Hmph." She reached out as one of the drink tables drifted by, effortlessly snaring two crystal tulip-shaped glasses filled with two different liquids. She kept the champagne for herself, and handed Peter the sparkling water. "I need to mingle," she said. "But I'm keeping an eye on you, and I want to see you smiling." Her voice became mockingly stern. "Or there will be words later, young man!"

Mary Jane smiled as she drank, ruby lips parting to grant a glimpse of flawless white teeth. Despite himself, Peter smiled, too. Formal receptions weren't his idea of fun—but being with Mary Jane was, no matter what the setting. The fact that someone else was footing the bill didn't hurt either.

"Yes, ma'am," he said, raising his glass to his own lips. After a quick sip, he kissed her, then watched her disappear into the surrounding throng. She had been excited about the evening, eager for a night on the town and well aware that there were many contacts to be made at such gatherings. As an actress and model, she was very aware of how many opportunities relied on chance meetings and casual conversations. A reception like this one was a gold mine for someone with her networking skills. In a sense, Peter knew, she was on the clock also, though she wasn't letting it get in the way of enjoying herself.

He shrugged, then started as a newcomer caught his eye. He raised the camera to his eye, and peered through its viewfinder. It was a nice little Nikon, not as small as the miniature camera he often used, but small enough to be discrete and loaded with very fast, fine-grain film, suitable for flashless indoor photography. A familiar face came into view, thoughtful features framed with brown hair going white at the temples—Reed Richards, leader of the Fantastic Four, the world's premiere super hero team, had just entered the room.

Peter pressed the shutter once, waited a second for the film to advance, and pressed it again for luck. This time, he caught both Richards and his attractive wife Susan, better known as the Invisible Woman and another member of the FF. The two of them moved into the surrounding crowd, shaking hands and exchanging greetings as they passed from Peter's line of sight. He was glad that he had spotted them; photographs of the famous couple weren't exactly a scarce commodity, but shots of them in formal attire were. If the *Bugle* didn't run the pictures, they would still make a nice addition to his portfolio.

A pity I can't walk up and say "hi," Peter thought with a smile. As Spider-Man, he had stood with the Fantastic Four on more than one occasion, but they wouldn't know Peter Parker from a hole in the wall. Still, their presence made him less apprehensive about not having his costume. *If something* does *happen, those two could probably handle it without breaking a sweat.*

Peter still wasn't sure about the focus of the evening. A few exhibit cases punctuated the room's spaces, and framed displays hung on the walls, but most featured old stuff that Peter had seen before—solar power collectors, desalinization systems, and other high-tech items from Stark Enterprises's futurist résumé. One large case in the center of the room held a full-size mock-up of Iron Man's armor. It was the original version, the heavy gray suit that had made Stark's bodyguard and corporate trademark look like a walking version of a Sherman tank. Massive and intimidating in its bulk, the suit seemed more menacing than heroic. As Spider-Man, Peter had met and worked with Iron Man several times, but those encounters had all been with the later, red-and-gold version of the super hero, smaller and lighter but more powerful than the original. Now looking at the original outfit, he found himself wondering how well the bulky suit had worked in battle. He didn't even consider taking a photograph of the display, however; there would be no market for it. The original armor, unbelievably advanced in its time, was nearly antique by contemporary standards.

Science and technology move fast these days, he thought. *Maybe too fast.* He glanced at his watch, then started edging towards the small stage at one end of the room. It was nearly time for the main event.

As if on cue, a new voice cut through the cocktail chatter and filled his ears. It was a remarkably neutral voice, vaguely masculine but devoid of inflection or character, and seemed to come from everywhere at once. A month before, Peter had read an article about Stark Enterprises's remarkable work with artificial intelligence systems and speech simulators; now he wondered if human lips shaped the words he heard.

"Ladies and gentlemen," the voice said, "your host for the evening, Mr. Tony Stark."

There was a polite smattering of applause as the man took the stage. About Peter's size and perhaps ten years older, he seemed utterly at ease as he looked out over the crowd of movers and shakers who were his guests. He was lean and surprisingly well built; he moved with an easy grace more befitting an athlete than the president and CEO of the world's most advanced technology company. His tuxedo almost certainly cost more than Peter Parker earned in an average month, and his neatly trimmed mustache and styled hair were more testimony to his affluence.

Peter edged closer to the stage. Doing so was easier than he would have expected, since the broadcast media representatives were sharing a common feed, leaving more room for print journalists—and there really weren't very many of those, either. Peter had the vague suspicion that even the *Bugle*'s presence had more to do with celebrities and networking than with actual coverage. JJJ wasn't really interested in scientific advances, and most of his staff took their lead from the boss.

"*Ad Astra*," Tony Stark was saying. He spoke to no apparent microphone, but something caught his voice, amplified it, and sent it out into the crowded room. "Most people know the meaning of those words. They're Latin, for 'to the stars.' Many of us who work in the aerospace industry—as Stark Enterprises does—have taken them as an informal motto." He smiled. "Too many people forget the rest of the sentence, however. The full form of the motto is, '*Per Ardura, Ad Astra*'—'Through work, to the stars.' I am very pleased to announce that tomorrow, after a great deal of work, Stark Enterprises will take the next step on the road that will lead us to the stars—again." He gestured upwards.

Peter suddenly realized that the house lights had dimmed, so slowly that the transition had been barely noticeable, until the room was barely lit. Now as Stark paused and pointed, the murals that had decorated the room's ceiling abruptly faded and vanished, followed by the ceiling itself—if either had ever actually been there. Where, a moment before, floral patterns and painted waterfalls had intertwined, there was only the darkness of a night sky, punctuated by stars. The countless points of light were constant and untwinkling, as they might be when viewed from orbit, unmasked by Earth's atmosphere. The effect was breathtaking.

Holograms, Peter thought. Either the ceiling had been a hologram, or the starscape was—and from twenty feet below, it was impossible to tell which was which. Despite himself, Peter was impressed. In his career as Spider-Man, he had seen some remarkable illusions, but this was as good as any in his experience. The technology behind it was, no doubt, worth a fortune in and of itself. He wondered where the projectors were, then thought again and wondered if there were any projectors. *Some kind of broadcast field effect?*

"Some years ago," Stark continued, "My organization placed in orbit the world's first privately owned space station, designed as a platform for industrial research and experimentation. This was—and is—the *Ad Astra*, still unique in human commerce."

As he spoke, another image became apparent in the space where the ceiling had been. It was an image that Peter had seen many times before, on magazine covers and television programs—and a few years before, on newspaper pages. It was a metal wheel, its broad rim connected by spoke-like passageways to a central hub. The hub itself was more of an axle, a long spire of steel that projected well beyond the rim's plane. The rod was studded along its length with radio antennae, smaller projecting rings, and other apparatus.

Peter had followed the news of the launch of Tony Stark's *Ad Astra* a few years before with great attention. He had been more than a little puzzled when coverage of the exciting new facility had ceased only a few months later. There had been rumors of problems, some whispered scuttlebutt of sabotage by Advanced Idea Mechanics, the criminal cartel better known as A.I.M.—but Peter had never heard any hard facts to back up that claim.

He raised his camera, and pressed the shutter control. As he took the picture, he wondered how well the film would record the illusion—if it was an illusion.

"This is the *Ad Astra*," Stark was saying. "Some twenty thousand miles above us, it is the single largest artifact ever placed in Earth orbit. With a total price tag of $800 million, it's also the most expensive." He paused, and smiled ruefully. "Unfortunately, for a long time now, the *Ad Astra* has been as inaccessible as the stars themselves. Certain technical problems have served to make it inhospitable to human life. Thanks to a joint venture between Stark Enterprises and Damage Control, Inc., that is no longer the case. I am pleased to announce that the *Ad Astra* is once more open for business.''

Peter knew about Damage Control. It was an industrial engineering firm that specialized in disaster remediation and emergency reconstruction work. Their services didn't come cheap, and outer-space work was likely to cost a hefty premium. He supposed that any fee had to be cheaper than building a new station, and Tony Stark certainly had the money to pay.

That didn't sound like the whole story, though—and it certainly didn't sound like enough of an event to justify the evening's festivities. Peter's journalistic instincts told him that there had to be more to tonight's events than simply announcing the reactivating of an old project. That wasn't the sort of event that Reed Richards would make time to attend.

''—first mission will be to serve as the test bed for Stark Enterprises's newest major initiative in the fields of applied cosmology and energy resource research. Ladies and gentlemen, I give you the *Infinity Engine*!''

Again Stark gestured, this time at the case that held Iron Man's old armor—or rather, the case that had seemed to hold the worn gray suit. Once more, the crowd gasped as apparent reality melted and vanished, revealing something else beyond it. Visible now inside the plastic display case was something quite different from the grim mass of Iron Man's battle suit. Instead, Peter could see—or seemed to see—something else, something elongated and graceful and very suggestive of NASA's space shuttle.

The model was perhaps four meters from tip to tail, and it was exquisitely detailed. Even from his vantage point near the stage, Peter could see hatches and panels and metal seams on the craft. The thing was long and lean, and its lines looked more aerodynamic than those of the NASA version. The nose came to a needle point, and delta wings fanned out from behind with curling tips unlike anything Peter had seen before. Ailerons punctuated the wings' trailing surfaces, apparently augmented by similar control surfaces on the tail assembly, so that the shuttle looked more like an atmospheric craft than like one intended for space travel.

Whatever it was, it sure looked fast, and many years beyond anything that the government's space program could offer. He knew that from personal experience. Only a few months before, he had visited NASA's Florida launch facility, caught up in a bizarre three-way adventure involving two old adversaries, Venom and the Lizard. During that visit, he had borne rather close witness to the shuttle and its associated launch equipment.

"More properly speaking," Stark continued, "what you see is the *Infinity Engine*'s mobile platform, the latest generation in Stark Enterprises's continuing series of reusable spacecraft. It seats ten. Later this evening, if you would like, I can provide you with some details on the craft itself." He paused, and smiled. "But not too many details, I'm afraid. My lawyers can be real sticklers about the improper release of proprietary information."

Polite laughter filled the room, but none of it came from Peter. He was no longer facing Stark, but continued to stare at the *Infinity Engine*'s sleek lines. A recessed collar ringed the hull just beyond the front view ports, its leading edges smoothed and shaped to reduce air resistance. It looked suspiciously like a docking ring. He was still gazing at it when the craft's apparent lower hull melted away, revealing complex mechanisms just behind the passenger compartment. After a few seconds, the hull turned opaque once more.

Another hologram, Peter thought. *The fun never ends.*

"This is the *Infinity Engine* itself," Stark continued. "A somewhat grandiose name, I will grant you, but a not-inappropriate one. The *Infinity Engine* is a mobile research platform, intended to tap into radical new energy sources, converting them into forms more convenient for use. I am pleased—very pleased—to note that the *Infinity Engine* embodies entirely new design and technological principles. I often speak of 'next generation' technology; my competitors do the same. This device, however, constitutes a quantum leap in scientific development. I am confident that future generations will look back on this creation as we look back on the inauguration of mass communications, or atomic energy, or the printing press, or even the wheel. This is a watershed event in human development, and a step over the threshold into a new age."

Big words, Peter thought. *But if anyone can back them up, it's Tony Stark.* For as long as the photographer could remember, Stark's various businesses had been the absolute leaders in making practical application of theoretical breakthroughs. Stark himself was a genius, and he employed many more, all dedicated to applying new findings to human needs. The Iron Man armor alone embodied countless advances in computer technology, microcircuit etching, energy storage, inertial propulsion systems, human/machine interfaces, force fields, and heaven only knew what else—and that was just scratching the surface. Iron Man might be Stark's most famous achievement, but there were others that were even more impressive to those who knew about them.

Antigravity, for example. Stark's team had taken antigravity out of the laboratory and made it work in the real world, turning what had been a scientific curiosity into a useful, though limited, tool. Now, looking at the *Infinity Engine*'s aerodynamic lines, he had to wonder if Stark had taken the next step, and found some way to make the anti-G field generators practical for large-scale use. Such an advance would make the craft much more energy-efficient for use inside the atmosphere, and make it correspondingly more maneuverable. *I bet NASA's green with envy.*

Model or mirage, the miniature *Infinity Engine* was moving now. It rose from its open-topped case in absolute silence, moving steadily towards the huge space wheel that hung above the crowd. As Peter watched, it aligned with the central hub of the space station, then moved closer and locked into place. *I was right*, Peter thought. *It's a docking ring.*

"In two weeks," Stark said, "the *Infinity Engine* will take its maiden flight and dock with the *Ad Astra*. There, the crew will conduct the first field experiments on the *Engine*'s systems, and perform final shakedown duties on the *Ad Astra* itself." He paused, and smiled. "The fine folks from Damage Control have done their work and done it well—but we want a chance to tidy the place up a bit before bringing it back online for full service."

Peter startled himself by speaking. He wasn't the only person he surprised; Tony Stark was visibly taken aback, and Peter could feel, even across the room, JJJ's sudden, angry glare. Photographers weren't supposed to ask questions, and they certainly weren't supposed to interrupt millionaire industrialists at formal functions. The words came from his lips, unbidden and unexpected, shaped by the bespectacled bookworm that still lived somewhere inside him.

"But why outer space?" He asked the question tentatively, and softly enough that he could almost have been speaking to himself—but he was close enough to the stage that whatever it was that amplified Stark's voice picked it up.

"Excuse me?" Stark paused again, and looked at Peter with something that was almost recognition—almost, but not quite. It was as if the older man were responding to some aspect of Peter instead of to Peter himself. "You have a question?" He spoke courteously, even respectfully, looking down at Peter only in the physical sense.

Acutely aware of the sudden silence surrounding him, Peter forced the words out. "Why outer space?" he asked. "I don't see any substantial number of solar collection panels, but outer space makes the most sense for solar power, since the air blocks out so many of the sun's rays. Anything else should work fine on the surface. Why spend the money to boost a piece of equipment this large into orbit? It can't be cheap, and keeping the facility on Earth would make access and study easier—right?"

Stark smiled. "Partly," he replied. "You're right; the *Infinity Engine*'s primary emphasis won't be on solar energy, though the crew will work some on that, too. Their main work will be studying a radically new energy source, by drawing directly on a previously unidentified subset of the quantum field." He said the words lightly, even calmly, but his eyes showed that he knew their import.

Wow, Peter thought. That explained why ESU's physics contingent had turned out in such force. His own field was biochemistry, but he liked to keep up with other disciplines as well. If Stark was serious, he was talking about tapping into the underlying structure of the universe itself, the substrate that lay beneath all other forms of energy and matter. In essence, if it worked, the *Infinity Engine* would be the final proof of Einstein's

Unified Field Theory. This was major news, indeed—
and Peter had the uncomfortable feeling that he was only
one of a minority of people in the room who realized
just how major.

Stark continued, speaking now to his larger audience
as much as to Peter. "For various technical reasons,
drawing on the quantum field is much easier in a low-
gravity environment. The *Ad Astra* is just high enough
in Earth's gravity well to do the trick, at least for pre-
liminary studies. In future years, we may have to go
further out—but I don't think that will be necessary for
a long, long time." He paused again, then glanced at
Peter, and did something surprising—he winked. "However, my young friend here has made a good point.
Parked in orbit, the *Infinity Engine* is relatively far
away—or is it?"

As he spoke, the panels on the *Infinity Engine*
mockup swung open, revealing a parabolic transmission
antenna that suddenly emitted a brilliant beam of yellow
light. The ray split the darkened ballroom, tracing a path
along wall and floor. The effect was spectacular. Several
times, the beam paused momentarily in its track, surrounding first one guest then another in a pool of light.
The selection seemed random; Peter watched as the
mayor, and Mary Jane, and Reed Richards, and then
some anonymous bureaucrat blinked politely in the
glare. The light skimmed though the crowd, splashed
against one wall, then the next, shone briefly on J. Jonah
Jameson as he nibbled a canapé, and then came to rest
on Peter himself.

"But neither the *Ad Astra* nor the *Infinity Engine* will
be inaccessible," Stark said. "They will be only a few
hours from the Earth's surface, thanks to recent advances
in spacecraft technology—and only moments away for

direct energy transmissions, which move at precisely the speed of light.''

Peter, blinking, thought he knew what the other man meant. In an instant, he saw the ramifications. They were breathtaking. If Stark could do it, if he could actually tap quantum energy and beam it back to Earth—

He could literally remake human civilization, Peter thought.

This was big, amazingly big, bigger than any news story had a right to be. Its nearly unprecedented nature suddenly made Stark's idiosyncratic guest list seem reasonable, even inevitable. This wasn't an event for the media, or for the scientific community, or for the government or the military. It was, indeed, a watershed event in human history, with the potential for unimaginable impact on every man, woman, and child on the planet, now and in the future.

The implications stunned him. He suddenly had some idea how some long-forgotten, anonymous caveman might have felt the first time that one of his fellows had created fire, or the wheel, or art, or even clothing. Those were the only precedents he could imagine, and he knew they weren't accurate. That long-ago witness could have had no idea of what he was seeing, no concept of the forces being set in motion as he watched. Peter thought he had some inkling, but he also knew that the reality would be far more dramatic than he could dream.

''I ask all of you to look forward with me,'' Tony Stark said calmly, as the house lights came on again and the ceiling wavered back into existence. ''Ten years from now, the *Ad Astra* will be one of ten orbiting stations, each tapping the quantum field for cheap, safe energy and beaming it back to Earth. My people already have constructed a prototype receiving station in the Southern Hemisphere. Twenty years from now, that prototype station will be one of a hundred, receiving the bounty that the *Infinity Engine* will harvest from sub-space and relay to them. In thirty years, all current, conventional power generation systems will be obsolete; in less than a century, burning fossil fuels and splitting plutonium atoms will be remembered as quaint barbarisms, the dangerous antics of a primitive people.''

The lights were back on now, and the ceiling's waterfall murals were visible to those who chose to look at them. Few did. The display case that had once displayed Iron Man's armor now held an image of the miniature *Infinity Engine* once more. Peter barely noticed and didn't care. Like the rest of the crowd, he stared spellbound at Tony Stark, his mind racing in response to the inventor's continuing remarks.

'' '*Per Ardura, Ad Astra,*' '' Stark repeated. '' 'Through work, to the stars.' Many talented men and women have worked long and hard to bring us to where we stand tonight: on the threshold of a new age. Their efforts will give us the stars, and the stars, in turn, will give us the energy we need to reclaim our world. Our children's children's children will live in a clean world, a world without hunger or want or thirst, as different from our own existence as modern day New York is from medieval Europe. You will meet some of these fine minds later this evening, but before you do, I ask you to join me in applauding them—in commending the boundless spirit of human creativity.'' He smiled again, more broadly this time. ''Because that, after all, is the true *Infinity Engine.*''

He brought his hands together, and the crowd followed suit. The applause began slowly and built, becoming louder and louder as it echoed through the room. Peter knew that some of the audience knew what they applauded, and a few even understood it—but that most could little imagine the miracles that Stark's words promised. It didn't matter; he applauded with the rest of them, joining with his fellow spectators in a celebration of human creativity and genius—and in anticipation of the new world to come.

Countless fathoms beneath the Atlantic Ocean's storm-tossed waves, *Barbarosa* moved inexorably along the lightless sea floor. A water pressure measured in tons heaved vainly against every square inch of the gigantic craft's surface, eager to surge in and crush the lives that *Barbarosa* sheltered. The metal hull, however, refused to yield; *Barbarosa* moved on through the darkness, unstopping and unstoppable, crushing all in its path.

Very nearly the size of an American Navy aircraft carrier, driven by nuclear motors and mounted on massive treads that gouged deep tracks into the seabed, *Barbarosa* was a community unto itself. Within the mobile command base's steel confines, five hundred souls lived their lives in servitude. Scientists and engineers ran tests and operated apparatus, working to implement their ruler's dreams. Soldiers and assassins trained, testing their bodies to the point of death—and beyond. Chefs prepared gourmet meals for their master and other, more pedestrian fare for their fellow rank and file. In *Barbarosa*'s clinics, doctors treated patients and readied them for new labors—or designated them unfit for service and marked them for execution. All of *Barbarosa*'s occupants wore the same colors, and all served the same master; all wore the uniform of Hydra, and all slaved to fulfill the demands of Baron Strucker, the founder and ruler of that criminal organization.

Wolfgang Von Strucker was a tall man, muscular in build and aristocratic in bearing. Beneath *Barbarosa*'s artificial lights, his pale skin seemed nearly as colorless

as milk, but his cold blue eyes still glistened with a
hellish vitality that belied his age. Strucker had led a
long and exceedingly adventurous life, from brutal military campaigns earlier in the century to a program of
world conquest in more recent years. An unpleasant biological accident involving an artificial germ called the
Death-Spore had literally revived him from the dead,
giving him the strength and stamina of a man a third his
age, along with the ability to inflict that same germ on
others, to agonizing and fatal effect. Strucker's body
bore many scars of battle, not the least of them the jagged metal prosthesis that glinted where his right hand
should have been. A desperate battle with a lifelong foe
had cost Strucker most of his arm below the elbow; now,
instead, he wore any of various Satan Claws, deadly re-
placements crafted by his scientists and charged with
deadly energies.

Seated now in *Barbarosa*'s command center, he
watched impassively as Garcia, his personal attendant,
polished the blade's glistening length. It would be the
work of an instant to activate the Satan Claw, to release
a bolt of deadly energy and force the worthless life from
the pudgy little man's body. The option was tempting;
an occasional, random execution did wonders for mo-
rale. He decided against it, however. Garcia had his uses,
and besides, now was not the time for simple pleasures.
There was business to attend to.

"Report," Strucker said. Even as the single word left
his bloodless lips, a video monitor in front of him flared
to life. Its glistening surface displayed a low-ranking
Hydra agent, standing at rigid attention.

"Hail Hydra!" the man said. He was Lyle Chesney,
one of the five agents Strucker had assigned to surveillance duties at the Long Island facility of Tony Stark,
the American industrialist. Strucker had long taken an

interest in Stark's operations, and that interest had been stoked by recent, unfortunate encounters with Stark's armored lackey, Iron Man. More important, however, were certain reports that had reached Strucker during the last few months, information regarding an experimental program that was entirely too promising to be left in the custody of its inventor.

"Report," Strucker repeated, not bothering to return the salute. He allowed a degree of impatience to enter his voice, and watched with faint pleasure as beads of sweat erupted on Chesney's face.

"It is as you said, Baron," the agent said. "Stark's project nears completion. He has announced it to the world, and even now moves into the last phases of preparation. The *Ad Astra* is back in service, and the *Infinity Engine* will launch tomorrow."

Strucker nodded. Since first hearing of Stark's experimental new energy source, he had followed the project's progress carefully. It was at least as promising as the energy chip that he had attempted to steal earlier in the year from his current chief rivals in the game of world domination, A.I.M. That attempt had failed, but this one would not. He had planned too well for failure. At any time in the preceding weeks, his men could have stolen the *Infinity Engine*'s secrets easily and tendered them to Hydra's custody—but that would have left his operation with the problem of actually constructing the device. The prospect had been both undesirable and daunting.

Certain recent events had reduced Hydra's available resources to levels that did not please Strucker. The ongoing conflict with the fools at A.I.M. had been a constant, annoying drain. The interference in that conflict by the armored super heroes, Iron Man and War Machine, had aggravated the situation. A debacle caused by his own rogue agent, Burton Hildebrandt, had cost him equipment and staff, as well. Fabricating the *Infinity Engine* would have been an unnecessary, unpredictable expense. Instead, he had chosen to let Stark do the work for him. There was no need to spend Hydra's money when he could spend someone else's instead.

"Excellent," Strucker said. "You have the launch schedule and orbital specifics?" He asked the question knowing the reply; Chesney would not have dared report otherwise.

"Yes, Baron!"

"Provide them to me within the hour, and return to your duties," Strucker said.

"Yes, Baron!"

"You have done well thus far, Chesney, and so I will give you this word of warning. Your assignment is a simple one, and your schedule is exceedingly precise. I hold you personally responsible for your phase of the operation. Any misstep, no matter how slight, will result in torments more terrible than any you can now imagine."

Chesney said nothing, but continued to stand at attention.

"That will change, however. Should you earn such attentions on my part, they will come only after similar attentions have been paid to your family and your friends—while you watch."

"I shall not fail you, Baron!"

Strucker smirked. "Of course not, Chesney. One way or another, you will please me, whether as a trusted lieutenant or as an evening's entertainment." He paused to make the meaning of his words clear. "Strucker out."

As the monitor image collapsed and disappeared, Strucker stood abruptly. The sudden movement caught his attendant by surprise. Garcia fell back as the Satan

Claw's molecule-thin edge bit deep into his hand, slicing through skin and flesh and bone like a razor might cut through paper. He gasped in pain but said nothing.

Strucker did not notice. If he had noticed, he would not have cared.

"Attention, all crew," Strucker said. His words rang throughout *Barbarosa*, carried by wire and speaker to every space on the vast craft. Everywhere within the moving fortress, his minions paused in their work, and attended to their master's words.

"The time has come! Notify all agents at all sites and alert the launch facility!" Strucker barked the words, like a field marshal might bark commands at his troops. "Commence Operation Infinity!"

—CHAPTER 2—

Tony Stark spent the remainder of his presentation introducing the crew and staff of the *Infinity Engine*, the three men and one woman who would take the craft into space and oversee its operations. Flight Commander Johnny Ramos was a tall, grinning man with dark hair who seemed to like himself entirely too much. Kellye Nakahara, a Japanese American who held three doctorates in various astrophysics disciplines, proved to be suprisingly young. Robert Powell was a specialist in cybernetic systems and feedback monitoring; and Douglas Deeley was a husky African-American test pilot, holding certifications in every commercial and almost every military aircraft in the world. Peter listened to the introductions with some interest and snapped a few photographs as they progressed.

He realized with surprise that he recognized all four names, and not all of them from scientific literature. Nakahara and Powell were only vaguely familiar, names that he had seen on seminar roll calls and in professional journals. He remembered trying to read an article by Nakahara in *Theoretical Physics Quarterly*, only to surrender halfway through a dozen pages of fourth-order differential equations. That had been particularly frustrating; Nakahara's piece had been a discussion of subspace phenomena, specifically Reed Richards's discovery, the Negative Zone. As Spider-Man, he had actually visited that weird pocket universe and lived to tell the tale. As Peter Parker, he couldn't even read about the place without it making his head hurt.

Ramos and Deeley were different. They each had a more general kind of fame. Peter remembered the taller of the two from the Empire State University basketball team. Johnny ''The Ray'' Ramos had been quite the local celebrity, the idol of regional high school students, and well remembered even by a non–sports fan like Peter. Ramos had graduated and moved on before Peter's first day of classes at ESU; he had never met the older man. He was surprised to see Ramos here now, and wondered briefly what career track had diverted the college sports star from the promise of a professional career and into a job at Stark Enterprises.

Deeley was famous, too, but in a different way. Peter had actually photographed him before, at another reception. That one had been to honor returning war heroes. The modestly smiling black man was one of the most decorated fighter pilots in modern history, with distinguished service in the Gulf War, the Panama Occupation, and the Transia Incursion to his credit. Universally well regarded, Deeley had racked up commendation after commendation before leaving the service for private industry. Peter suspected that there was more to that story, too. Most servicepeople with Presidential decorations spent the rest of their careers in the military, unless they had good reason to leave. Peter made a mental note to research the matter further in his spare time, if he ever had any. For now, however, he contented himself with pressing the shutter release again and again.

"Relax and enjoy yourself, son," a familiar voice said from behind him. "All work and no play, you know."

"Don't let Jonah hear you say that," Peter said, then turned to face Joe "Robbie" Robertson, the *Bugle*'s Editor-in-Chief. "He'll have kittens."

Robbie smiled. He was a rangy African-American man with white hair, in his mid-fifties, but he looked much younger. "Might be worth it, just to see that," he drawled. "But I mean it. You'll be here all evening, and part of the reason I suggested you for the assignment was that I thought you might enjoy it.''

''Thanks.'' Peter meant it. He had been wondering how he had drawn an assignment so far off of his typical beat. Peter had known and worked with Robbie for years and knew that such casual consideration was typical of the older man. ''I thought it was because everyone else was busy.'' He grinned.

Robbie grinned, too. ''Well, that was part of it,'' he said. He winked. ''At least, that's what I told Jonah.'' He paused. ''But seriously—what do you think of Stark's little bombshell?''

''It's not 'little,' and it's much more than a bombshell,'' Peter replied. ''Unless he's talking through his hat, Mr. Stark has just closed one book of human history and opened another. I can't think of anything that would make a bigger difference to civilization than unlimited, free energy.''

Robbie made a rueful look. ''Free for him, you mean. Water's always free to the guy who owns the faucet.''

His words were surprising, but they made sense. Peter hadn't considered that aspect of the situation. He had been so caught up in the wonder of the event that he hadn't stopped to think about some of the less-pleasant ramifications. One man in charge of the world's energy supply would be in a position to exert unprecedented influence on the course of human events. Everything he had heard about Stark suggested that he was an honest, ethical man.

But . . .

Robbie nodded, his thoughts apparently mirroring Peter's. '' 'Power corrupts . . . ,' '' he quoted, then looked serious. ''As I understand it, we're talking about absolute power here.''

Robbie was right, Peter realized. ''I hadn't thought

of that," he admitted. He thought a moment, wrestling with the issue. "But we're talking about science, too, Robbie. Advances always have consequences, and you can't put the toothpaste back in the tube."

Robbie smiled at the mundane metaphor. "I'm not talking about putting it back in the tube," he said. "I'm talking about watching who opens the tube very, very carefully." He shrugged. "That's for other minds to consider, though. The issue might even be part of the reason for tonight's function. By announcing the *Infinity Engine* this way, Stark's put it squarely in the public eye and presented it to a wide range of people. He's told the story from his side, and he's sidestepped any measures the government could take to silence him."

"I hadn't thought of that," Peter said again. It made sense, though. His opinion of Stark's tactics went up a notch.

"Well, don't think about it too much now. Have fun, but do your job. I don't want to rely on publicity hacks. Take care of the personality snaps for the Society page—I know you can do it—but make sure you get some good ones of the displays, too."

"Will do, Chief." Peter made a mock salute.

"Don't call me 'Chief,' " Robbie said wryly, then turned and drifted away into the crowd. In seconds, he was exchanging pleasantries with Johnny Ramos.

Good old Robbie, Peter thought. *Always on the job*.

He moved through the crowd himself. Now and then a familiar face came into view, and he said a word or two of greeting before moving along. Some he knew from college, or from the news; a surprising number were professional contacts from his own career in the media. Barney Bushkin, from the competing *Daily Globe*, was in attendance, and so was Joy Mercado, one of the *Bugle*'s star reporters. The two were conversing amiably enough, a sight that Peter suspected would send J. Jonah Jameson into orbit, with or without antigravity and rockets. Meanwhile, Reed Richards and Kellye Nakahara chatted quietly in one corner, under the watchful eye of Susan Richards. Peter drifted closer, thinking he might hear a snatch or two of mathematical dialogue, but the subject of conversation turned out to be good Mexican food and where to find it in New York. Once or twice, Peter found himself uncomfortably close to JJJ's sphere of influence; each time, he edged carefully away. He spent enough time dealing with the irascible publisher during the work day, and there was no way he was going to let such contact spill over into the evening. He noticed with a grin that others apparently felt the same way. JJJ always tried to dominate whatever audience he could find, and his concerted efforts made turnover high.

A very familiar voice cut through the chatter. "Peter! Hey, come on over here! I've got someone I want you to meet!" Mary Jane's green eyes peeked over a tall man's shoulders, and she waved at her husband.

Peter obeyed, and barely managed to keep shock and surprise from his own face when MJ's companion turned to face him. He took the extended hand and shook it, his mind racing. He knew the other man.

Rather, Spider-Man knew him.

"Peter," Mary Jane said, "This is Duncan Huxtable. He's a television producer. He thinks he might be able to use me." She paused and gestured. "Mr. Huxtable," she said, "This is Peter Parker. He's my *husband*." She put a noticeable emphasis on the last word, and Peter suddenly knew what kind of conversation his wife had been having with the alleged Duncan Huxtable.

Spider-Man had met the other man a little over a month ago, late in a complex adventure involving intel-

ligence agents, power blackouts, Hydra and A.I.M., and
the incredible Hulk. The man wasn't a television producer, and his name wasn't Duncan Huxtable. He
worked for a clandestine American security agency,
Strategic Action For Emergencies, or SAFE. Spidey
knew him as Joshua Ballard.

"Hey, Tiger, pleased to meet you!" Ballard pumped
Peter's hand once, twice, then released it. He played the
part of a sleazy show-business type remarkably well,
enough so that Peter had to wonder how much of it was
an act and how much of it was for real. "You're a lucky
man, my friend!"

"I like to think so," Peter said carefully. He moved
closer to MJ and stood next to her. He draped one arm
around her warm shoulders and pulled her closer to him.
Mary Jane could take care of herself, but this situation
looked like it merited extra attention from the watchful
husband.

Plus, he liked having her beside him.

"Do you work in news, Duncan?" Peter asked the
question in a light tone, but he was seriously interested
in the response. Obviously, Ballard was undercover, and
it wasn't hard to guess why. He wondered if Stark knew
that SAFE had planted an agent at the reception.

Ballard nodded and lied with easy finesse. "Yup. In-
dependent producer, mostly cable, but we've got a network magazine ready to launch next season." He
paused, and eyed Peter carefully. "Have we met before?" he asked.

"Silly man," MJ interjected. "You tried that one on
me, too."

Suddenly on his guard, Peter ignored Ballard's question and offered one of his own. "And you think MJ's
right for the job?"

"No, no, no—not for that project, anyway." Ballard

shook his head. "But our production company has some other irons in the fire, and MJ here might be right for some of them." He grinned, apparently conceding that his cause was lost, at least for the moment. "Here," he said. "Let me give you my card, and we'll talk later."

Mary Jane took the proffered bit of paper, then pointedly passed it to her husband. "You know, Mr. Huxtable," she said, "You might want to talk to Peter, too. He's in the news media. He's an experienced photographer. You may have seen his work."

Ballard looked closely at Peter, then smiled. This time the smile was a real one, as if he had resolved some minor issue that had been troubling him. "Of course," he said. "I knew that there was something familiar about you. You're *that* Peter Parker."

A feeling of relief swept over Peter. Sometimes there were advantages to being a minor celebrity in his civilian identity. Ballard had met him before, of course, under very different circumstances and in very different roles. Ballard had managed to escape Doctor Doom's castle stronghold in Latveria, and make his way back to New York in time to help resolve some very thorny problems. The SAFE operative was good at what he did—good enough that he might recognize Peter Parker as Spider-Man, and too good for Peter to allow that to happen.

"Guilty as charged, Duncan," Peter said easily. "That's me."

"I've seen your work in the papers, and I got a copy of your book for Christmas last year. Very nice, very attractive." Ballard grinned. "Well, I hope you'll excuse me, but I see someone else I know. Give me a call sometime."

"Of course." Peter and Mary Jane said the words in perfect unison, and watched as Ballard made a beeline for a statuesque blonde wearing a black formal gown.

Once he was safely out of earshot, MJ allowed herself a polite shudder. "What a creep," she said.

"Not really," Peter replied. "He's actually a very good, very brave man, pretending to be a creep."

MJ looked up at him, puzzled. "I don't understand."

"Neither do I, honey, but I'll tell you what I know later." Peter looked at the card closely. It was a professional piece of work, just what he would expect from a SAFE cover ID, featuring a business name, a sporty little logo, and two telephone numbers. He wondered just which phones those numbers would ring.

The evening had just become significantly more complicated.

"Peter," Mary Jane said, a warning note in her voice. "You're zoning out on me again."

He smiled and hugged her close. "Not really," he said. "Just thinking. Want to take a look around with me? I have to get some shots of the displays."

MJ nodded. "Okay, but let me track down one of those flying saucer snack trays first. I'll catch up."

"Okay," Peter agreed. Putting on an awful Southern drawl, he added, "Snag me some of them thar little bitty hot dawgs, okay? I love them things."

Mary Jane didn't bother to reply.

Peter moved closer to the *Infinity Engine* display. At close range it was even more impressive, somehow embodying a perfect grace more like a living thing than an artificial construct. He leaned closer, tracing its lines with his eyes. Even with his nose against the surrounding plastic case, he couldn't tell whether display was a model or a hologram. Its edges were hard and distinct, without the telltale fuzziness that marked most such illusions. On the other hand, it didn't *look* like a model. It was perfect in its detail, with none of the errors or omissions that were part of even the most perfect miniature model. Everything was absolutely to scale. He could even see microscopic rivets holding access panels shut, and view what looked like full control panels glinting behind smoked-glass windows. It was as though Stark had built the *Infinity Engine* to scale, then physically shrank it down to size.

If anyone could do it, Peter thought, *Tony Stark could.*

"Beautiful, isn't it?" The words could have been his own, but the man who spoke them was Tony Stark.

Peter came to sudden attention, nearly dropping his camera in surprise. Stark had appeared behind him. Close up, the man had an undeniable personal magnetism that Peter found almost overwhelming. His blue eyes, piercing and direct, nonetheless held humor and compassion, and his nonchalance bespoke a remarkable self-confidence. It was easy to see at least some of the reasons for Stark's success and social prominence.

Now he was flanked by two associates who were silent as the industrialist spoke. One of them was a strikingly attractive red-haired woman, with dancing blue eyes and full red lips set in a serious expression. She looked a little bit like Mary Jane, and Peter wondered if Joshua Ballard had paid her a visit yet this evening. The other was a heavyset man with brown hair. He was muscular and fit, but looked very ill at ease in a Navy blue tuxedo. Peter felt a sudden rush of sympathy.

"I don't believe we've met," the millionaire industrialist said. "I'm Tony Stark."

"Uh, yes, of course you are. I mean, I know." Peter flushed, then reached forward and took Stark's hand, noting its firm and confident grip. "Peter Parker, *Daily Bugle*."

"Yes, I know." He seemed to mean it too.

"You do?" The calm assertion startled Peter. He

wasn't used to recognition, and to get it from someone as famous as Stark was doubly surprising.

"Of course," Stark said. "*Webs*, right?" His question referred to a book collecting some of Peter's more famous Spider-Man photos, published to minor success a few years before. It was the same book that Joshua Ballard had mentioned earlier. Stark smiled, and gestured at his companions. Peter took their hands in turn.

"Bethany Cabe," Stark said, gesturing at the redhead. "My Chief of Security. The burly fellow is Harry Hogan, my personal trainer and one of my oldest friends."

Bethany Cabe murmured some noncommittal pleasantry. "You can call me 'Happy,' " said the big man, who looked anything but.

"Wow, this is an honor, Mr. Stark," Peter said. "I—"

Stark shook his head. "Please, it's 'Tony.' " He smiled. "You ask good questions, Peter."

"Oh, you mean, back there? I'm sorry I interrupted, but I was very curious about some of the things you said." He smiled wryly. "Too curious for my own good, I guess."

"No apologies, Peter. As I said, you ask good questions. That's the basis of the scientific method," Stark said. "And, unless I miss my guess, you're something of a scientist yourself. Correct?"

Peter nodded, his camera and assignment suddenly forgotten. "That's right," he said. "Graduate studies at ESU. Biochemistry, with core studies in viral mutation and DNA synthesis."

"Those are good subjects, and important ones, but I suspect they aren't the full extent of your interests."

Peter laughed. "No, just the limits of my official ones. One of my professors called me an 'autodidactic polymath' once. I'm interested in almost everything, and I read fast. I even tried to work my way through one of Doctor Nakahara's articles once. It was about subspace anomalies.''

''Good heavens, you've got my respect for that,'' Stark said. ''I hire other people to do that kind of thinking for me, and I have to pay them well to keep up with her.'' He paused. ''But tell me, Peter, why the camera? How does someone with your scientific aptitude end up taking news photos?''

Peter shrugged, and a bantering tone entered his voice as he spoke. ''You see, Tony, there's this thing called 'money.' Mr. Jameson is kind enough to give me little bits of it for my photographs, and I use it to pay my bills. I've been doing it since high school, and things have worked well so far.''

''Ah, yes, money. Filthy stuff.'' For the second time that evening, Stark winked at Peter. ''Never touch it myself. That's what the staff is for.''

Happy Hogan rolled his eyes at the sarcastic comments, but Bethany Cabe continued to say nothing. Peter wondered what she was thinking. Unlike MJ's expressive face, her composed features gave no hint of the thoughts behind them. Peter had the impression that she was carefully studying every word and every movement around her, either out of a sense of duty or simply because she liked doing it.

Stark gazed speculatively at Peter for a long moment, long enough to make him think that the wisecracks might have been a mistake. They were more Spider-Man's stock in trade than Peter Parker's, but sometimes the two roles blurred together. He was just beginning to think that his audience had come to an end when Stark spoke again.

"Tell me, Peter, have you ever done work as a lab assistant?"

"Sure. I interned with Henry Pym." The reference was to one of the world's most renowned biochemists, who had been known by more than a few other names during his long career as a super hero. A stroke of luck during Peter's undergraduate years had resulted in a few sessions in Pym's lab, and he never failed to mention them on the rare occasions he felt like name dropping.

"Think you'd like to do more?" Stark said the six words so casually that it took Peter a moment to realize that he had been offered a job.

"I—" Peter stammered. "I—sure!"

Stark reached into one pocket and pulled out a slender, supple wallet. He opened it, revealing several plastic rectangles—each one the exact shade of platinum. No cash was in evidence. *He really doesn't touch the filthy stuff*, Peter thought. "Here you are," Stark said and extended his card. "Fax me your résumé. I may be able to do something for you, if you're interested."

"Sure! I'd be very interested!" Mentally, Peter was turning cartwheels at the prospect of doing work in one of Stark's state-of-the-art labs.

Stark continued. "Earlier this year I bought another company, Peter. Its name is Odyssey Designs, based in Manhattan. It's basically a one-horse show, operated by another old friend of mine, Cosmo Haberman. He's working on some of the calibration software for the *Infinity Engine*, and he could use another pair of hands to help him out around the place."

Peter stared at the card, tempted now to hand it back, suddenly afraid that he was in over his head. "Um, I hope I haven't given you the wrong impression," he said reluctantly. "I'm a quick study, but I'm not *that* good.

The stuff you've talked about tonight is way, way out of my league.''

"Of course it is, Peter," Stark said. "It's out of my league, too. I told you, I just hire other people to do that kind of thinking for me. I just worry about putting the pieces together.''

"Then—''

Stark smiled. "You get to worry about putting the pieces away,'' he said. "Cosmo has had some setbacks in the last year or so. He needs someone to help out around the lab for a few months, so that he can catch up again. You might get to do some real work, but mostly, you'll put things away and clean up after him. I believe the term is 'good learning experience.' Plus, you'll get to learn more about the *Infinity Engine*, and I think you'd like that.''

"Sure! I sure would.'' Peter smiled broadly and put Stark's card in his wallet, next to the one that Joshua Ballard had given him.

"Tell him the rest, boss.'' The friendly growl came from Happy Hogan. "The kid's got to worry about some things that you don't.''

"Of course. Peter, the hours are flexible, so you can set your own schedule. If you'd like, I can probably arrange for academic credit at ESU, since SE funds an internship program there.''

"The rest, boss,'' Hogan rumbled. "The moolah. The dinero. The long green.''

"And there's a stipend,'' Stark said. He mentioned a number.

Peter stared at him for a long moment.

"Will that be satisfactory?'' Stark asked, apparently honestly concerned about Peter's reaction.

"That—that would be great,'' Peter said, literally stunned by the sudden turn of events. "More than great." It sounded like a dream job, and the figure that Stark had quoted would go a long way towards retiring his and Mary Jane's more pressing debts. "But why?"

"Why what?"

"Why are you doing this? I mean, you barely know me, and you're offering the kind of opportunity that other students would give their eyeteeth to get."

"Don't be silly. The opportunity isn't what matters, it's what you do with it. And as to why—well, let's say you remind me of someone I knew a long time ago." Stark paused, then reached out and rested one hand on Peter's shoulder. "And you ask good questions." He paused again. "And anyone who can put up with J. Jonah Jameson has the kind of patience this job needs."

"You know JJJ?" Peter wasn't sure he liked the sound of that. The *Bugle*'s publisher, annoying and intrusive as he was, was nonetheless an important source of income for the Parker household. The lab position would probably qualify as moonlighting in JJJ's beady little eyes, and wasn't something he was likely to approve. Never mind that Peter was a freelancer; JJJ had a nasty habit of viewing people as property.

"Jameson and I belong to some of the same clubs," Stark said. "We've exchanged a few words." He didn't seem very pleased to admit it.

Peter extended his hand again. Anyone who didn't like JJJ was okay with him. "You've got a deal, then, Tony!"

"Deal? What kind of deal? What's going on here?" Another voice, grouchy and annoyed and more than a little unwelcome, joined the conversation. It was Jameson, with an unhappy MJ in tow. In her left hand, a small saucer held four cocktail franks.

"Parker!" Jameson, barked the word. He was a stocky man with wiry hair and a bristling mustache scarcely wider than his nose; just now, he looked like a walking bundle of anger—but that was par for JJJ's course. "I'm paying you good money to take pictures, not to do business—" His words broke off as he recognized the other members of his audience. "Oh, hello, Tony," Jameson said. "Didn't see you there. Sorry. Hope I'm not intruding."

Tony nodded. "Jonah," he said. His tone was polite but distant.

JJJ fixed Peter with a steely glare. He didn't look happy, but that was typical too. "Now, what's this about a deal, Parker? And why are you lollygagging around here, when you should be out taking pictures?"

"Just a moment, please." Stark's voice, though calm and measured, made it clear that he would brook no further interruption. One of the flying drink trays had drifted close. He reached for it, and glanced at Peter. "Champagne?"

Peter shook his head. "I don't drink," he said. "Never picked up the habit."

"I did," Stark replied, ruefully. He plucked two glasses of mineral water from the tray's gleaming surface and handed one to Peter. "A toast," he said. "To new friends and new business!"

"And to a new age," Peter said, then raised the glass and drank. The bubbles ticked his throat as they went down, but they weren't a tenth as amusing or satisfying as the exasperated expression on JJJ's face.

It had been a remarkable evening already, and the night was still young. He wondered what the future would bring.

Summer's last full moon hung low in the night sky, bathing the village of Doomstadt with a ghostly luminance. The sky was a black bowl inverted over the sleeping countryside, dotted with stars that barely twinkled as they shone. There was a reason for their easy visibility. Latveria was still a rural land, a country of villages and farms. No cities marred the countryside, so there were none to cast their light upwards and mask the beauties of the night sky. Doomstadt, the nation's capital, was tiny by foreign standards; now, hours past curfew, it was shuttered and dark. Even the atmosphere itself did less to obscure the stars than it did over more industrialized nations. The air here was purer and cleaner, scrubbed clean of the toxins and pollutants that drifted in from other, less civilized lands.

Victor Von Doom had seen to that.

From his castle's central tower, Doctor Doom gazed out over the sleeping nation that was his by right of conquest. A gentle breeze found him in his vigil, caught the trailing edges of his broadcloth cloak and hood. The fabric danced and fluttered in the cool night, but he did not feel it. The heavy steel armor he wore shielded him from such trivialities as the elements. Many times he had stood here, unmindful of furious storms or freezing gales, considering the nation and the people he had made his own.

Doom had spent much of his youth in the rolling hills that surrounded his castle. He was a member of a gypsy tribe that wandered through most of Eastern Europe. It was in this land that he had first known love, and loss, and hate, all born of lesser minds than his. In his own way, he loved the tiny nation, and cared for the humble folk who dwelled within its borders. Since his coronation years ago, he had worked to make Latveria's lot a happy one. By his measure, he had succeeded. His people lived in comfort; they ate wholesome food and they breathed clean air, and they had productive work to fill their days. They were secure, their borders

protected by Doom's might and their streets guarded by
Doom's army of internal security robots. Nearly immune
to the vagaries of politics and the global economy, tiny
Latveria ranked among the world's most prosperous
nations.

By royal decree, his people were happy, content to
pay the one small price that such prosperity demanded.
That price was their freedom. Doom ruled Latveria with
an iron hand, a steel fist that meted out swift and inar-
guable justice to all in his kingdom. Unlike denizens of
other nations, Doom's people voiced no mawkish rhet-
oric of personal liberty and self-expression. Order ruled
supreme here, untrammeled by other concerns. Doom's
word was law, and the law was good. Silent, sleeping
Doomstadt was testimony to that.

The events of recent weeks had made him become
increasingly aware that the world beyond deserved such
peace and prosperity, as well. He had already taken steps
to ensure that such would be so.

Beneath his steel-shod feet, heavy slabs of granite hid
titanium steel support members and reinforced armor of
Doom's own creation, sufficient to make the castle proof
against a multimegaton nuclear strike. Within the ancient
structure's many levels, anonymous men and women
toiled with absolute devotion, doing Doom's will. Serving as his hands, they crafted the tools that Doom needed
for his campaign of conquest. Somewhere in that laby-
rinth, an automated intelligence system monitored countless frequencies, assessing reports from Doom's agents
throughout the world.

Now that same system noted one specific transmission, isolated a single sentence, and compared it to a list
of search criteria. The name matched, as did the point
of origin. A content analysis module verified meaning.
The computer pulled up a file voiceprint and compared

it to the incoming signal for final verification. An excerpt of the message then emerged from the monitor again, riding radio waves to a bone-induction speaker inside Doom's armor. The entire process had taken less than a second.

Baron Wolfgang Von Strucker's voice sounded in Doom's ears. *"Commence Operation Infinity!"* Only three words, spoken to someone else in Hydra's insipid subsea base, but they were enough.

Behind Doom's mask, his ruined features smiled. It was time. The American industrialist, Stark, had long since taken his place on the chessboard, along with members of that nation's intelligence community. Now at last, the German had made his play, an opening gambit as obvious as it was inevitable. It was Doom's turn.

He turned away from the vista of Latveria and strode through an open door to his castle's interior. The time for reflection had ended; the game had begun.

There were pawns that demanded his attention.

"I just hope you know what you're doing, Tony," Bethany Cabe said. The previous night, she had worn a shimmering black evening gown to the *Infinity Engine*'s public unveiling, but today she was just as beautiful in a slightly severe business suit that vaguely suggested a military uniform. There was a reason for that; the previous night had been at least partly pleasure; today, she was all business.

"I almost always do," Tony said easily, as he sat before a flickering systems monitor display. It showed the *Infinity Engine*, perched atop a rocket booster. The shuttle's tip protruded about twelve meters above the rim of an underground launch silo at Stark Enterprises's Long Island facility. Judicious use of antigravity field generators meant that the whole assembly needed only about forty percent of the motive thrust that NASA would have used for an equivalent payload, and made practical the launch from a site so near the city. ''What are you worried about this time?'' He spoke in an casual tone of voice that belied the careful attention he paid his monitor.

They were in his private suite of offices, deep inside the Long Island complex. Not too terribly far away, in the control center, other men and women labored over control panels and computers. Educated hands moved switches and knobs, performing the thousand last-minute duties that went into a successful rocket launch—or even an unsuccessful one. Part of Tony wanted to be there with them, shepherding his pet project through to fruition, but he had decided against it. His staff did their jobs well, and to make them work under his personal supervision would have been insulting, to say the least. For now, he was content to watch from a distance.

''Doing it this way,'' Bethany said. ''In the public eye. Announcing the *Infinity Engine* at the last minute, at a public function, after months and months of secrecy. You moved the launch date up two weeks too. The software isn't even complete yet.''

Tony shrugged. ''The time was right. Besides, only one person can really keep a secret,'' he said. ''Too many people know about the *Engine* already, and it's too big to keep under wraps. If more than one person knows about it, everyone has to. That's the nature of this particular beast.'' Numbers danced on his cathode-ray screen, each one giving way to a smaller value.

''I still don't like it,'' Bethany said. She spoke with a directness she had learned in her years with Tony, both as his former lover and as his current Chief of Security. Those two roles had accustomed her to speaking her mind, at least in private. Similarly, he had few secrets from her; she was one of only a handful of people who knew that he was also Iron Man. "Too many people would like to get their hands on that thing," she said. "You should have at least waited until after the launch. They didn't make a press announcement the night before the first nuclear test at Alamogordo."

Tony looked up and smiled at her. "That's the government's way of doing things," he said. "I'm not the government."

She didn't say anything, but simply stared at him levelly.

"And besides, I had to," Tony continued. "Or I would have been working for the government, and I didn't want to do that."

"What do you mean?"

"Like I said, only one person can really keep a secret. Even before last night, enough people knew about the *Engine* that the feds knew too. I've had visits and phone calls from every government security agency—"

"I didn't know that," Bethany interrupted. "They're supposed to go through me."

"Oh, these weren't official visits," Tony continued. "Or so they assured me. They just wanted to help me see this project to completion." He made an angry sound. "You weren't around in those days, Beth, but a few years ago, Congress held hearings and tried to take the Iron Man armor away from me."

"I know about that."

"Then, later, S.H.I.E.L.D. did its best to pull the whole company out from under me, pleading 'national security.'" S.H.I.E.L.D. was the Strategic Hazard Intervention, Espionage, and Logistics Directorate, a top-level security agency that Tony himself had helped found. "You remember how much fun that was."

Bethany nodded. She had been on hand for that bit

of unpleasantness. "So what are you leading up to?" she asked. "Any evidence that something like that was going to happen again?"

"Nope." Tony shook his head. "No evidence. Just rumors, and a bad feeling. There's a new agency on the block, SAFE."

Bethany nodded.

Stark continued, "They're too much of an unknown quantity for my tastes."

"So you jumped the gun, based on nothing more than rumors?"

Tony looked back at the display screen and its countdown. The numbers were smaller now, well into the single digits. Launch was seconds away. "This is too important, Beth," he said. "I don't want it buried in some minor bureaucrat's bottom drawer. The world had to know about it. That's the best way to make sure the *Engine* ends up in the right hands."

"Yeah, well that may be true," Bethany said. "But you're making it harder to keep it out of the wrong ones."

The number on the screen dropped to zero. The ground trembled slightly beneath Tony's feet, even here, deep inside his private, heavily shielded offices, as the massive booster rocket ignited. Bethany's words still sounded in Tony's ears as the *Infinity Engine* threw itself skyward, rising from the launch silo on a column of flame and smoke.

At about the same time, somewhere in South America, another, unmarked rocket did the same.

— CHAPTER 3 —

"**G**ot everything?" Mary Jane asked the question sleepily, surprising Peter and making him look up from his careful study of the refrigerator's skimpy contents. For once, he had risen earlier than her, and he had tried very hard not to disturb his still-sleeping wife. Not for the first time, the effort had failed.

Now she stood framed in the kitchen doorway blinking at him, a bed sheet wrapped around her graceful curves. The clinging fabric did less to conceal her charms than it did to display them. Drowsy green eyes gazed out from a face that was all the more beautiful for not being made up, and her red hair was a tangled mane, tousled and friendly looking. This was the way that Peter liked to see her best. The rest of the world could share the carefully groomed image of Mary Jane Watson-Parker, model and actress, but only her husband got to see the real thing.

"Did I wake you?" He asked the question in a contrite tone of voice. "I tried not to. I was just packing a lunch." It was the first day he was to report to Odyssey, following a series of telephone calls on Friday and over the weekend. He was still amazed that things were coming together so well and so quickly. JJJ had been suspicious when Peter invaded the *Bugle*'s offices in search of a fax machine for his résumé, but the publisher hadn't managed to ask the right questions.

"Lunch," MJ said drowsily. "Made you one. Here." She brushed past him and reached inside the refrigerator, her delicate fingers reaching unerringly for a small zippered case that looked like a medium-sized camera case. "Here," she repeated, apparently not fully awake yet, but awake enough to function. "Lunch. Mmmm, good." She thrust it into his hands with enough force to rock him back slightly on his heels. It was still cold from its night in the icebox. "Don't leave containers behind like last time. Need them back."

Peter looked at her warily. It was like being served by a zombie. *She usually isn't this bad in the morning,* he thought. On the other hand, maybe she was. MJ usually got up long before he did, so he wouldn't know. "Yes, ma'am," he said, taking the gift of the undead. "What's in it?"

"You'll find out." MJ smiled, but it was a generic sort of smile that hid more than it told. She kissed him on one cheek. "Surprises." She tottered back towards the bedroom, her sheet trailing like a bridal train. "Time to go now," she said in a dreamy monotone, and Peter wasn't sure whether she meant it was time for him to go to work, or time for her to go back to bed. She turned in the doorway and paused, looking back at her husband.

"You're in costume," she said, beginning to sound somewhat aware. "Why?"

Despite himself, Peter laughed. Ordinarily, MJ was one of the most observant people on Earth. The fact that she had managed to talk to him and hand him his lunch and kiss him without noticing that he wore most of Spider-Man's costume meant that she was sleepy, indeed. As he replied, he picked up one of the two web-shooter assemblies that rested on the kitchen counter and continued putting himself together for the day.

"I'm running late," he said, sliding his left hand through the web-shooter's wrist band. Like a watch strap, it stretched and widened, then contracted again as it settled into place on his forearm. Instead of a watch, the band held pressurized capsules containing the adhesive polymer compound that turned into Spider-Man's webbing upon contact with the air. More cartridges of the stuff waited in compartments on his belt, hidden beneath the colorful tunic of his costume.

"Always late," MJ said, still groggy but less so now, and also undeniably correct. Peter's many duties had a brutal impact on his schedule. She watched as Peter carefully aligned the web-shooter's nozzle, and flipped the round actuator switch forward so that it rested in the palm of his hand, where a single fingertip tap would activate it.

"Yeah, well—I live a busy life." Peter said the words lightly, but they were true. Classes would begin again in a few weeks, but in the meantime, he still had plenty to juggle, balancing his careers as Spider-Man and *Bugle* photographer with the duties that marriage brought. The temporary Odyssey job would almost certainly make things more hectic. He donned the second web-shooter and shrugged. "Maybe I need to take some time-management courses," he said. "If I can find the time."

Mary Jane laughed at that one. She sounded fully awake now, which meant going back to bed was out of the question. MJ wasn't the type to lay about all day, as attractive as the prospect might be. "Yeah," she said. "That's a good idea. You could carpool with Spider-Man to them, too."

"Har har har." Peter picked up the case that held his lunch, and the slightly larger one that held his civilian clothes. He looped their straps around his shoulders and arrayed the cases on his back, where neither could interfere with his freedom of movement. He performed the ritual with the ease born of much practice; he had been Spider-Man for long years now and could get ready for the role in a matter of seconds.

Mary Jane came close. "C'mere, you big galoot," she said. She wrapped her arms around Peter and kissed him again, this time on the lips. After a long moment, she pulled back, all traces of sleep gone from her eyes. "There. That's better."

"I'll say," Peter said, meaning it. He donned his gloves. "I'll call if I get the chance."

"Okay, but don't be surprised if I'm not here. There's another casting call out in Queens, and I don't know when I'll be back."

"The toothpaste thing?" A month before, at about the same time as the Hulk's most recent visit to the Big Apple, MJ had tried out for a toothpaste commercial. Callbacks had been promised, but none had come. "I thought that was a wash."

"It was, and it wasn't. The agency scrapped the idea, but liked me enough to call and tell me so. The same production company is doing an infomercial for one of those telephone psychic things. I might get to be someone whose life was changed by a single telephone call." She paused. " 'Calls cost $3.99 per minute. Age eighteen and older, only,' " she quoted, in a stern but singsong voice.

"I know some real psychics," Peter said. "I could give you some tips." He pulled Spider-Man's mask over his head, hiding his still-boyish features behind its webbed pattern.

"Don't bother," MJ said. "You'll just spoil the effect with dumb ol' facts."

"Yes, ma'am!" Peter saluted smartly, then stepped to the window. "I'll still call, if I get the chance. Good luck." He slid the sash up and let the cool air of morning spill inside before looking back at her. "I love you," he said.

Then he was gone.

* * *

The whole world had turned to crap.

It had happened fast. Only a few minutes before, everything had been on track. Each member of the squad had done his job, no more and no less, and had done it on schedule. The impact grenades and the gas bombs had done their part too, detonating flawlessly, with precisely the desired results. By Morrie Erikson's count, a hundred and one different things could have gone wrong during the operation, but none of them had.

Item number one hundred and two was an off-duty cop with dreams of being a hero. Many things had happened when he had made the scene, none of them good and all of them fast. Now, three minutes in his past, two of Morrie's best men lay in pools of blood near the armored car, either dead or dying. Morrie didn't really care which.

The cop was another story. The cop was history. Morrie had seen to that himself.

He cursed, and spun the steering wheel frantically, weaving in and out of traffic. Tires squealed against the dirty asphalt of FDR Drive as a small imported car got out of Morrie's way. Its driver made a gesture and yelled several four-letter words. Then the other man saw the look on Morrie's face and the gun in his hand, and fell silent. Morrie kept driving. Traffic was surprisingly light for a Monday morning. He was making good progress, all things considered.

"Gonna die." The words were little more than strangled gasps. They drifted forward from the car's back seat, punctuated with wet, bubbling noises that Morrie didn't like at all. "Gonna die." The gasp became a sob. "Don't wanna die."

"Shut up," Morrie barked. "I'm driving, here!" He didn't look back as he spoke. He was, as he said, too busy driving, and besides he knew what he would see.

Some unexpected humanitarian urge had made him put David Quick in the back seat himself, after the younger man caught a bullet with his left lung.

"Hurts, Morrie. It hurts." Quick moaned, more loudly than Morrie would have thought possible at this point.

"It's supposed to hurt. You've been shot. The cop shot you. Now shut up, or I'll shut you up, good." Morrie snarled the words, and he meant them. Quick's complaints were getting on his nerves.

A doughnut delivery van suddenly loomed large in the windshield. Morrie cursed again and snapped the wheel to one side, hard. There was almost enough space to the van's right for the car to pass—almost, and then not quite enough, as the other driver realized what Morrie was trying to do and moved to block him. Morrie didn't know why, but he didn't care either. It didn't matter.

Metal shrieked and the car shook as Morrie forced it into the not-quite-wide-enough space between van and curb. The weathered gold paint of the 1972 Plymouth Satellite met the van's cheerily decorated side panels. Sparks flew. The side-view mirror tore free. Chips of friction-burnt paint ricocheted upwards and through the open window to find and sting Morrie's left cheek. He didn't notice. The car's right tires had found the hard concrete of the roadway curb and were doing their best not to tear themselves apart against it. If they succeeded, he knew, the fast, hard ride was over.

Behind him, Quick moaned.

Morrie punched the gas again. At the same time, the doughnut van pulled away slightly. Its driver had apparently realized that Morrie wasn't playing games. The Satellite shot forward, grinding against the van. Metal continued to shriek as the two vehicles slid against each other. He could feel his own car's side panels give under the unrelenting pressure, but they didn't matter. Only the tires did.

The doughnut van moved further to the left, trying to get away. Morrie's car pulled forward, its big V-8 engine roaring. He was clear of the curb now, but not about to take any chances. He kept bearing left as he pulled alongside, then past the van. The painted image of the doughnut company's cheerful mascot filled his window, then moved behind him as Morrie pulled ahead. To his right, the curb receded.

Morrie let himself sigh with relief. He was going to make it. In another moment, he would make it.

A sudden impact resonated through the Satellite, a heavy shake that jarred the entire vehicle. The car slowed as something dragged heavily at it. Morrie wasted a split second looking out the side window, turning his head to see what had happened.

The Satellite's rear bumper had found, met and locked with the van's front one. The other driver couldn't keep up and probably didn't want to, so his decelerating van pulled at the getaway car and slowed it. As Morrie watched, the red line of the speedometer slid to the left, marking lower and lower numbers.

"Gonna die," Quick gasped. "Hurts!"

"I told you to zip it!" Keeping one hand on the wheel and both eyes on the road, Morrie pointed his revolver at Quick. It was a .357 Magnum, a Smith & Wesson Model 19, not his favorite weapon but a good one. He drew back the hammer. "Last warning, Quick," he snapped. "Shut up!"

Quick shut up.

Morrie set his gun down on the front passenger seat, next to the three remaining gas bombs and the small leather case that held half a pound of high-carat, jewelry-

quality diamonds. Split four ways and sold on the underground market, the gems would have yielded enough
to support Morrie and his men for many years. That
didn't seem likely now.

Morrie snapped the wheel from left to right, then
back again, trying to wrench the bumpers free. He kept
accelerating, wincing in sympathy as the engine strained
futilely against the van's drag. The Satellite was a good
car. It had a big engine and good shocks, and it moved
quickly in response to his demands. After twenty-five
years, it was still a better car than almost anything else
on the road. He hoped it was good enough.

Left, then right, then left again. He rocked the wheel
back and forth. His ears filled with a grinding noise as
the two bumpers pulled at one another. The speedometer
reading continued to drop as the car slowed. A new
sound cut through the din of tortured metal. It was the
wailing shriek of police sirens, far away now but getting
closer.

He was running out of time.

Still trying to pull free from the van, Morrie grabbed
one of the gas bombs. He used his teeth to pull the pin
free and spat it out, careful to hold the release lever in
place. He put the bomb in his left hand and got ready
to throw.

Out of the corner of his eye, he saw something move
in the distance. He could see it for only a fraction of a
second, high above street level and moving between the
tall buildings that bordered FDR Drive. It was red and
blue, and it moved from point to point with an easy
swinging motion that Morrie found unsettling.

He knew what it was. More importantly, he knew
who it was. That was the problem with pulling a job in
New York. Sooner or later, some creep in longjohns
would make his presence known.

Morrie reached out the window and dropped the gas

bomb. It fell directly in the path of the doughnut van.
He didn't hear it hit the asphalt, but he heard it explode
to release billowing clouds of tear gas that would blind
and sicken anyone who breathed it. Morrie gripped the
steering wheel tightly, pointing the car straight ahead,
and braced himself.

Behind him, brakes shrieked and rubber squealed as
the van's driver tried to stop before sliding into the white
cloud. Horns blared angrily and the police sirens became
louder. Now Morrie could hear the rhythmic beat of helicopter blades getting closer fast. More police, or reporters.

The Plymouth's big engine strained. The speedometer
needle continued to drop. The gas pedal was flush
against the floor now, and his wheels spun against the
asphalt as the drag increased. He began to worry about
the tires again.

There was a wrenching noise, the raw, sharp sound
that metal makes as it bends and tears. Either the doughnut van's bumper had torn free, or the Satellite's had. It
didn't matter which. The Satellite surged forward, bucking and swerving in its sudden freedom. Morrie had to
struggle to keep moving in a straight line.

Cars and trucks did their best to get out of his way
as the car rocketed forward. Morrie snapped the wheel
from side to side again, weaving in and out of traffic.
The speedometer needle edged upward and Morrie
smiled tightly. Things might work out, after all. If he
could make it to the next exit, if he could find a side
street, if he could detonate the last of the gas bombs
before the police or anyone else caught up with him—

If.

Something came down on the car from above, something heavy that hit hard and made the roof sag under
its sudden impact. The car jolted and shook, and the

steering wheel twisted in Morrie's hands. He cursed and snatched up his gun again. He knew what had happened, knew who had arrived.

A masked face appeared in the windshield, suddenly peering in from above. White eyepieces, set against a red and black field of what looked like webbing, stared at him from beyond the glass. A gloved hand waved, then gestured for him to stop the car. The newcomer might have spoken, but Morrie could not hear him through the glass.

"Spider-Man!" Morrie made the name a curse.

He brought his gun up and fired, aiming for the super hero's head. The bullet smashed through the glass, shattering it instantly. Fragments filled the driver's compartment in a hard, jagged rain. The bullet hadn't hit Spider-Man, though. The masked man had dodged at the last possible moment. Cold morning air whistled through the windshield's empty frame. Morrie raised his gun and trained it upward, in a straight vertical.

Spidey was still on the car roof. The thin metal would offer no more resistance to bullets than the glass had. If he shot enough times, if he shot fast enough, he might be able to—

"What is it, Morrie?" Quick's tortured voice cut thought the shrieking wind. "What's happening?"

Angry beyond reasoning, Morrie looked back at the wounded man. "Shut up," he screamed, turning to train his gun on the pale form in the back seat. "*I told you to shut up!*"

A new voice spoke. "Fun time's over, Junior." The words were flippant, but the tones were strong and commanding. "Put the gun down before you hurt someone with it." Morrie had never heard the voice before, but he knew whose it was. He looked forward and tried to bring his pistol back in line with the shattered windshield, but he moved too late.

Spider-Man had stepped down onto the still-moving car's hood. He straddled the windshield frame as he reached inside the car. Already, he had one hand wrapped securely around the steering wheel. Now he reached in with the other. Morrie yelled in pain as Spidey tore the gun from his grip. Gloved fingers closed, and gun fragments rained from between them.

"Stop the car," Spider-Man commanded. "Stop the car, and I'll make this as painless as I can."

Morrie snarled, more in rage than in fear. Hoping to shake Spider-Man off the hood of the car, he grabbed the wheel with both hands and wrenched it to his left— or tried to. Locked in the super hero's iron grip, the wheel wouldn't budge.

"Nope," Spidey said. He sounded remarkably patient for someone perched backwards atop a moving car in city traffic. "Not that. The brake is what you want. I can't reach it, but you can."

For an instant, Morrie considered obeying. His right foot moved to the brake pedal, hovered above it. It was all over. The sirens were louder now, and the air fairly shook with the beat of helicopter blades. He might be able to deal with Spider-Man, or with the cops, but not with both.

A horn blared. The car had drifted into the left lane, dangerously close to a dump truck full of broken concrete slabs. Spider-Man's hand twitched, the steering wheel moved a few degrees, and the slowing car glided back into the right lane. Spider-Man had corrected its course without even looking.

Morrie wondered how he had been able to do that. Eyes in the back of his head? Or the same way he had dodged the bullet, a few moments before?

"C'mon, c'mon, c'mon," Spider-Man ordered. "I don't have all day."

"Yeah, I bet you don't," Morrie sneered. Spurred by anger, confusion and fear, he moved his foot back to the accelerator. It was time to go for broke. A blue sedan loomed ahead of them. If Morrie could ram it fast enough and hard enough, maybe Spider-Man would—

He pressed the pedal. The Satellite's engine roared in instant response. It was a great car.

"Nice try, Chuckles," Spider-Man said, sounding angry for the first time. "I told you, I don't have time to screw around." He reached inside the car with his free hand, to grip the gearshift lever. Before Morrie could even try to stop him, he moved it two notches up, until the selector needle pointed at "R."

The letter that stood for "reverse."

Morrie heard a new and different grinding sound as the car's transmission tore itself to pieces. The V-8 raced for an instant, then fell silent. As suddenly as if it had struck a brick wall, the battered car came to a wrenching halt, lurching and spinning as it did. Anchored securely to the roof and hood, Spider-Man seemed barely to notice, but inertia threw Morrie forward, fast and hard. As he hurtled forward, he saw the fingers of Spider-Man's free hand curl together.

Morrie heard the masked man say, "Told you." Then he heard nothing at all, as his chin found Spider-Man's fist, and darkness claimed him.

Odyssey Designs proved to be a small suite of offices on the seventh floor of a ten-floor building, apparently constructed sometime in the 1950s and not modified much since then. The woman who opened the door introduced herself to Peter as Anna Marie Sanchez, office manager and administrative assistant. He had spoken

with her twice on the telephone and was pleased to see
how closely her appearance matched the mental image
her voice had created. She was a Latina with reddish
hair, a bit over five feet tall and had striking features
that meant she had probably once been quite beautiful.
Now in late middle age, she was still handsome, attractive even in her annoyance. "You're late," she said.
"That's not smart, being late on the first day of a new
job."

She was right, Peter realized. His little adventure on
the FDR had used up all of the time he had hoped to
save by web-swinging to work, and then some. He
sighed. It wasn't the first time that Spider-Man's needs
had gotten in the way of Peter Parker's, and it wouldn't
be the last. At least the police had been cooperative and
had given him no trouble for trying to leave once they
made the scene. He wasn't always that lucky.

"I'm sorry," he said. He thought about the battered
Plymouth and about driving it backwards, guided by his
spider-sense. "I'm really sorry. Traffic's bad, and I had
some trouble with my ride."

Anna Marie shook her head. "I'm not the one you
need to apologize to," she said. "At least, not for being
late. You manage to keep yourself hired, then you can
apologize to me."

"Huh? What do you mean?"

"We really need someone here, Peter. *He* needs
someone, and he won't admit it. You'll be the third lab
assistant in four weeks—if he doesn't notice that you're
late."

"The third in four weeks?" Peter didn't like the
sound of that.

She nodded. "You'll understand when you meet
Doctor Haberman. He can be—" She paused, as if considering her words carefully. "He can be difficult." She

paused again, and corrected herself. "He can be *very* difficult."

Tony Stark's words came back to Peter then: *"And anyone who can put up with J. Jonah Jameson. . . ."*

"Let me guess," Peter said. "He's crusty, but lovable."

" 'Crusty' might not be the right word," Anna Marie said. She opened the door that separated her office from the rest of the suite. " 'Lovable' might not be, either. But I'll let you decide." She led him through the door and down a long, narrow hall, past closed doors that apparently opened on empty offices. "Layoffs," she said, guessing his thoughts. "We had to lay off most of the staff when their contracts ended. The government isn't buying much of our kind of work these days. If Mr. Stark hadn't bought into the company, Odyssey would have closed its doors for good. As it is, we'll consolidate with the parent firm in another month."

Peter had to wonder about that. Over the weekend, he had done a little bit of research at the ESU library on Odyssey Designs and Cosmo Haberman. Odyssey had been founded several years before, to sell sophisticated scientific software to the federal government. It had apparently been a casualty of recent spending cutbacks. Haberman was the company's founder and chief shareholder; it must have been heartbreaking for him to watch his company dwindle and nearly die.

If Haberman's business track record wasn't especially impressive, the same couldn't be said of his academic experience. According to his entry in *Who's Who In Applied Non-Relativistic Physics*, he held two doctorates from MIT, one in subatomic particle physics and one in software design. He had studied with Reed Richards at State University and again at Yale, and worked with Henry Pym on applied cybernetic systems. His patents included several key artificial intelligence circuits and something called a ''quark enumerator'' that Peter didn't even want to think about. Haberman's name also appeared on the paperwork for Stark Enterprises's antigravity field generators. Indeed, he had worked for Stark for much of his career, leaving only when another company, Stane International, succeeded in a hostile takeover attempt. Now, the wheel had turned again; Tony Stark had taken his company back, and with the acquisition of Odyssey Designs, he had taken Haberman back as well.

Things must be looking up for the old guy, Peter thought, as Anna Marie waved him around a corner and through an open door into Haberman's private laboratory. There, an emaciated, bald figure sat hunched over a computer keyboard, slowly and painstakingly striking one key and then another with palsied fingers.

''Doctor?'' Anna Marie spoke slowly and carefully. She sounded apprehensive as she stepped into the office. ''Doctor Haberman?''

''What? What?'' The voice was thin and querulous, and the words were slightly slurred. Peter had heard people speak like that before. ''What? What is it you want from me?''

Anna Marie shrugged and shot Peter a glance that said, *I told you so*. Aloud, she said, ''There's someone here to see you, Doctor Haberman.'' Now she spoke briskly, in a businesslike voice that promised little patience with difficult old men. ''This is Peter Parker. Mr. Stark talked to you about him.''

''Parker? Yes, yes, of course.'' Haberman spun in his desk's chair, turning away from the computer screen that displayed a complex circuit design. Frosty blue eyes peered out from behind thick lenses that rested on ruddy cheeks. "Tony told me about you, and I saw your résumé." He still seemed to have trouble speaking, and the drooping left side of his face verified Peter's suspicion; at some point in the fairly recent past, Haberman had suffered a stroke.

Haberman stood, and Peter immediately wished he hadn't made the effort. Instead of extending his right hand in greeting, the older man used it to lean heavily on an ornate walking stick. "Yes, yes, most impressive," Haberman said, his slurred lisp overlaid slightly with a vestigial German accent. "Interesting fields you have chosen, good fields. Much work will be done there in the years to come." He stepped over to a work table and began sorting through the papers that covered its surface. For a moment, Peter wanted to help, and then decided against offering. Haberman looked like a man who preferred doing things for himself.

"And you worked with Henry Pym," Haberman continued. He had apparently found what he was looking for, a few pages that Peter recognized as his own résumé. "Such a fine mind Henry has. You are very fortunate."

Peter felt the tension begin to ooze out of him. Even Anna Marie began to look a little relieved. His tardiness had been forgiven; things were going to be all right.

"Not for very long, sir," Peter said. "Just a few summer weekends in his private lab."

Haberman nodded. "And your grade transcripts— most impressive. I know several of your professors, they have good things to say about you. I spoke with them, you know."

Peter smiled.

"You will go far, Mr. Parker," Haberman said. He paused. "But you will go far somewhere else. I have no use for a sluggard."

Peter stared at him, stunned by the sudden reversal. "But—I—"

Haberman continued speaking, as if Peter had said nothing. "You were told to be here at 9:00," he said. "That was more than half an hour ago." He made a spitting sound, and tore Peter's résumé in half, then let the scraps of paper fall to the floor. "I have no use for you. Get out of here."

"But—" Peter and Anna Marie spoke the word in perfect unison.

"*Get out!*" Haberman nearly screamed it, the still-expressive right side of his face contorted in fury. "I'm an old man! I'm weak! But I can make it to work on time! Get out of my sight! You make me sick!"

Peter began to move towards the door. This wasn't going well. Silently, he cursed the holdup man he had intercepted on FDR Drive. Part of him cursed Spider-Man too, for his devotion to his work. Stark had given him the chance of a lifetime, and fate had conspired to take it away from him.

He wondered how he would tell Mary Jane. She had been so excited at the great career opportunity.

"I guess I'd better be leaving, then. It was nice meeting you," Peter said sadly. He turned to look at Anna Marie and froze at what he saw.

The woman's lips were set in a straight line, and the muscles of her jaw were clenched in fury. A red spot burned on each of her cheeks, and when she spoke, her words began in a low, urgent tone that brooked no denial. "No, Peter," she said. "You stay right where you are."

Peter stayed right where he was.

"As for you, 'old man,'" Anna Marie continued, turning to face Haberman. Her voice raised in pitch and volume as she spoke, the words coming one after another like hammer blows on an anvil. "As for you, you ungrateful, impatient, condescending, arrogant, petulant—"

She yelled at him long and hard, switching from English to Spanish and then back again. Haberman stood and took her invective, unblinking, as the woman who managed his office shrieked at him.

Finally, when she paused to take a breath, he picked up where she left off. "Foolish woman," he snarled, his weak reedy voice suddenly strong with anger. "I have put up with your nonsense long enough. How dare you—" His tirade easily matched hers in length, if not in speed or volume. Haberman's proclamations were peppered with German syllables and phrases, words that Anna Marie Sanchez probably didn't understand—but with meanings she could obviously guess.

Peter certainly could. None of them were nice.

They went on like that for the better part of half an hour. At first, Peter was embarrassed and uncomfortable, feeling like a child might feel when his parents fought. After a while, however, he managed to feel some small degree of amusement. It was almost funny to listen to the matching tirades, to listen to trilingual vituperation that surrounded but did not affect him. Sanchez and Haberman had obviously had this fight before, or others like it; they tore into one another with a venom and zeal that he found surprising. Now and then, one or the other made reference to him, using such terms as "that worthless sloth" or "that sweet young man." Neither combatant seemed to realize that he was still in the room— unless he edged towards the door, when they would both break off their tirades and order him to stay. There was much agitated discussion of perceived shortcomings and inadequacies, of failures and presumptions. Tony Stark's name came up once or twice, too. Haberman was ranting about heartless viragos and Anna Marie was shrieking some word in Spanish that had too many vowels when the argument abruptly stopped, as if suddenly someone had flipped a switch.

The silence was deafening.

Peter looked at Anna Marie, and then at Haberman. They looked back at him, then at each other.

Haberman shrugged. "I have twelve years of *The Journal of Seventh-Dimensional Topology* in the library," he said to Peter. He sounded resigned to a particularly unpleasant fate. "I bought them from Kellye Nakahara. Sort them, catalog them, and shelve them. Anna Marie will show you where. Then come back, and I will give you something else to do." He paused. "You won't like it, but I will give you something else."

He sat back down, and began tapping the keyboard again. The audience was over.

Peter looked at Anna Marie. She pressed a finger to her lips and shook her head, then gestured towards the still-open door. As they walked down the hallway together, he finally said, "Does that happen much?"

"Once in a while. That was the worst in a long time, though."

"Oh. Um, thanks."

She looked at him. "Don't thank me. It's good for him, gets his blood pumping. Since the stroke, he has difficulty communicating. He lives too much in his own world. He needs to get out of it once in a while, or one day he'll go in there and stay. I don't want that to happen."

"Well, still—you really went to bat for me back there. I appreciate it."

She laughed. "I wasn't doing you any favors, Peter.

I did it for myself. I have too much to do around here, and I'm too busy to play nursemaid to a cranky old man who can't put his own toys away.'' She sighed and looked sad. ''No matter how much I used to like him.''

''Oh.''

She opened another door, on a room crowded with stacks of magazines and crates of books. Huge, shape-less mounds of paper perched on every flat surface that was level, and on a few that weren't. ''Here,'' she said. ''This is what he calls his 'library.' Part of it, anyway.''

Peter said it again. ''Oh.''

Anna Marie smiled. ''Hey,'' she said. ''It's a dirty job, but someone's got to do it. Not right now, though. I've got some papers you need to sign, and you'll probably want to put that lunch in the refrigerator.'' She paused, as if noticing something for the first time. ''Those cases aren't both lunch boxes, are they?''

''That Sanchez woman, she's sure got a mouth on her,'' Lyle Chesney said. ''Knows how to use it, too.'' He was a short man with eyes that seemed too big for his face and lank colorless hair that looked more like fungus. Just now, he was slumped behind the steering wheel of what looked like an ordinary package deliv-ery van parked in the alley behind the building that housed Odyssey Designs. He wore a uniform that was not his own, the distinctive fatigue-like outfit of a prominent parcel delivery service. A pair of head-phones and a long wire connected his ears to the dash-board, and from there to the small parabolic antenna on the van's roof.

''Yeah, well.'' The words came from the van's rear compartment. Eustace K. Winwood, Chesney's lieuten-ant on this assignment, answered without really answering. Instead, he busied himself with the bank of sensitive listening and recording equipment that filled the van's rear. His fingers danced along the fingers and knobs like those of a piano virtuoso, coaxing the very best readings possible from each of the many listening devices that the two had planted in the Odyssey suite.

"No, I mean it. You listen to this, you'll hear some pretty wild stuff. She's got Spanish curse words I never heard of." Chesney tried to pronounce one of them, but failed.

Winwood finally rose to the bait and joined the conversation. "What about the old guy?"

Chesney snorted. "Him, I don't like listening to so much. He curses good too, but he sounds too much like the boss. Too German."

Winwood, finally satisfied with his settings, squirmed into the empty front passenger seat. He pulled a set of headphones from his jumpsuit and plugged it into the dashboard. "Yeah, I can see how that would upset you. You've gotten a few dressing-downs from the Baron, right?"

Chesney didn't say anything.

"Right?" Winwood repeated it.

Chesney still didn't reply, but gazed steadily at Winwood with his oversized eyes.

Winwood gave up, and changed the subject. "What about the new guy?" he asked.

"Name's Parker," Chesney said. "I think he's some kind of file clerk."

"Is he gonna be any trouble?"

Chesney shrugged. "Don't see how he can be, my friend. He gets in the way, he dies. Simple as that."

"Yeah. Simple."

"Hail Hydra, Eustace."

"Hail Hydra right back at ya, Lyle."

The two men brought their right hands together in an impromptu, awkward "high five," and settled back in their seats.

Their shift had just begun.

— CHAPTER 4 —

The week went reasonably well, all things considered. A nickel-and-dime thug named the Eel escaped police custody and tried to play in the big leagues by kidnapping an oil heiress; Spidey put a stop to that foolishness, and Peter Parker sold photographs of the action to the *Bugle* for a modest sum. MJ didn't get the infomercial gig, but she did find work doing voiceovers for radio spots, thanks to her experience looping dialogue for *The GigaGroup* cartoon show. She also came in and had lunch with Peter on Tuesday, met his coworkers and was suitably impressed—positively by Anna Marie, negatively by Haberman. There weren't any more arguments at the lab, other than a few minor skirmishes. Anna Marie kept herself busy, concluding a thousand and one bits of minor business as Odyssey Designs closed out its contracts and prepared for final, full incorporation into Stark Enterprises. Peter managed to completely reorganize the library in only a few days, thanks as much to his own attention to detail as to Spider-Man's strength, speed, and stamina. His next assignment proved to be tidying up Odyssey's software files, which at least got him back out in the main lab, where he could chat occasionally with Haberman, when the disgruntled scientist felt like speaking.

The older man both baffled and infuriated him. Anna Marie had worked for Haberman for ten years, both at Odyssey and at Stark before that. She said that he had been a different man since the stroke, and Peter could believe her; it was hard to believe that anyone would choose to work closely with the venomous thing he had become. Peter realized that there must have been a time when Haberman had been, if not a saint, at least likable. Now, hampered by the failure of his own body, frustrated and angry in the midst of his own collapsed business, Haberman did little but work, bark orders, and complain. Some days, he came very close to being a monster.

But he was also, undeniably, a genius. Wizened and gnome-like, he sat for long hours in front of his computer, meticulously but oh-so-slowly giving substance to his visions. On occasion, he allowed Peter to review and proofread long runs of printed out programs; each time, Peter came away from the experience stunned by the elegance and complexity of the man's work.

"Everything must fit together," Haberman told him, in a rare moment of loquacity. "The problem with the *Engine* software, it is so complex that all parts perform many, many functions. The operating software and the calibration systems, the transducer algorithms and the feedback loops, they are not distinct modules, like they would be in another system. They gray into one another, so that every part is also the whole."

Peter nodded. There was considerable truth in that. In some ways, Haberman's software coding reminded him of DNA models he had reviewed in college, sinuous and intertwined, built of simple components but almost infinitely complex in their totality. "Tony mentioned that you were working on the calibration system," he said.

Haberman sighed, and made an unhappy sound. "Such sloppy thinking. There is not a single line of code in the software that does not support all system segments, and so there are no system segments. Tony, he knows better. I am disappointed in him for that."

"Maybe he was trying to make it easier for me to understand," Peter said, trying to exonerate his patron.

Haberman laughed then, the only time Peter ever heard him do so. "More foolishness. You do not need someone who talks down to you. You merit better than that.'' Then he turned in his chair again, and began tapping the keys once more. The rest of that day, all he had for Peter was a series of inarticulate grunts.

As the days passed, Peter became more and more aware that Haberman's current work had less to do with correcting actual errors than with endlessly refining already operational systems. Twice, they uploaded new software to the *Infinity Engine* via the remote satellite link at Stark Enterprises; twice, Haberman pronounced himself satisfied, only to return to his keyboard and begin work anew. Peter thought he understood the man's mania for perfection, and told Anna Marie so over lunch on Friday.

''He's dealing with fundamental forces here,'' he said, biting into the turkey-and-cheese croissant that Mary Jane had packed for him. ''He's afraid of the consequences, if anything goes wrong.''

Anna Marie shook her head, and looked in disgust at the prepackaged entree she had brought from home and microwaved for her own meal. ''This is awful,'' she said. ''I need to start packing my own lunch—if I can ever find the time.'' Anna Marie had told Peter about her five children. Four of them were in their teens. They occupied most of her off-duty time, especially since her husband's death three years before. ''And you're wrong about Doctor Haberman.''

''How so?'' Peter finished his sandwich, and reached for a small plastic container of sliced kiwi fruit and white grapes. Taped inside the cover, he found a short note from MJ; he unfolded and read it silently, then blushed.

''Aw, you're so cute when you're all red like that,'' Anna Marie said, laughing. She reached out and pinched his cheek. ''It must be so nice to be young and in love.''

"Yeah, yeah," Peter said, embarrassed. He twisted away from her. "What about the mad doctor?"

Suddenly serious again, Anna Marie continued. "Think about it, Peter. The stroke, the business situation. His body has failed him." She tapped her forehead. "He's lost something upstairs, too; not much, but something, and he knows it. Problems that used to take him minutes to solve now take an hour or more. And in three months, all that will be left of his Odyssey will be a name on old letterhead and a business trademark registered to Stark Enterprises."

"I thought he liked Stark," Peter said. "Tony sure seems to like him."

"Oh, they do like one another. They've known each other for many years, and he knows that Tony has saved him. This isn't charity, either. He's absolutely the best man for the work he's doing. He just hates that it had to happen this way." She paused. "Everything's going wrong for him, Peter. He wants this *Infinity Engine* thing, whatever it is, to be perfect. He just wants *something* to be right."

She was right, Peter realized, eating his fruit in silence. He couldn't do anything about the stroke or the business situation, but he could make the lab work easier. He found himself promising Anna Marie that he would do his best to get Haberman at least that much satisfaction out of life.

Lyle Chesney set his headphones aside as his dashboard communicator buzzed. He took a quick glance at his own reflection in the van's rearview mirror. He hadn't shaved that morning, but there was nothing he could do about that now. He contented himself with hastily running a comb through the lank hair that clung to his brow. The boss could be a real stickler about personal grooming, and there was no sense in courting disaster.

A panel slid open, revealing a recessed video screen. Baron Strucker's scarred features glared out from it.

"Hail Hydra!" Chesney said.

"Report." The voice crackled through the dashboard speaker.

Chesney felt a thin film of perspiration form on his brow, as it almost always did in Strucker's presence. He much preferred dealing with Hydra's ruler through intervening layers of management and command, but he didn't have any choice now. Strucker had taken personal charge of this assignment, for reasons known only to him. Chesney hoped he would change his mind about that at some point.

"Surveillance continues as directed, Baron," he said. "No change. Haberman is still working on the calibration system software."

"No progress?"

"It's not clear, sir. They've provided two upgrades to the orbiter so far, and Stark's people have accepted both, with thanks—but Haberman keeps working."

Strucker grimaced. "No matter. Our own people can complete any final changes, and time grows short."

"Yes, Baron."

"Take the information we need, then liquidate the old fool. He owes us something for this delay, and there is no sense in allowing him to serve anyone else."

"Yes, Baron," Chesney said. "What about the others?"

"It matters not." Strucker sneered. "Very little will matter, once this operation is complete. Do as you think best, Chesney." He snickered, making it clear that he thought Chesney's best would be very poor indeed.

"Yes, Baron!"

"And Chesney," Strucker continued. "Do not let me

ever again see you unshaven, if you value your paltry life. You are a disgrace. Were you in uniform, I would have you shot.''

"No, Baron! I mean, yes, Baron! Hail Hydra!"

The screen went dark before the last words left Chesney's lips. He turned in his seat, to face an amused-looking Winwood, who peered out from the van's crowded rear compartment. "What's so funny?" Chesney asked angrily.

"Nothing," Winwood replied. His eyes said differently. "I take it we've got orders?"

Chesney nodded. "Yup," he said. "Come on up front. We've got places to go and people to kill."

As Winwood squirmed his way into the front seat, Chesney turned the van's ignition key, and pressed a concealed button. There was whirling thunder as several powerful turbine engines roared to life. Their pitch and volume rose, then dropped when the craft's transmission system engaged.

"Ready?"

Winwood grinned in agreement. He tapped a holstered energy pistol that hung at his side, similar to the one that Chesney wore. "Always, my friend. This eavesdropping gig was becoming a drag."

Chesney flipped another control lever, activating the huge, fan-like blades arrayed along the van's underside. Slowly at first, but then more swiftly, the disguised hovercraft lifted itself from the alley's dirty pavement floor.

"Going up," Chesney said. "Next stop, seventh floor. Ladies' lingerie, notions, and scientific secrets."

"And death," Winwood reminded him as the craft rose on a cushion of air. "Don't forget that."

The argument started a little more than an hour after lunch. It came suddenly and without any warning. Up until the moment it began, things had been going well. Peter had finished with the software files and had proceeded to his new assignment: comparing a series of actual readings from the still-orbiting *Infinity Engine* against Haberman's projections. It wasn't as easy as it should have been; Haberman's endless revisions to the operating software and to its report formats meant that there was no longer a one-for-one correlation between data fields in the real and projected listings. Peter's job was to identify and highlight apparent discrepancies, then present them to Haberman for verification.

The work was slow going. To aggravate the situation, many of Haberman's projections were in his crabbed handwriting, almost unreadable to someone unfamiliar with it. Peter sat at a work table near Haberman's desk, fifteen feet of folded green-bar computer paper at his right, stacks of Haberman's notes to his right. Methodically, he shifted his attention from one to another, making a check mark for each match, circling each pair of numbers that disagreed. There were many more hits than misses; Haberman's math was almost flawless.

Nearby, Haberman sat at his desk, still tapping one key after another. Peter was concentrating so hard that he scarcely noticed when the physicist paused in his labors. Peter glanced up briefly and saw Haberman staring at the screen, having apparently reached a sticking point in his work. Peter didn't say anything, but returned to his own labors; the physicist had long since let it be known that he would ask for any help he needed.

Peter watched from the corner of one eye as Haberman reached for a box of diskettes. The old man began flipping through its contents, pausing now and then to glance at a label, then continuing. Peter knew that box's contents well; it was part of the lab's software files, and held backup copies of various test algorithms. He had spent one entire morning reviewing and labeling each diskette.

Haberman said something, softly. Peter couldn't hear it clearly.

Haberman repeated the word. "Sloppy," he said.

That doesn't sound good, Peter thought. Out loud, he said, "Can I help you, Doctor?"

Haberman fixed him with a surprisingly steely glare. "These disks," he said. "What have you done with them?"

Peter had explained the files' organization to Haberman the previous day, but he didn't mind doing it again now. "They're alphabetical by application type," he said, "then in reverse order by date. They should all be there."

"Should be, but they are not!" Haberman's voice rose. "The secondary regression sequence from six weeks ago, where is it!?"

"Um, I'm sure it's there," Peter said. "Here, let me look." He reached for the small case.

Haberman threw it at him. Rather, he threw the box's contents, swinging his good arm in a lazy arc that sent the diskettes flying in Peter's general direction. "Here," he snarled. "You want to meddle with my things, you take them!"

Effortlessly, guided more by reflex than by anything else, Peter dodged the barrage of plastic. The same speed and agility that allowed Spider-Man to sidestep bullets let Peter avoid the flying diskettes easily. He even caught two of them in midflight, a spontaneous demonstration of dexterity that seemed to enrage Haberman even more.

The older man began to curse. Veins stood out on his forehead and his eyes bulged in their sockets as he ranted at Peter. It was as though a storm, long building, had finally broken, and there was no stopping the pent-up torrent of abuse. He said things about Peter, about Peter's presumed skills, about Peter's parents and friends and loved ones. He said things in German and in English, and a word or two in Spanish that he must have picked up from Anna Marie, perhaps even unknowingly.

Peter stared at him, aghast. What had seemed vaguely amusing on Monday was horrifying now, especially since it was directed solely at him. The fountain of abuse gushed on and on, and he wondered how Anna Marie had been able to put up with it on an even semiregular basis.

He looked at the diskettes he had caught. A familiar word on one label caught his eye. He examined the diskette more closely. "This is it," he said.

Haberman kept ranting.

"This is it," Peter said. He spoke more loudly this time, and let a week's worth of tension finally enter his voice.

Haberman's invective continued, punctuated with angry gestures.

"I said, *this is it!*" Peter shouted angrily at the older man, instantly ashamed of doing it, but unable to help himself. "Here's your blasted regression sequence!" He thrust the disk forward.

Haberman interrupted his tirade and looked at the proffered disk, squinting to read the label. He made his spitting sound again and slapped at the diskette. "Where was this when I needed it?" he demanded angrily.

The square of plastic few from Peter's fingers and spun into away into some corner of the lab. He watched it sadly, trying to compose himself, but finding that he could not. Hot anger boiled up inside him, and his fingers balled into fists, instinctively. Long years as Spider-

Man had taught him much about controlling his temper, but even his iron discipline had its limits.

Behind him, a door opened. Anna Marie Sanchez, drawn by the conflict, entered the room. "What's going on here?" she asked.

Before Peter could answer, Haberman did it for him. "Your lapdog, here," he said. "Your pet, your serf, your toy, your Mr. Peter Parker, he has ruined my files! Ruined them!"

"I—" Peter managed to force out only a single syllable.

Anna said something unpleasant and loud to her employer. Haberman said something louder. Peter felt the long muscles that corded his arms and legs bunch and knot as tension built within him. He wanted to say something, but couldn't think of anything that was worth the effort. Around him, the argument built, and moved from topic to topic with breathtaking speed—but always coming back to him as its subject. With meticulous skill and precision, Haberman cataloged Peter's many alleged sins; with less precision but more passion, Anna Marie defended him. Neither would let Peter say a single word on his own behalf.

Finally, his own anger exploded. "That's it!" he said. "I've had enough!" He spun on one heel and headed for the door through which Anna Marie had so recently entered.

"And where do you think you're going?" Haberman roared the question, with a volume and vigor surprising for a man of his age and condition. Anna Marie looked like she wanted to ask the same thing, but didn't.

"Out! Anywhere but here! Anything's better than this!" Peter yelled the words, and he meant them, too. Just now, the prospect of a half-dozen super-villains seemed more attractive than spending another minute in this rage-filled room.

"Peter—please, you—" Anna Marie started to say, a pleading tone lending texture to her own anger.

Haberman interrupted her. "Look what you've done," he shrieked. "You've driven him away with your foolishness!"

Anna Marie said something in reply, but Peter did not hear her. He was already in the outer offices, moving with quick, sure steps towards the elevator. He paused only long enough to retrieve his lunch container from the suite's refrigerator.

He didn't want to have to return for it. He didn't want come back for anything.

Lyle guided the van upward, past the sixth floor and into position, while Winwood perched himself it its open doorway, drawing his pistol as he did. When the van door was level with the seventh-floor window that he knew opened on Cosmo Haberman's private lab, he took careful aim and fired a low charge with maximum dispersion. The glass shattered inward with a satisfying sound, and Winwood leaped through the breach. Lyle set the disguised aircraft to hover on auto-pilot and followed his partner inside.

Surrounded by glass fragments but unharmed, Haberman and Sanchez stared at him in stunned silence. The Parker kid was nowhere to be seen.

"Nobody moves, nobody gets hurt!" Lyle said the lie easily; he had said it many times before. "You're in Hydra custody now!"

"Who are you? What do you want?" The Sanchez woman asked the question angrily. She had gathered her wits with remarkable speed, considering the unusual entrance the intruders had made.

Lyle answered her with the back of his hand, lashing out with an easy blow that caught her square in the mouth and spun her around and down. The fall slammed her against a desk; her head hit a projecting handle as she fell, to sprawl apparently unconscious on the floor.

"Shut up," Lyle barked at the motionless woman, then turned his attentions to Haberman. "I want the access codes, old man—and I want them now!"

"A-access codes?"

"Don't play dumb," Lyle snarled. "We know who you are, and we know what you're doing here. Give us the access codes to the *Infinity Engine*, and we'll let you live!"

To Lyle's surprise, Haberman balked. Whether from courage, contrariness, or simply confusion, the Hydra agent would never know, but the old man shook his head. "No," he said. "No, I will not do that!"

Winwood stepped behind Haberman, closer to the scientist's desk. He opened a small zippered canvas bag and began scooping papers, diskettes, and notes from the desktop and shoved them indiscriminately into his sack.

"Now, old man!" Lyle raised his energy pistol. "Now, or there's just hot plasma where your head used to be!" He hadn't expected any resistance, and time was of the essence. The same camouflage that made the van almost unnoticeable at street level cried out for attention at the craft's current elevation. He wanted to finish the job and get out of town, fast.

"No! The *Engine* is not for such as you!"

Lyle tried another tack. He lowered the pistol and trained it at the woman, still slumped and motionless on the floor. "Okay," he said. "Give me the codes, or the woman gets it!"

"You can't—they are not complete," Haberman said, haltingly. "They won't do what you want."

Lyle's trigger finger tensed and tightened, squeezing his gun's trigger just enough to move it halfway back it its track. Another quarter inch, and the gun would fire. He sneered. "Last chance, old man!"

"Lyle!" That was Winwood. He sounded pleased with himself. "Look at this!"

Lyle looked. Winwood had drawn a leather case from Haberman's desk drawer and opened it. Twelve record-able CD-ROMs sat nestled inside, glistening under the lab's fluorescent lights. A thick sheaf of instructions in tiny print was clipped to the case's inside cover.

"You can't take those," Haberman said, querulously. "Those aren't for you!"

Lyle laughed. "Maybe not for me," he said. "But there's a bald man with a scar who will be mighty happy to see them!" He reached for the case. As he did, he looked away from Haberman and Sanchez for a moment.

It was only a split-second—but it was enough.

Anna Marie Sanchez suddenly came back to life. Her left leg kicked out, without any warning. The heel of her shoe smashed into Lyle's knee. He cried out in pain, stumbled and almost fell. As he did, his pistol erupted in a flash of energy. The wild shot blasted a hole in the office ceiling, and fragments of cork tile rained down on all three of them.

Lyle snarled and brought the gun around to train it on her again. He moved fast, but he didn't move fast enough. By now, the woman had half-risen, and was reaching with her right hand for the one desk drawer that Winwood had not opened.

Lyle didn't like the looks of that. She seemed to be going for a gun.

Sanchez managed to open the drawer and reach in-side. Winwood, moving quickly, slammed it back shut with her fingers still inside, making her cry out in pain.

"Uh uh," the Hydra agent said. "Not today, lady!"

Neither man had noticed that Anna Marie's left hand was still moving. Now, its fingers found the base of a lamp. She bought the desk accessory up in a savage trajectory that smashed it into Winwood's angry face, making him cry out in pain.

"Bad move, lady! Really bad move!" Lyle yelled the words. He aimed his energy pistol at her.

"*No!*" That was Haberman. Moving faster than Lyle would have believed possible, the scientist threw himself into the line of fire. The pistol buzzed once, and energy erupted from its muzzle to sear a hole in Haberman's chest about three inches below his left collarbone. An electrical smell joined with the stink of burning flesh to fill the air.

"Doctor Haberman!" The anguish in Anna Marie's voice turned the name into a cry of sorrow. "No! Oh, please, no! *Madre de Dios!*"

Haberman remained standing for perhaps a second, balanced by some fluke moment of equilibrium—then he fell. His frail form sprawled across Anna Marie's body and knocked her back to the floor.

It took Peter three minutes to wait for, board, and ride an elevator to the building's lobby. It took him fifteen seconds longer than that to gather his wits, and muzzle the fury that raged within him. It wasn't easy; Haberman's scornful and completely unjustified words still rang in his ears. The old man had been so vicious, so—

Pathetic. That was the word he was looking for. Standing in the elevator lobby, he thought about Haberman. The scientist was emotional and impatient, but maybe those were the qualities that he needed to cling to his life so tenaciously. Peter wondered, not for the first time that week, how he might have fared in similar circumstances. On the verge of business bankruptcy, betrayed by his own body and brain, Haberman had nonetheless clawed his way back to productive work in the laboratory. Even in his present state, he was performing first-class work in a rarefied discipline that had been mastered by only a few dozen of the world's finest minds.

Under similar circumstances, would Peter have been able to do the same? He doubted it.

He thought about Anna Marie's words. "He just wants *something* to be right," she had said. He thought about the pleading sound in her voice as he stormed out of Haberman's lab. He thought about her troubled eyes gazing into his over lunch, and about the promise he had made, to help Haberman get whatever satisfaction he could get out of life.

Peter took a deep breath. He turned on one heel, to face the elevator doors again. Their polished metal surfaces seemed to mock him. After a long moment, he pressed the up button, wondering if he had made a mistake.

I guess I'll know soon enough, he thought.

The elevator doors opened again, and Peter stepped inside. He pushed the button for the seventh floor.

"Monsters!" Anna Marie Sanchez, still pinned under the collapsed Haberman, shouted the word. "Monsters!"

"Shut up," Lyle snapped. "Shut up, lady, or I'll shut you up!" He looked towards Winwood, who was pulling spool after spool of microfilm from a small cabinet on one office wall. "Hurry up there," he said.

"Yeah, yeah, yeah. I just want to be sure I get everything."

Haberman groaned, a faint sound that Lyle barely caught. Anna Marie stifled a sob as she heard the muffled whimper of pain.

"Still alive, huh?" Lyle stepped closer to the two of them. "Not for long, I'll bet. You must hurt pretty bad."

Pain-glazed eyes stared back up at him. Haberman didn't reply. He seemed to devote all of his remaining energy to forcing air in and out of his lungs.

"A doctor, oh God, you've got to let me call a doctor." Anna Marie's anger gave way to pleading. "Please, let me call a doctor for him. Take whatever you want—just let me call a doctor."

"Nah, don't think so."

"Oh, please. He's an old man, he's hurt, he's dying."

Lyle shrugged. "That's the idea," he said. He bought the butt of his pistol down, hard, on Anna Marie's skull. Her eyes closed instantly and she collapsed without another word. It was no act this time.

Haberman moaned again. Each breath was a muffled gasp of pain.

"You wanna kill her, or should I?" Winwood asked the question in a laconic tone of voice. The other Hydra agent had finished his search and was zipping his sack shut.

"Nah." Lyle smiled. A thought struck him. He leaned close to the two figures sprawled at his feet. The woman could not hear him, so he spoke to the man, who could. "She's not going to die right now, old man," he said. "You saved her. We're gonna let her live."

Haberman's breathing became marginally less strained.

"Of course," Lyle continued. "She's going to live in a world where Hydra has the *Infinity Engine*. And we're gonna have it, because you didn't stop us. Think about that, Pops, as you die."

The agony that clouded Haberman's eyes gave way for a moment to other emotions, ones that Lyle recognized with pleasure: sorrow and despair. Lyle grinned, and stood again. "Think about it," he repeated.

"We have to get out of here," Winwood said. "We're running late."

The two men stepped back into the waiting van. Lyle lingered for a moment, smiling as he gazed back at the dying man he had left behind.

"The Baron isn't going to like this," Winwood said. "He likes clean jobs, no loose ends."

Lyle shrugged. "Strucker left it up to me," he said. "Now shut up, and let's get out of here."

The hovercraft moved away from the window.

The elevator went up more slowly than it had come down, but Peter didn't mind. It gave him another few moments to gather his wits, and rehearse what he would say upon his return to the Odyssey suite. It wasn't going to be easy. He knew from experience that dramatic exits made subsequent entrances almost impossibly difficult—but he had to try.

As the elevator passed the third floor, he felt a slight sense of unease. At first, he attributed it to nerves, but the feeling increased and became more intense as the elevator continued to rise. Along about the fifth floor, it condensed into something troubling and distinct. It became a familiar throbbing sensation that had been his all-too-frequent companion since that fateful afternoon when a radioactive spider's bite had changed his life forever.

It was his spider-sense, the ESP-like warning signal that alerted him to immediate danger. Something was wrong—seriously wrong.

Peter moved between the elevator's doors before they

opened completely. Three bounding strides carried him the length of the hallway. He yanked the suite's door open without turning the knob, and ignored the shriek of splitting wood as the bolt ripped from its recess in the doorframe. He rushed inside.

The spider-sense buzz grew stronger. He charged down the hallway, negotiating the maze of deserted hallways with lightning speed. As he got closer to Haberman's office, he heard a roaring sound, the kind that turbine engines made.

What was happening? What had he *let* happen, while he nursed his hurt feelings?

The roaring sound dropped, and began to fade, as though its source were moving away. The spider-sense buzz faded too, but Peter didn't slow down. Instead, he only moved faster.

He turned the final corner and charged into Haberman's personal office, only to draw up short in his tracks at what he saw there. Horror and fury swept through him. A few minutes before—a lifetime ago—the lab had been a tidy, if noisy place. Now, ragged glass fragments and charred bits of cork ceiling tile littered the place, and wind whistled in the empty frame of a shattered window. Worse, Anna Marie lay sprawled on the floor, pinned unmoving beneath another limp form that whimpered as it took shallow breaths.

Haberman.

Peter leaned close. A single glance at the red wound on the old man's chest told the story. Spider-Man had seen enough of death to recognize its imminent presence. Anna Marie was merely unconscious, but Haberman was dying.

Gently, Peter moved the man from atop his assistant. Partway through the process, Haberman looked up at Peter. Recognition glimmered in his nearly closed eyes.

His hand frail and colorless, came up and rested, feather-light, on Peter's shoulder.

"What happened?" Peter spoke the questions clearly and slowly. He knew that he would have only one chance to ask them. "Who did this?"

The dying man's reply was a single, barely audible word, little more than a gurgling noise. Peter could barely hear it over the pounding of his own pulse in his ears.

"Hydra."

"What did they want?"

Haberman said another word, but it was in German, and Peter could not understand it. The scientist made another sound, something too soft to be called a gasp, and convulsed. A faint smile spread across Haberman's face. Then the labored breathing stopped, and the out-stretched hand fell.

Peter was moving, even as Haberman's fingers hit the floor.

In Latveria, Doctor Doom listened carefully to words spoken by a fool to his master, a man who was only marginally less foolish. Strucker, however, could at least claim some degree of accomplishment. His underling could not.

"Hail Hydra!" That was the voice of the lower echelon Hydra agent, intercepted and unscrambled by one of Doom's many communications monitors, then relayed to him via satellite link.

"Report." That was Strucker. Doom did not need the voiceprint validation his computers offered. He had heard the other man's voice many times before.

"We've got the codes, sir!"

"Bring them to me!"

"Yes, sir!"

"And Haberman?" Strucker spoke as though the man were an inconsequential detail, an attitude that irritated Doom. He knew of Haberman. The man was a scientist, with knowledge and perceptions that Strucker would never possess. In another, happier time, Doom might have allowed Haberman to serve him.

"Dead." Doom had expected that answer, and Strucker no doubt expected it too. Hydra's leader could boast a certain functional efficiency in his planning, after all.

"Good. Return to base."

Doom turned his attentions from the intercepted conversation. His computers would record it, and he could review the remainder later, if necessary. He did not think that that would be the case. For now, he shifted his attention to one wall of his castle's command center. There, a schematic map of the world's surface met his gaze, marked with indicators of various colors and sizes. Each one represented a potential threat to Latveria's security, or a possible impediment to Doom's campaigns. Military bases, secret strongholds, super hero headquarters, enemy bases—specific symbols and colors denoted each. Somewhere in the Atlantic Ocean, a green star pulsed. It had moved slowly but perceptibly over the last six hours. The green star was *Barbarosa*, Hydra's mobile, subsea fortress.

Doom considered the display carefully. Strucker's plans had entered a new stage of implementation and demanded response. Now it was Doom's turn to act.

— CHAPTER 5 —

It was Peter Parker who heard Cosmo Haberman's last words, but it was Spider-Man who launched himself through the breach that Hydra's assassins had made in the Odyssey building's north wall. Peter had spent a scant ten seconds listening to that aged physicist die, and perhaps that long changing into his costume. Now, as Spider-Man threw himself out into the empty space above the crowded city streets, he twisted and turned in midair, looking for some sign of whoever had done the deed.

He looked—and he found.

A block away, perhaps twelve stories above the Earth, he saw what looked like an ordinary package delivery service van cut its way through the dirty New York sky. Despite the background of traffic noise, he could hear the roaring wail of the incongruous vehicle's engines. He had heard that sound before; moments ago, it had echoed from Odyssey Designs's suite. He had not recognized it then, but now, with his eyes to help him, he knew what kind of a craft his quarry rode. A month before, during an adventure with SAFE and the Hulk, Spider-Man had ridden in a somewhat similar vehicle.

A hovercraft, Spidey thought. *Disguised. That makes sense. Camouflaged on the ground, but a fast way out of town when their job is done.*

He suddenly knew what their job had been.

Twisting some more as his body followed the trajectory defined by his own muscle power and by gravity, he considered the possibilities with sudden, grim clarity. Hydra had killed Haberman and injured Anna Marie; no doubt, they would have tried to do similar damage to him, if he had been there. The infamous organization didn't do such things without reason. They wanted something, and it was fairly obvious what that something was.

Spidey finished his twist and flip. He felt gravity tug at him, and saw his moment of opportunity. He brought his left hand up and pressed the palm activator, hard. In response, the web-shooter on his wrist fired a long, looping line of viscous web fluid at the decorative façade of a bank building midway between him and the fleeing hovercraft. It caught and it held, condensing instantly into the super-strong polymer cord that he used as his main means of transport. Spider-Man gripped the newly formed web-line with both hands and pulled, hard. The web went taut, humming with tension as it instantly translated his double yank into sudden, emphatic momentum. He flew forward and up, toward his quarry.

Spider-Man was in luck. For some reason, the flying van wasn't moving very fast. Maybe the driver thought he was safe from pursuit, or maybe he was having trouble with the thermal updrafts that danced and whirled among the city's skyscrapers and made above-ground travel a tricky proposition. More than once in his career, Spidey had been buffeted in midswing by a sudden slipstream, or nearly forced from a building ledge perch. He was sure that such currents would give problems to a hovercraft as well, especially one as boxy and nonaerodynamic as the delivery van. He didn't really care what the reason was for the craft's slow progress, however; he just hoped his luck would hold for another moment.

He shot another web-line, this one from his right wrist. The last swing had closed a third of the distance between him and the fleeing Hydra agents and brought him perhaps another five stories above street level. The next one did the same.

One more, he thought. *Just let me get one more good*

swing, before someone thinks to look in the rearview mirror.

Obviously, Hydra was after the *Infinity Engine*. He thought about what Haberman had said. The craft's operating system was a single, organic whole. Anyone who had the calibration software had the whole system—and anyone who had the whole system had the *Infinity Engine*. Spider-Man shuddered to think what kind of damage Hydra could do with an unlimited source of free energy. Then the image of Haberman, frail and dying, rose in his mind again, and hot anger swept aside all apprehension.

This wasn't about the *Infinity Engine*. It was about Cosmo Haberman. It was about a weak old man, shot down like a dog.

Ahead of him, the pitch of the strange craft's engines changed, as the bizarre vehicle increased its speed and elevation. Further ahead, the skeleton of an incomplete high-rise hotel marked the city's skyline. Around it, other gaps and foundations yawned as the chase led him toward a construction site. *Fewer buildings, less turbulence*, Spider-Man thought. *Easier flying. They're getting away.*

No.

Shoot webbing, grip it, pull—Spider-Man repeated the triple action, working hard enough this time to make his shoulder joints ache even as his muscular body swung through the muggy air. The arc he cut this time was enough to do the job, but just barely. As his upward swing reached its peak, he released the web-line and fired another, at a new target. This time, the blob of web fluid struck the van's rear bumper. Spidey knew what would happen next. He gritted his teeth and hung on for dear life.

The flying delivery van bucked and rocked as Spider-

Man added his weight to its burden. Almost instantly, the strange craft accelerated, shooting upwards and forwards at almost twice its previous speed, even as it adjusted for the sudden change in weight.

Well, if they didn't know I was on their tail before, he thought, *they sure know now*. Hand over hand, he began drawing himself up and along the line towards his quarry.

The van accelerated some more. Now it darted and dodged between buildings and down side streets, changing course with dangerous speed and surprising suddenness. Behind it, at the end of his lashing web-line, Spider-Man did his best to hang on as he kept climbing. It was like a deadly game of crack-the-whip, played for very high stakes. They were already high enough that a fall would be fatal, even to someone with his enhanced strength and resilience, and the van's driver was doing his best to shake Spider-Man loose. Worse, each sudden course shift threatened to smash him against building walls that were at least as unyielding as the pavement below. Only his spider-sense and his superb muscle control let him avoid most of the potential impacts. Once, both failed him, and his head grazed a flagpole hard enough to make his eyes tear and his ears ring.

Spidey kept climbing. Wind shrieked in his ears and perspiration pasted his mask to his face. His whole world became a lone, long strand of webbing and the need to put one hand before the other along its gray length. Another thirty hand-lengths or so, and he would be close enough to leap and board the van.

Close enough to get his hands on the monsters who had killed a harmless old man.

His spider-sense buzzed. Ahead of him, the delivery van's rear doors swung open. Working hard to compensate for the herky-jerky nature of his ride and focus,

Spider-Man saw a man framed in the opening. The man was not dressed as a Hydra agent. Rather, he wore the familiar uniform of a delivery service. Like a window washer, he wore a safety strap to keep himself inside the van. Behind him, Spider-Man could see, not parcels, but banks of electronic equipment.

In the man's hands, he saw a pistol.

Maybe this wasn't such a great idea, Spidey thought.

The man fired the weapon once. A searing bolt of plasma split the air inches from Spider-Man's head. The miss was due as much to a last-second dodge by Spider-Man as it was to the turbulent trajectory of his path through the sky. He knew that he was a hard target.

He worked to be a harder one, twisting and dodging as he dragged himself along the web-line's taut length, closer and closer to the flying van.

The man assumed a marksman's stance, both hands wrapped around his pistol's grip. He fired another bolt, then a third. Spider-Man dodged them and kept climbing. The man yelled something; Spider-Man could not hear what he said and did not care. Ten feet, twelve, fifteen—almost close enough. He tensed himself for the final effort.

The man turned and faced the van's interior. He yelled something more. Spidey was close enough now that he could hear a word or two, even over the shrieking wind and the roaring hovercraft engine. "Yeah, yeah," the man said, apparently to a companion. Then he turned to face Spider-Man again.

Twenty feet, twenty-three, twenty-four—Spider Man was close enough now. He had to be close enough. He gripped the line in another double clutch, let the muscles of his arms and back tense and tighten, then yanked on the line as hard as he could.

His spider-sense screamed.

The man fired his energy pistol again—but not at Spider-Man this time. Rather, he shot the weapon at the blob of adhesive that anchored the web-line to the van's bumper.

Spider-Man watched with something very much like horror as the gray polymer burst into flames, boiling and melting as the blast seared it—and parting as the force of his own pull stretched the damaged stuff past its breaking point.

The man shouted something more, but Spider-Man could not hear him. Already, the pair was too far away for the words to carry. Ahead of him and above him, the van's rear doors slammed shut, and the disguised hovercraft raced upwards into the sky.

From nearly fifty stories below the plummeting Spider-Man, the dirty gray asphalt rushed up to greet him.

"Good. Return to base." Strucker spoke the words, then watched as Lyle Chesney's face faded from the view screen. He took pleasure in seeing it vanish; the blank slab of polished glass it left behind was more pleasing to his eyes than were the field agent's slack-jawed features.

"Garcia." Strucker said the name, and watched as his personal attendant did his best to come to attention.

"Yes, Baron!" As with Chesney, Strucker often considered the slovenly, heavyset Garcia a disgrace to his Hydra uniform. Now, for example, the fool had evidently managed to hurt himself; one of his hands wore a bandage instead of a standard-issue green glove. Unlike Chesney, however, Garcia had skills that went well beyond basic competence, including a certain basic administrative efficiency that Strucker found useful. For as long as he continued to please Strucker, the pudgy man would continue to live.

"Field Operative Chesney is about to provide us with the *Infinity Engine*'s access codes. Before that happens, I need a context in which to use them. Meet with the Intelligence and Science divisions, and prepare for me a list of appropriate strategic targets that fall within the range of Stark's space station."

"Yes, Baron!" Garcia saluted, bringing his bandaged hand up in a sharp angle. "Hail Hydra!" He headed for the office door without waiting for Strucker's salute. He was moving fast, like a man who knew full well the consequences of moving slowly.

Strucker returned his attention to reams of reports and analyses. Before Chesney's call, he had been reviewing a backlog of detailed notes on past campaigns that had failed. Hydra had made mistakes in the past; he would brook no further ones in the future.

Backed by the power of the *Infinity Engine*, his will would reign supreme.

Spider-Man fell. Wind shrieked in his ears and tugged at the fabric of his costume as he plummeted through the dirty, muggy air. He fell fast and he fell hard, tumbling and twisting as he fell into gravity's eager embrace. For a split second, he glimpsed the still-accelerating hovercraft as it vanished in the distance, but he forced all consideration of that tantalizing image from his mind.

Hydra will have to wait, he thought grimly. *I've got more pressing matters to deal with.*

His spider-sense still screamed as he fell, a useless warning of imminent danger of which he was only too well aware. With a conscious effort, he pushed the worst of the signals aside and tried to think. Still, intermittent warning signals flashed through his mind like angry lightning as he considered his options.

They weren't many, and they weren't good. He couldn't catch himself with his web; anchoring his line to a building would simply change his angle of descent, slamming him into a vertical surface instead of to the ground's horizontal one. Two lines anchored to opposing walls would balance each other—but they wouldn't do him any more good than a single one. At the rate he was falling, such a cold stop would probably tear his arms out of their sockets. He was too high and falling too fast to weave any kind of a safety net or cushion, and not high enough to create and use a parachute, as he had on some other occasions.

As Spider-Man's thoughts raced madly, his body twisted and turned in midair, moving almost of its own volition into a horizontal orientation. He spread his arms and his legs wide. Presenting the greatest possible surface area to the shrieking wind meant that his rate of acceleration, if not his actual descent, slowed, buying him a few more precious seconds. That was what parachutists did, he knew, delaying as long as possible the moment when they had to pull their rip cords. Unfortunately, Spider-Man was no parachutist.

Just now, however, he was certainly a skydiver.

Essentially, what confronted him at the moment was an elaborate physics problem, more complex and more demanding than any written exam—and with more dreadful consequences for failure. He was falling. He had to shed the energy of his descent and slow himself before he stopped, or he was a dead man. An old joke drifted, unbidden, to the surface of his mind: *It's not the fall, it's the sudden stop at the bottom.*

Spider-Man angled himself into the rushing wind. He tilted his hands like an airplane's wing flaps, holding them rigid against the wall of air. The trajectory of his fall changed from a straight perpendicular to a sloping angle. The hovercraft's track had doubled back on itself, so that the construction site lay directly ahead once more. If not otherwise interrupted, his new trajectory would end somewhere inside the incomplete building. He had seen his only chance. It wasn't much of one, but with luck, it would be enough.

It had to be enough.

Large sections of the high-rise were incomplete. The place was little more than a steel frame at its uppermost levels. Just now, the building was essentially a structure of space rather than one of substance, an aggregation of huge openings delineated and defined by an elaborate steel lattice.

Still moving at a terrific rate of speed, Spider-Man shot through a gap in what would one day be the east wall of an office on the building's twenty-third floor. He passed though it at a descending forty-degree angle, twisting and turning to avoid contact with the steel support members. His fingers found the activator buttons in his palms, and webbing spat from both wrists. The two strands found and clung to a single horizontal beam as Spider-Man passed beneath it. The webbing caught and hardened instantly, then drew him up short.

Spidey gripped the twin lines and grunted in pain as his downward, angled momentum abruptly translated itself into a closed circle, with its radius defined by the two lengths of webbing. Once, twice, three times he let inertia carry him around the girder, in a spiraling track that grew tighter as his webbing wound itself onto the steel beam. The initial shock of transition slowed him some, and wind resistance slowed him more, but not enough. Half a second before he could have slammed into the steel axis of his impromptu Ferris wheel, Spider-Man released the two lines and let himself be thrown further into the building's incomplete interior. He was still moving fast—but not as fast as he had been moving moments before.

Again and again, he executed the maneuver. He did it more times than he could count, orbiting the building's metal bones in slower and slower spirals, twisting and turning and angling himself to avoid slamming into any of the beams. He had no time to think about what he was doing, only enough to do it. Because he had no other choice, he let himself be guided by instinct and spider-sense rather than by any conscious decision-making process. His path carried further into the metal cage that was the future building's interior. The place's lower levels were more finished than the upper ones, so he shot through the increasingly narrow gaps between interior support members, and had to avoid the occasional floor slab. Twice, his transit carried him near enclosed areas, apparently construction shacks for the building crew; twice, he avoided them at the absolute last instant. The rollicking monkey-bar ride carried him back and forth as well as down, so that his course followed a zigzag trajectory into and out of the structure's interior—but also downward.

Always downward.

The spiraling gyrations slowed as he expended more and more of his momentum. Each dodging maneuver became less elaborate than the last, each successive gap, though narrower, became an easier target because he was moving more slowly. Finally, the moment came when he had shed enough energy to dispense with spinning webs and could use his hands instead to slow his progress. For the last few orbits, he grabbed posts and pipes and cables, working to slow his descent more and more. A final somersault and a double flip, and he came to a breathless halt inside an empty, unfinished office suite on the building's ground floor.

The poured concrete slab floor felt feather-soft as Spider-Man slumped dizzy and motionless on it. His breath came in panting gasps and his pulse pounded in his ears while he waited for the world to quit spinning around him. Slowly, near-panic gave way to conscious consideration once more.

Never again, Spidey thought. *I never, ever want to do that again.*

Of course, it beat the alternative by a country mile.

Deep beneath the main building of the Stark Enterprises complex, in Tony Stark's private laboratory, a buzzer sounded. Seals parted with a hissing sound, and one bay of the fabricator unit slid open, to reveal a red-and-gold helmet, approximately twice the size of the current version of Iron Man's mask. Faint wisps of chemical vapor vanished into the fabricator's ventilator hood while the helmet's thin layer of refractory glaze hardened and fused. The buzzer sounded again as that process completed itself, a different tone this time, then the signal fell silent.

Tony barely noticed. He was seated at a nearby workbench, and wore protective goggles and thick insulating gloves. Before him, a miniature plasma cannon assembly, half-completed, lay forgotten on the bench's surface. A half-dozen specialized tools and test probes were arrayed around it, equally forgotten. Ordinarily, Tony's private work in the armory lab held his complete attention. It was here that he designed and endlessly refined the suits of armor that he wore as Iron Man. It was complex work that he usually found completely absorbing.

Not today. Several thousand miles above Tony, the *Ad Astra* and the *Infinity Engine* flew together silently through the void; several feet before his face, a bank of video monitors told their story. Tony stared at the monitors, almost hypnotized by the data and images they displayed. Later today, the craft would return to Earth and its sensors would become available for hands-on examination. For now, Tony contented himself with a remote view.

It had been a very successful week of test runs and adjustments, far more successful than Tony had dared hope. Onboard the *Engine*, Nakahara and Powell had put the system's energy taps through their paces, drawing power from the quantum field with seventy-three percent efficiency—nearly ten percent greater than Tony had anticipated, and many times more efficient than the most effective conventional power generation systems. Better still, it was "clean" energy, in a new sense of the word, pure and focused and falling entirely within the preselected wavelength ranges. The calibrated transducer system that Cosmo Haberman had labored over for so very long was a triumph of software engineering, and each revision that the physicist provided set new benchmarks of excellence. Tony watched as new readings danced across one screen, and made a mental note to congratulate the older man in person.

He smiled. Buying Odyssey Designs had been a good decision. He had missed working with Haberman, and the old grouch had adjusted with almost unbelievable speed to the *Infinity Engine* project. The massive stroke that the older man had suffered earlier in the year had barely taken the edge off of his remarkable intellect. Tony hoped that the *Engine* would prove to be just the first in a new series of collaborations with the genius who had given so much to Stark Enterprises in years gone by.

"Excuse me, Tony." A perfectly modulated, vaguely masculine voice interrupted his thought. It was HOMER, the Heuristically Operative Matrix Emulation Rostrum, the artificial intelligence system that resided in Stark Enterprises' supercomputer mainframe. HOMER had many functions; not the least of them was serving as Tony's personal lab assistant. "The new head piece assembly is ready now," HOMER said. "It has been ready for precisely three minutes and seventeen seconds."

"Thank you, HOMER," Tony replied. He pushed his chair back and stepped over to the fabricator port. "It's easy to get distracted around here."

"I quite understand," HOMER said, but Tony hoped he didn't. HOMER's other responsibilities included overseeing most of Stark Enterprises' manufacturing and prototyping facilities, and monitoring the experiments that went on, constantly, in the various labs and test beds. Tony didn't like to think what might happen if HOMER's personality ever evolved enough to allow him to become derelict in those duties.

Tony lifted the head piece assembly from the fabricator's open bay. Cool to the touch, it had a satisfying heft that he found reassuring. Much of that weight came from heavy plate armor and compressed-metal radiation shields that encased the unit's cybernetic pickups and sensory relay circuits. This particular helmet was intended for a new version of his outer-space armor, one of the many customized Iron Man suits that Tony had built to serve various purposes. This newest one embodied some promising new control interfaces suggested by Robert Powell's work.

Some ten meters from the main fabricator unit, the rest of the red-and-gold suit of armor waited for its head. Tony stepped over to it, and placed the helmet on the articulated test dummy's head. The new component snapped into place easily.

"Integrity?" Tony asked the question without addressing it; he knew who would reply.

"One hundred percent, Tony. All seals are functional, to thirty atmospheres." HOMER operated the test dummy, as he operated so many other pieces of lab apparatus. Later, if he wanted, Tony could get detailed hard-copy printouts of the specific data, but for now, HOMER's assurances sufficed.

"What about rad levels?"

"I've run the emulator twice," HOMER said. "The collapsed metal shields are holding up nicely—interior background count is less than half that of sea level."

Tony smiled tightly. That was one of the big problems with space travel. Beyond the protective layers of Earth's atmosphere, the levels of certain exotic radiation types could reach disturbing levels. Other, earlier space explorers—Reed Richards among them—had found that out the hard way. The problem before him now was to find some way to screen out the radiation without sacrificing Iron Man's mobility, and the new shields seemed to be the solution. They were dense enough to do the job, and compact enough that the armor could remain relatively maneuverable.

He gazed at the stocky suit before him. It stared back at him with empty eyes. Larger than his original Iron Man armor, this latest version of the space exploration model wasn't just an armored suit; it was a miniature space ship in humanoid form. Its legs were the size of tree trunks, and they hid tanks of fuel and oxidants sufficient to launch the whole thing into orbit.

Tony had crafted and worn many suits of armor over the years, since that unpleasant afternoon in Southeast Asia when he had donned the very first version. Some of them had been general-purpose combat models; others had been specialized units with assigned goals. This

new prototype fell into the latter category. He had prepared other, similar space suits, but this was the first one
to include the new layers of protective shielding, as well
as the new control interfaces; he was eager to test both.

"Tony." There was something different in HO-
MER's voice, some faint quality that suggested emotion.
"I have Ms. Cabe on line. She says that she must speak
with you."

Tony frowned. He had left instructions that he was
not to be disturbed when in his private lab, but HOMER
and Bethany both knew when to break that rule. "Put
her on, HOMER."

"Tony? This is Bethany." His security chief's voice,
crisp and businesslike, hung in the lab's cool air. "I have
bad news."

"What is it, Beth?"

"Doctor Haberman is dead, Tony. We just had a call
from the city."

Dead? Cosmo is dead? Beth's words struck him like
hammer blows, and the thought thundered through Tony's brain. He had spoken to the older man mere hours
before, a spirited discussion of regression values and test
readings that had reminded him of his many years working at Haberman's side. He realized with sorrow that his
last discussion with the scientist had been what many
would term an argument.

"What happened, Bethany?" Tony asked the question in a soft voice. "Another stroke?"

"No. It was murder. We aren't sure exactly what happened yet. Ms. Sanchez was unconscious for most of it,
and now that she's awake, she's close to hysterical.
She's shaken up, but intact. Someone broke in and shot
Haberman. It looks like a professional smash and grab."

"God." With great effort, Tony bundled up his grief
and sorrow, and set them aside. There would be time to

mourn later; for now, he would have to satisfy himself with trying for justice. "What were they after?"

"We don't know that either, but it's a safe guess they wanted the *Engine*'s software. That was all he was working on." Bethany paused. "Tony," she said. "I'm sorry. I know you two were close."

Tony stepped away from the test dummy and back to his workbench, where the video monitors still flashed their messages. "Yes," he said, but he was speaking only to let Bethany know he had heard her. "We knew each other for a very long time." He thought for a moment, then continued. "What about Parker?"

"The lab assistant? What about him?"

"You didn't mention him. Is he okay?" Tony hoped so. He had given the young man the job as a favor, in part because Parker reminded him of himself. Now he hoped that his casual gesture had not laid the groundwork for tragedy.

"As far as we know. He wasn't there when the police arrived—but we don't even know if he was working today. I'll follow up and find out what happened to him."

"You do that, Bethany. Keep me posted on how things develop."

"I will."

A movement on one screen caught his eye. The *Engine*'s main output level suddenly dropped dramatically, plunging to zero in an instant. Tony stared at the screen, startled, as other values followed suit. One by one, environmental readings, background counts, navigational data, communications and all the rest dwindled and went blank.

What the hell was happening up there?

"Excuse me, Tony." That was HOMER again. "Something is wrong with the *Infinity Engine*'s telemetry downlink. I have one hundred percent failure on all incoming readings. I'm shifting to secondaries now."

Bethany, still online, spoke. "I guess that tells us what they wanted from Haberman."

And what they got, Tony thought grimly. He wondered who had done the job. The *Infinity Engine*'s operating system was almost unimaginably complex; anyone who was able to override and subvert it no doubt had considerable assets and expertise.

"No success, Tony. One hundred percent failure on the secondary monitors, as well. The control interface has been completely overridden." HOMER paused briefly, apparently accessing some other portion of his complex artificial personality. "There is some distress in the command center. The personnel there request your immediate presence. They are quite strident in that request."

Tony stared at the newly completed suit of armor. "Overall systems report on the new suit, HOMER," he said. "Now."

"One hundred percent, Tony. The software has been loaded, and all systems check."

"Still there, Bethany?" He asked the question, knowing the answer.

"Yes."

"See to the guys in Mission Control. Call the feds, too. Try to keep a lid on things for me."

"What about you?" Bethany's voice held a familiar note of annoyed concern. Tony realized that she knew the answer to her question, too—she had known him too well for too many years.

"I'm sending Iron Man up," he said, suddenly calm. He knew what he had to do now. He removed his gloves and eye protectors. "I'll report back as soon as I can."

There were some things a man had to do for himself.

*   *   *

Neither Abner Sinclair nor Erasmus Krelm knew what time or day it was when the security robot came for them. Both men knew only that they had already spent far too long in the dungeons of Castle Doom. Neither had any way to know the precise span of time; deep underground, isolated in Spartan, windowless cells, it had been easy for them to lose track. During their imprisonment, they had discussed their likely fates many times. Sinclair was of the belief, or perhaps the hope, that their captor had forgotten about them. He thought that they would languish in their cells forever. Krelm, however, was certain that Latveria's ruler had some special, unpleasant fate in store for them, and that their day of execution would surely come.

As the seven-foot tall purple security robot opened their cell doors, both men began to suspect that Krelm's theory was about to prove correct.

The robot ignored their questions and pleas. It bathed and dressed the two men with silent efficiency, clothing them once again in the uniforms that they had worn when captured. In minutes, Sinclair wore the green robes of Hydra and Krelm was dressed in the yellow jumpsuit of A.I.M. All they lacked were their respective masks. The two men had been members of a team composed of agents from both organizations assigned to raid Castle Doom's secrets. Sinclair and Krelm's designated role had been to wait in the wilderness for a rendezvous with members of the assault squad, and then to escort them to safety beyond Latveria's borders.

That rendezvous never came, and neither did safety. True to their duties, Sinclair and Krelm had waited long hours past their deadline, to no avail. In the last pale minutes just before dawn, Doom's mechanical security forces had captured the two agents and imprisoned them in Doom's dungeons. They had languished there ever since.

Until now.

The two men exchanged fearful glances as an elevator lifted them and the robot from the dungeon's depths to the castle's higher levels. They had dreaded this moment since their initial capture, wondering when they would join their fellow operatives in death—or worse. The wrath of Doctor Doom was legendary, and the whispered tales of his vengeance were many, varied, and unpleasant. The two men saw no reason to expect mercy at his iron hand. The stress of the situation had even allowed them to forge something of a friendship, despite the traditional rivalry of their organizations.

The elevator doors opened. Not wanting to, but having no other real choice, Sinclair and Krelm stepped out of it. Their robot escort kept pace with them as they walked into a lavishly appointed receiving room. Tapestries and lush carpets made a stark contrast with the grim confines of their cells. A detailed mural decorated the room's vaulted ceiling. Paintings and ornaments punctuated the walls, and several marble sculptures stood on small pedestals. The only piece of furniture was a single massive, ornate chair, set in the room's precise center. A man sat in it now. He wore gray steel armor with a flowing green broadcloth tunic and hood. Intense blue eyes ringed with puckered scar tissue stared out from behind a grim, death's-head mask.

The man in the chair was Doctor Doom.

The security robot placed its heavy steel hands on Sinclair and Krelm's shoulders, forcing the two men to drop to their knees before the armored monarch. The prompt was unnecessary; something about Doom, even seated, made both men want to kneel, to drop their heads and avert their faces from the ruler's steady gaze.

Doom spoke, without preamble or salutation. "You two have enjoyed the hospitality of Castle Doom for some weeks now," he said. His voice was a resonant bass that echoed faintly in the small room. "Latveria has fed and sheltered you and asked nothing in return. Now the time has come for you to repay my courtesy."

Neither Sinclair or Krelm said anything. There seemed to be no reply they could make.

"You will perform a task for me," Doom said. "It is a simple thing, the work of minutes. Complete it, and your debts will be paid, your sins against me expunged. I will allow you both to leave the castle and find lives in my nation, in my service."

Sinclair spoke. "We have to stay here? In Latveria?"

Doom ignored him, and continued. "If either of you refuses to do my will, or if either fails me, both will die."

Krelm looked up and asked, "What do you want us to do?"

Doom's masked face turned some microscopic percentage of a degree of arc in Krelm's direction. His stormy eyes found the captive A.I.M. agent's frightened ones. "The organizations that you represent have caused me some small inconveniences in recent times," Doom said. "Your deceased compatriots invaded my home and disrupted my people. Strucker and A.I.M.'s vaunted 'Scientist Supreme' must pay for that effrontery. You will be my instruments of revenge against them."

"But we weren't working for them on that," Sinclair said, haltingly. "We were working for someone else. Our master was Burton Hildebrandt."

This time, Doom took notice of his words. "A distinction without meaning," the monarch said. "Hildebrandt was a renegade, but it was Hydra and A.I.M. that moved against me, and so it is Hydra and A.I.M. that will pay." He paused. "Hildebrandt has paid, too, with a very dear coin of his own."

Sinclair and Krelm didn't like the sound of that.

In response to some unspoken command, another robot entered the room. It carried two compact pieces of equipment that Sinclair and Krelm recognized immediately. The twin devices were miniature satellite uplink communicators, issued to the agents by Hydra and A.I.M. before their ill-fated mission. Doom's security robots had confiscated the units from them upon capture. "Each of you will send a message for me to your respective organizations," Doom said. "You will speak the words I give you to speak, and no others. Afterwards, I will release you." He continued his instructions in a calm, matter-of-fact voice that brooked no further interruption.

Sinclair and Krelm glanced at each other nervously. Doom had not waited for any agreements or objections, but that was not surprising.

After all, they had very little choice in the matter.

— CHAPTER 6 —

The attack came when Iron Man was still some ten or twelve seconds below the lowest reaches of the stratosphere. Something huge and gray and vaguely humanoid hurtled at him through the cold air, moving faster than anything its size and shape had a right to move. Tony Stark had only a split second of visual display before the thing smashed into Iron Man's metal form.

The impact made Iron Man tumble and roll through the thin air of the upper reaches, his upward momentum deflected sideways and down. Immediately, the suit's automated correction system kicked in firing steering jets and shifting the vanes in the main boot thrusters to control and impose a new trajectory on his tumbling form. Tony let the suit worry about keeping itself aloft; he had other things to concern him.

He caught a glimpse of his assailant as it spun and turned for another attack. It was a robot, maybe three meters tall, crafted of gray steel plates that mimicked the contours of human musculature. Metal spikes studded its arms and legs, and emotionless optic sensors stared out at him from a vaguely skull-like face. Tony recognized it instantly, even before Iron Man's inboard threat assessment system screamed a warning.

It was a Dreadnought.

Criminal scientists had developed the Dreadnoughts as robot stormtroopers, mechanical commandos in the campaigns of Hydra, the world's most feared terrorist cartel. Hydra, in turn, had sold the robot's design and schematics to the Maggia and a few other clandestine organizations. Several had fielded their own, customized versions. For the moment, however, Tony set aside the issue of who owned this particular robot.

There were more pressing issues at hand.

Iron Man's gloves came up as the robot raced toward him again. The repulsor ray projectors set in each gauntlet irised open and spat at the onrushing Dreadnought. High-energy plasma bolts splashed against the thing's gray skin, searing its armor without penetrating it. The force of the double blast was enough to slow the thing but not stop it. It kept coming, driven forward by a twin jet assembly mounted on its back, a new addition to the robot's basic design.

In response to Iron Man's blasts, the Dreadnought raised its own hands, revealing fingertip nozzles that Tony knew were linked to chemical tanks somewhere in its interior. Now a pressurized mixture of hydrazine and liquid oxygen spewed forth from them, erupting in a gout of fire that suddenly seemed to be everywhere. There was no time to dodge the incandescent blasts. In effect, the robot had turned its hands into flamethrowers, and turned Iron Man's world into flame.

Not good, Tony thought. *Not good at all*. He watched the suit's outside temperature gauge climb steadily as the fiery onslaught continued. He knew from experience that the Dreadnought's blasts could vaporize steel, if given enough time to do their work.

He couldn't let them have that time. There were lives depending on him, three men and a woman trapped in orbit above. He realized now that the telemetry blackout signaled no accident, no equipment failure or natural mishap. It was enemy action, plain and simple.

Tony thought he knew who the enemy was.

The temperature readout kept climbing, but its rate of ascent slowed as the armor's thermocouple system activated itself. The thermocouple converted a substantial percentage of the fire's heat energy to electricity and stored it, creating a net cooling effect. This was only a stopgap measure, however; inevitably, the system would overload and shut down, and Iron Man would be back where he started, seconds away from meltdown. The situation was bad, and it could get much, much worse.

This particular suit of armor wasn't a combat unit. He had designed it for space exploration and rescue and retained only a basic menu of offensive and defensive systems. Everything else had been stripped out to make more room for fuel supplies, guidance computers, and radiation shielding. The oversized suit's bulk and specialized systems made it difficult to maneuver quickly, and the unexpected, brutal nature of this battle didn't make things any easier.

Worse, this Dreadnought was some kind of deluxe model, apparently customized for this battle. For some reason, it was invisible to the armor's proximity detection systems, so that Tony had to rely on visual contact. It was also bigger than the versions Tony had encountered before, though built along the same lines, and it had the added capability of flight. The thing probably had other new capabilities, as well.

Fire gave way to thunder as the robot shut down its flamethrowers and drove a spike-studded fist into Iron Man's face. The hero's head rocked back, then forward as the armor's automated compensation servomotors rode with the force. The helmet's face plate flexed and bent, but held. The robot's fist pulled back and smashed at him again. This time, Iron Man's head moved aside and dodged the blow, but just barely. That was one thing that hadn't changed; this Dreadnought's personality emulator still mimicked the fighting techniques of a boxer, just like the original versions did.

Two could play that game. Tony brought Iron Man's hands together, then swung them in a smashing uppercut. The double blow caught the Dreadnought just below its chin, but barely fazed the robot. *They're building them better these days*, Tony thought. *Last time around, that would have taken the thing's head off.*

The Dreadnought's mouth opened. Tony knew what that meant, and moved to compensate. A single mental command cut the fuel flow to Iron Man's boot thrusters, and the armored figure dropped down and away as the Dreadnought vomited liquid Freon gas at him. He managed to avoid the worst of the spray, but not all of it. The freezing stuff splashed against his still-superheated armor's skin. It boiled away instantly, but left a spider-web pattern of microscopic fractures as its legacy. Below Tony's left eye, a miniaturized display flashed a warning. The suit's structural integrity was severely compromised, to an estimated seventy percent. Silently, Tony wished he were using a different suit of armor. This one couldn't take much more punishment. Desperately, he considered his options.

They weren't many. The Dreadnought was bigger and faster than Iron Man—at least, bigger and faster than this particular version of Iron Man. It was more maneuverable, too; Tony Stark had built the space exploration armor for brute thrust, and not for midair combat. The Dreadnought's jet pack—

Jet pack. Tony considered the implications. His Iron Man armor was relatively self-contained, using a fuel and oxygen mix to drive its rockets. The Dreadnought's jet, however, was an air breather; it needed to take in oxygen in order to work. Tony wondered what its operation ceiling might be, how high an altitude the thing could reach before shutting down. Even the most effective supercharger wouldn't work in the upper stratosphere. There just wasn't enough air there to do the job.

The robot approached again. Tony reached out with Iron Man's hands and clamped them onto the Dreadnought's neck assembly. Red steel fingers dug deep into the gray metal, locking in place. The robot did not seem to care as its skin split and tore under the pressure. Iron Man's boot jets flared, driving the two metal forms further upward. Locked together, they rocketed into the stratosphere. *If I can take out the thing's propulsion system*, Tony thought, *I've got a chance to beat it.*

The Dreadnought struggled in Iron Man's grip, trying to tear itself free. For a moment, Tony thought it would use the flamethrowers again, but that didn't happen. *Maybe it's out of gas.*

Then the robot tried something else. Its left hand came up, wrapped massive fingers around Iron Man's right wrist, then gripped and squeezed hard enough to crush through the armored glove. Warning signals rang in Tony's ears as the Dreadnought exerted more pressure. *The suit can't take much more of this.* Grimly, he resolved to continue the desperate gambit, at least for the moment. It was his only chance. If he could get the Dreadnought high enough, its propulsion systems would shut down, making the thing easy pickings even for this noncombat suit of armor.

Red metal split and flaked, then peeled back as the Dreadnought pushed upwards. Iron Man's servomotors squealed in protest as they tried to resist the inexorable pressure—tried and failed. The fingers of Iron Man's right hand came free from the Dreadnought's neck as his arm moved up and bent backwards.

Too strong, Tony thought. *Whoever built this one did a good job.*

The pressure continued. Iron Man released his left hand now, and clawed at the Dreadnought's fingers, but to no avail. The robot kept forcing Iron Man's right arm backwards, in a twisted arc that ignored the natural limitations of the human skeleton.

Suddenly, the robot's jet-pack hesitated, gulping for oxygen and finding none in the rarefied air. It shuddered, flamed one last time, then failed. As it did, the robot used its free arm to clutch at Iron Man, reinforcing the grim embrace that held the two together. A moment before, the robot had sought release; now it held on, relying on the armor's rockets for flight. Iron Man's thrusters moaned in the thin air and drew upon internal oxygen supplies as the load increased. Tony noticed, but he didn't care. It didn't matter anymore. Nothing mattered except breaking the thing's grip, before the thing's grip broke Iron Man.

Iron Man's knee came up, driven by exoskeletal muscles and by the thrust of a boot jet. The knee slammed into the Dreadnought's pelvic region, rocking the robot but not damaging it, or dislodging the steel fingers that now dug even more deeply into Iron Man's wrist. His right arm bent into a tighter arc, and the metal of the joint turned white with strain.

Iron Man brought his free hand up and pressed it against the robot's optic receptors. Desperately, he fired a blast of repulsor rays directly into one artificial eye. His reward was an explosion, as the Dreadnought's head disintegrated into ragged fragments. The robot didn't even seem to notice.

Blast, Tony thought. *The main processor wasn't in the head.* There had been no reason to assume that it would be, other than simple human prejudice. It was probably inside the heavily armored thorax segment—and Tony already knew that the thing's chest armor was invulnerable to his available repulsor.

The pressure continued to build as the robot pressed harder. Metal found its limits, then exceeded them. Steel laminates and titanium alloys wrenched and tore, and triple-reinforced shoulder joints screamed in protest, then parted.

Tony screamed too, as Iron Man's right arm tore loose from his body.

Still holding the detached limb by the wrist, the Dreadnought swung its grisly prize like a flail, smashing it down on Iron Man's head again and again. By now, the surrounding air was too thin to carry much sound, but Tony's helmet receptors caught the ringing impact of steel against steel and relayed it to his ears. Chips of sundered metal tore loose and fell through the air, glinting like diamonds in the bright sunlight.

Distress signals shrieked in Tony's ears and system alerts flashed as he brought his remaining arm up again and pressed the palm repulsor flat against the twisted metal where the robot's head had been. *This is it*, he thought. *All or nothing.*

The repulsor flared, spitting high-energy plasma into the Dreadnought's insides. Apparently, they were more vulnerable than its exterior; certainly the beam found something that it could destroy—something important, evidently.

With a spasmodic lurch, the Dreadnought released Iron Man and fell. It thrashed and tumbled as it fell, spinning end over end into the distance below, taking Iron Man's arm with it. Tony watched it fall, ignoring the damage alerts that his armor shrieked at him. He had no time for them now. The two combatants had moved upward during the battle, higher and higher into the stratosphere. Now as the robot fell, it passed again through heavier, denser layers of air, relatively rich in oxygen. If its jet-pack was still functional, if any of its computers still worked, there was still a chance it could recover.

Tony couldn't let that happen.

Iron Man dropped down a few hundred feet, keeping pace with the falling Dreadnought but also keeping a safe distance from it. Image enhancing systems in his helmet tracked the damaged robot, assessing it carefully. The thing thrashed and writhed as it fell, either in response to false control signals from its ravaged interior, or in some futile attempt to save itself. The turbines, however, remained dark and lifeless, even as the two humanoid figures dropped into the troposphere and found an abundance of available oxygen. Tony sighed in relief. Some of the robot's motor control systems might work, but its flight unit did not. The threat was over.

He was monitoring the jet-pack so closely that he almost did not notice what happened next. The robot's empty hand clawed the shrieking air, as if reaching once more for Iron Man. For an instant, he thought that the flamethrowers would roar to life again, but they did not. Instead, the Dreadnought's fist closed and clenched, in a gesture of menace that seemed futile but was not. The ten metal spikes studding the robot's fingers tore loose and threw themselves at Iron Man.

The thing's not dead yet, Tony thought, cursing. The Dreadnought's capabilities included firing its spikes with bullet-like force. Ordinarily, they wouldn't be much of a threat to Iron Man, but this particular armor was in bad shape. The earlier combination of heat and cold had made its outer casing brittle and weak. That was why the Dreadnought had been able to tear off the arm. If the slugs hurtling towards Iron Man now connected, if they contained any kind of explosive charge—

He sent more fuel to the boot thrusters, and tried to commence evasive actions, but the attempt was too little and too late. The outer space armor wasn't very maneu-

verable in the best of times, and having an arm torn off
didn't help matters much.

The first of the ten spikes caught him in the chest,
digging deep into his weakened armor before exploding.
Six of the remaining nine whistled past, but the last three
found their targets.

Some twenty thousand feet above the Earth's surface,
and some two hundred feet above the plummeting foe
who still clutched his severed arm, Iron Man exploded
in a cloud of shrapnel.

When the attack came, Kellye Nakahara was in the *Ad
Astra's* main lab complex taking inventory of the space
station's automated testing equipment. When an attack
by an A.I.M. technovirus had rendered the station un-
inhabitable, Stark's people had been forced to evacuate
and mothball the place. But they had left behind an
amazing array of very expensive hardware, surrendering
it to the tender mercies of the technovirus. One of her
duties on this trip was to run systems checks on the
reclaimed equipment and assess what could be salvaged.
There wasn't much; A.I.M.'s biological weapon had
done its work well, infecting and destroying most of the
lab's control processors. The corrective measures taken
by the people from Damage Control had eliminated the
cause, but not its effects. Most of the forcibly retired
hardware was worthless junk.

Now taking inventory, she was surprised to realize
how much of it would have needed replacing, anyway,
thanks to the passage of time. State of the art upon installation, much of the stuff was hopelessly obsolete
now. *Funny how big a difference a few years can make*,
she thought, not for the first time. Recommissioning the
Ad Astra would be a very costly process; replacing the

quark enumerators alone would run well into the millions of dollars.

A vibration rumbled though the steel deck plates beneath her feet. At first, she thought that Ramos had fired the space station's steering rockets again; that was one of his duties, to make the series of course corrections that would lift the *Ad Astra* to a slightly higher orbit and make the *Infinity Engine*'s operations that much more efficient. After a moment, however, the rumbling sensation stopped, and she knew that something else had happened. A rocket burn, even a controlled one, would have continued for long minutes. Besides, this had felt sharp and abrupt, as if something massive had struck the space station.

A meteor? Unlikely, she knew, since large ones were actually quite rare. Besides, no alarm had sounded. Still—

Kellye raised her on-board communicator to her lips and punched the button that would connect her to the control center. "Johnny?" she asked. "What's going on up there?"

There was no answer, only a whisper of static.

Kellye shrugged, and pushed another button. This time, she was rewarded with a laconic drawl from the *Infinity Engine*'s test module.

"Powell here."

"Bobby!" She grinned. He hated it when she called him that. A week alone with her fellow crew members had taught her most of the three men's quirks. "What's going on? Did we hit a pothole?"

"I dunno, but I felt it, too. I think it shook one of my fillings loose." He paused. "It felt like a botched docking, but we're not scheduled for visitors."

"Have you talked to Johnny?"

"Nope, not since the last burn. He said something

about checking the linkages in the receiving bay, though. Why?''

Kellye shrugged again. There was no point in paging Ramos if he was in the receiving bay; since it served as the station's docking area, it was heavily shielded and insulated, and beyond the reach of her portable communicator. ''Just curious,'' she said. ''I guess if it were something serious, we'd know by now.''

''It is serious.''

It took Kellye a second to realize the new voice hadn't come from her communicator, but from somewhere behind her. She spun around in time to see a uniformed man step in though the open hatch, his gloved fingers wrapped around the butt of an odd-looking pistol. She had never seen him before.

She had seen the uniform, however. The man wore a green tunic and trousers, with boots and gloves and a mask of similar colors. Strips of yellow trim came over his shoulders and down the front of his shirt, approximating the shape of the letter ''H.''

''Who are you?'' The question burst from her lips, but she knew the answer. She simply could not believe it.

''As far as you're concerned, lady, I'm Hydra.'' The masked agent grinned. ''And, as of right now, you're property.''

The woman known as Number One had given up much in the climb to her present rank as A.I.M.'s Scientist Supreme. By hook and by crook, she had made her way to the top. She had done it by forging alliances and then breaking them; by making crucial discoveries and stealing credit for those made by others; and by finding weaknesses in others and exploiting them ruthlessly. The cutthroat corporate culture within A.I.M. had demanded such tactics, and she had employed them willingly. Her family and friends, her sex, and her very identity—all had been sacrificed on the altar of her career. Now, as a subordinate's report faded in her ears, she had to wonder if the prize had been worth the price.

Hydra had stolen the *Infinity Engine*. That much was obvious, even based on the sketchy information at hand. Hydra agents had slain a key programmer, and less than an hour later, the experimental craft's telemetry signals had vanished. Moreover, a Dreadnought robot had apparently destroyed Iron Man while the armored super hero was *en route* to the orbiting craft, although Number One was not entirely willing to credit that report. She knew that Strucker hated Tony Stark and Iron Man both with a passion; the theft of the inventor's greatest accomplishment and the simultaneous death of his champion had to be linked. It was impossible not to associate the two events with one another, and to further connect both of them with Hydra.

She wanted to sigh, but did not allow herself to do so. She did not dare. Surrounding her, in ring after concentric ring of desks and workbenches, sat the assembled upper ranks of A.I.M. Though all labored silently at their assigned endeavors, she knew that each also listened carefully for any sign of weakness—of humanity—on their leader's part. She knew this from experience; there had been a day when she sat where they sat, and waited like them for a moment of weakness, for the opportunity to create an opening and take it. She did not want to give them that chance.

So. Hydra had the *Infinity Engine*. That was unfortunate. It was a prize her own organization had coveted, but had been unable to steal. It had been a bad year for A.I.M. Two major initiatives, the energy chip and the orbiting research center, had been destroyed, in part due to the efforts of Iron Man and some other super heroes. Worse, an attempt to re-create one of A.I.M.'s greatest achievements, Modok, had ended in utter disaster. The new Mental Organism Designed Only for Killing had rebelled and led a small army of synthetic life forms against A.I.M., against humanity in general, and against his creators in particular. In the ensuing disarray, another small group of agents had seceded from A.I.M. and entered into a partnership with renegade Hydra agents that had also ultimately failed, costing the parent organization many assets and much expertise in the process. Number One had hoped to delay further campaigns for at least a few months until she could regroup her forces and lay the groundwork for future endeavors.

The subordinate, Agent ZYX-319, remained before her, still waiting. Number One could not see his— her?—eyes behind the obscuring mesh of the standard A.I.M. mask, but she knew that the agent watched her no less carefully than any of the others. "Do you have anything else to report?"

"Yes, Number One." ZYX-319 answered her question, but did not volunteer the information. To do so would have been a gross violation of A.I.M. protocols, which were loosely based on scientific technique with some tailoring to allow for political reality. To give information without being asked to do so, at least within A.I.M.'s innermost circles, could be interpreted as a challenge to established authority.

Behind her mask, Number One allowed herself to smile. Challenges to her rule would come; that much was inevitable. They would not come from a witless drone like ZYX-319, however. "Go ahead," she prompted.

"We have received a report from Field Operative

Erasmus Krelm,'' ZYX-319 said. ''He is a prisoner within Hydra, but he has managed to obtain a communicator. He wants to come home and offers valuable data in return for his rescue.''

Krelm. That was a surprise. Number One had never expected to hear the agent's name again. Krelm had been one of Wanda Frants's people, a member of the splinter group that had joined with Hydra agents in an attempt to duplicate the Hulk's power and contend with Strucker for control of Hydra. The last that Number One had heard, Krelm had vanished somewhere inside Latveria, having taken part in a disastrous raid on that tiny nation. She had presumed him long since dead.

''What does Krelm offer?'' She disliked saying the name; she was accustomed to using only A.I.M. designators, but field operatives were allowed to retain their civilian identities.

''Intelligence data on Hydra's inner workings. Key access codes and security procedures. Strategic data.''

That sounded promising, but that was all—promising. It was the kind of data that a captive A.I.M. agent of Krelm's skills might be able to gather, but it was not enough to risk A.I.M.'s limited resources on an all-out rescue attempt. Krelm would know that. Number One thought for a moment.

''What proof does Agent Krelm offer?''

''He was able to intercept recent internal communiqués,'' the agent said. ''Baron Strucker is preparing for a major demonstration or initiative. Krelm does not know what. He knows that Strucker requested a list of strategic targets and their coordinates. Krelm says that the list includes this installation.''

That wasn't good news. Strucker hated A.I.M. and had sought to destroy the organization many times over the years, and would doubtless use any weapon at his disposal to carry out that goal—including the *Infinity Engine*. His enmity was one reason that Number One moved A.I.M.'s main headquarters from place to place so frequently. The idea that Hydra knew its current location did not please her. She wondered where Strucker had gotten the information.

From Krelm? No, that was impossible. The renegade had gone missing long before the latest move. Still, the fact that Hydra knew where A.I.M. made its home meant that she had another traitor in the ranks. Again, she wanted to sigh; again, she resisted the temptation. Finding the presumed traitor could wait. Now there were other measures to take.

"Place the station in War Mode," she said. She spoke loudly this time, and her voice carried throughout the command center. "Further orders will follow."

Instantly, the agents who sat in the Security Ring dropped their current endeavors and went to work. Number One heard a dozen whispered commands from masked lips, a frantic shuffling of papers and the click of countless switches as her people prepared for battle and defense. A.I.M. was heavily fortified, but she did not look forward to facing Hydra's challenge, especially if Strucker had the *Infinity Engine* in his clutches.

"What of Krelm?"

The question came from ZYX-319, surprising Number One. She wondered briefly if she had been wrong in her evaluation of her subordinate. For the moment, however, she set the question aside. "Krelm can look to himself," she said crisply. "You are dismissed."

Number One watched as ZYX-319 left the room, and made a mental note to continue watching the agent in the days to come. The unsolicited question had been an affront to protocol: she wanted to determine whether it had been accidental or deliberate. Until then, she would allow the agent who had asked that question to continue living.

Number One was A.I.M.'s Scientist Supreme, after all, and part of science was knowing the reasons for events—even executions.

Kellye Nakahara had often wondered what she would do in a hostage situation. It was a hard thing not to consider; she was an attractive woman who traveled a great deal on business, and she read newspapers and watched television newscasts. She worked out frequently, and knew a thing or two about self-defense, so she had always thought she would be able to handle herself well if it became necessary. Now the reality was proving to be somewhat different than she had expected.

The Hydra agent knew his business. He handed her the plastic shackles and stood well back from her as she donned them. "Cuff yourself, behind your back. Clamp them on tight," he commanded, keeping his pistol trained on her. "I'll know if you don't."

She obeyed. There didn't seem to be any alternatives, except for getting herself killed—and there didn't seem to be much point in that. She tried to remain calm as she fastened the shackles. Once, she thought she was going to drop the restraints, but then she caught them, and clicked the fasteners. The Hydra agent stepped closer now, and verified that she had obeyed his orders.

Her mind was racing. What had happened? How many Hydra agents had gotten on board, and how? What did they want—the *Infinity Engine*, or something else? The *Ad Astra* itself was a pretty valuable piece of property, after all, especially now that it was functional again. What had happened to Ramos, Powell, and Deeley?

She asked some of the questions aloud, but to no

result. Her captor was very nearly silent. He walked five paces behind her to their destination, too far away for her to try anything but quite close enough to shoot her if she tried to flee. He didn't say much, except to bark an occasional command, as the two of them made their way through what seemed like miles of corridors and passageways. Finally, he opened the last hatch and gestured for her to precede him into the command center.

What she saw answered some of her questions immediately. A half-dozen uninformed Hydra agents scurried among the control consoles, looking like giant green rats in a maze as they assessed the complex equipment. They whispered among themselves, using technical terms and what were obviously code phrases that she did not recognize.

Johnny Ramos was there, wearing handcuffs very much like hers. He sat on the deck in one corner, looking none the worse for wear, except for a split lip and a disgusted expression on his face. A Hydra agent stood over him.

"Johnny!"

"Hello, Kellye," he drawled in reply. "They got you, too, huh?"

His words were cut off by a green-gloved backhand. "Silence," the Hydra agent snarled. "I told you, no talking!"

Johnny looked back up at him. "Aw, take a hike, pal," he said. "You need us, or we'd be dead by now."

The man slapped him again, then gestured at Kellye. Obediently, she settled to the floor next to Johnny and tried to make herself comfortable. She didn't have much success in the effort.

Johnny's captor conferred with Kellye's escort. As the two masked men spoke, she whispered urgently to her fellow crew member.

"What happened?" she asked.

Johnny shrugged. "I was in the receiving area when the big airlock cycled. I barely got out in time. The next thing I knew, a shuttle the size of a Winnebago had docked, and the James Gang here had piled out."

"That's not possible! The bay won't open without—"

"Silence!" One of the Hydra agents barked the word. "Speak when you're spoken to, and you'll live!"

"I don't believe you," Johnny said evenly. "We're witnesses, and Hydra doesn't have much use for folks like us."

"Ordinarily, that would be true." The words came in another voice, as a third Hydra agent came close. Unlike his fellows, this one wore no mask. He was a tall man, with blond hair and good features. His voice, measured and confident, carried the tone of command.

Must be the boss, Kellye thought. *Or at least the site manager.*

"That is not the case just now, however," the blond man continued. "Today, we want witnesses—but we only need one. Obey, and you will live."

Kellye surprised herself again, by speaking. "We won't cooperate, you know."

The man down looked at her. "I could prove you wrong," he said calmly. "You would be amazed how easily I could make you do anything I want you to do." He grinned, a mask of affability settling on his handsome features. "But not today. Like I said, we don't need you."

He turned to one of his subordinates. "What of the other two?" he asked.

As if in answer, three more Hydra agents entered the room. Two of them were of normal height and build, and wore standard Hydra uniforms—but the third was a different matter altogether. Bigger and bulkier than the others, he was several inches over seven feet tall, and wore a modified hood that covered his features completely. The green fabric of his uniform strained to contain his barrel chest.

He's the size of the Hulk, Kellye thought.

"Where have you two been?" The blond man asked the question with an annoyed tone in his voice. "You're seven minutes behind schedule."

"Sorry, Section Leader," one of the agents said. He had a split lip, worse than Ramos's, and blood trickled from his nose. "He put up a bit of a fight, and we had to call in some muscle."

Put up a bit of a fight? Muscle? As the trio of newcomers came closer, Kellye could suddenly see that there were not three, but four. The big guy had the fingers of one hand dug deep in the neck of another man and was dragging him into the room, like a cat might drag its prey.

The man was Robert Powell.

The giant Hydra agent came closer and released his limp burden a few feet from the other two captives. Powell fell to the floor with a thump and lay unmoving. Kellye leaned closer to his inert form, and gasped in dismay. Powell's eyes were closed, and his face dark and suffused with blood. He didn't seem to be breathing, and his neck was twisted at an angle that looked terribly, terribly wrong.

The Hydra section leader looked at the dead Powell, and then at Kellye and Johnny. "Like I said," he told them. "We don't need you; we just want you."

"They'll come for us, you know." Kellye said the words with a confidence that she did not feel. "When we don't report, they'll come for us. This is a Stark

Enterprises project, so Iron Man is probably on his way already.''

The blond man looked at her and laughed. ''Funny you should mention that,'' he said. Still gazing at her with an intensity she did not like, he spoke to someone else. ''Run the feed from the surveillance monitor, and run it now! You know what I want to see!''

An image formed on the elevated monitor on one wall. The section leader watched Kellye as she watched it.

It was low-resolution footage, apparently taken from some distance. It showed the familiar red-and-gold form of Iron Man as he rocketed through a cloudless sky. Kellye had seen him many times before. Now, however, there was something wrong with his proportions, something bulkier and less aerodynamic about his armor. Then the figure's orientation changed so that Kellye could see, to her horror, that one arm had been torn from the flying figure. Bits of debris hung from the empty socket, and fluid gushed from it.

He seemed to be dropping lower and lower. It was hard to tell without points of reference, but the super hero seemed to be in a controlled descent. As he moved, the camera moved with him, until another metal figure came into view. This one, more severely damaged, was vaguely humanoid, but much larger. Its head was missing, but it still had arms and legs that twitched and writhed as the it fell through the air. As Iron Man came closer, one of the thing's hands came up, and the massive gray hand at one end clenched into a fist. Kellye thought she saw something fly from it, or several somethings, but she could not be sure.

A second later, Iron Man exploded. He exploded with great force, erupting into a ball of fire and smoke that hung motionless in midair for a second, then dropped.

The screen went blank.

The blond man smiled. "Case closed," he said. "Now, shut up."

Kellye slumped back against a wall, while Johnny made some kind of a moaning sound. The last of his bravado had apparently fled, and he leaned back and closed his eyes. Kellye didn't blame him. There didn't seem to be much else they could do.

The blond Hydra agent looked to his men. He pointed at the dead Powell. "That's three," he said. "Where's the fourth one?"

Yes, Kellye wondered. *Where's Deeley?*

CHAPTER 7

As Iron Man exploded in the upper reaches of the stratosphere, an anguished cry rang out in the cool confines of the Stark Enterprises armory lab. The sound of the scream echoed for a long moment, then gave way to silence, broken only by ragged breathing. Then—

"Tony?" HOMER's voice, ordinarily neutral, somehow managed to sound concerned. "Tony? Please respond."

Tony Stark, seated again at his work bench, took another gasping breath and replied. "I'm here, HOMER," he said. "I'm okay." He reached up and unfastened the miniaturized virtual reality headset he wore. He blinked as his blue eyes adjusted to the lab's indirect lighting.

"I was becoming concerned," HOMER said.

"You're not the only one," Tony said grimly. He pushed aside the hair behind one ear. His fingers searched for and found the small electrical jack there, and tugged a miniature connector free. He set the VR headset aside. "I ran into trouble."

An attempted assassination some years before, followed by an experimental radical therapy, had left Tony Stark with a nervous system composed largely of artificial materials. It had taken him many months to learn how to live with the fine mesh of techno-organic circuitry that had interwoven itself with his nerves and muscle. Once he had learned the basics, however, the implants had revealed new abilities to him. Now, for example, cybernetically engaging the VR unit allowed him to operate Iron Man's armor by remote control, essentially beaming his consciousness into the suit from a distance. The Dreadnought had managed to destroy several million dollars worth of hardware, but nothing else.

The remote control process wasn't without its drawbacks, however; the feedback was startlingly real. Tony massaged his right shoulder, working some sensation back into his traumatized arm. Through the cybernetic link, he could "feel" damage done to the armor—at least to a limited extent.

Not limited enough, he thought. He flexed his fingers, relieved to see them respond. Already, most of the stinging pain had faded from the length of his arm. He reached for his suit jacket.

"I am aware of your difficulties," HOMER said. "I monitored the battle."

"We have to do something about signal lag, HOMER. Another split second, and I could have saved the suit." That was the main problem with the process; operating by remote control decreased reaction time and increased vulnerability, in a line that tracked with the distance of separation.

"Yes. The microelectronics division has proposed a new processor that looks promising."

"Good. Where's the Dreadnought?"

"At the bottom of Long Island Sound."

"Send someone out to get it." Tony said. "Anything else?"

"Yes. Mrs. Arbogast reports that the authorities are anxious to speak with you regarding the *Infinity Engine*." There was a pause, as HOMER again checked something. "They would like to discuss Iron Man, as well."

Somehow, HOMER's words weren't surprising.

"It isn't your fault. You can't blame yourself." Those were the words that Mary Jane wanted to say, and they were accurate—but she knew that they were the last ones Peter wanted to hear, so she did not speak them. Instead, she gazed at his troubled features for a long

moment, her green eyes finding and locking with his brown ones as she waited for him to speak.

Finally, he broke the silence. "I should have been there," he said. His words were little more than a strangled whisper. "I should have been there, and I wasn't. He's dead, and it's my fault." He was seated on the couch in their living room, still in costume, but not wearing his mask. His left hand clutched the red, black and white piece of fabric. It was an incongruous image; Mary Jane's husband rarely spent much time at home in his work clothes.

"No," MJ said. "No, Peter. You can't let yourself think that way. You were Haberman's lab assistant, not his bodyguard."

Peter laughed, a bitter sound. "That's not the way it works," he said, his voice a dead monotone. "I could have kept it from happening, and I didn't. I let myself get mad at him, and now he's dead."

Mary Jane said it again. "No." She shook her head, making the red mantle of her hair ripple and course like a waterfall. "You could have been there, Peter, and you weren't—but that doesn't mean you *should* have been there." Her voice took on a pleading tone. "You've done so much, Peter—for the city, for the world, for me. But you can't do it all. You can't be everywhere at once. And you can't quit being human."

Peter didn't reply.

She sat beside him, took his right hand in both of hers. He didn't resist. The fingers that could rend steel effortlessly seemed nerveless and dead as she held them. "Peter," she said. "Listen to me."

He said nothing.

"You're a human being, Peter. So a radioactive spider bit you, so you have powers and abilities far beyond those of mortal men—you're still a human being.

You're a man, Peter—a *good* man." She paused, took a deep breath. "But being a good man means more than doing good. You have to let yourself be a man, first."

Peter looked at her, a puzzled look on his face. "What's that supposed to mean?" he asked.

"It means you're allowed to get angry, Peter. It means you're allowed to make mistakes."

He flinched at the last word, tore his hand from hers and stood. "This wasn't just a mistake, Mary Jane," he said. His words came in a torrent. "This was a man's life." He gestured at his costume. "That's the kind of mistake I can't let Spider-Man make. That's the kind of mistake that *made* me Spider-Man!"

Mary Jane knew what he meant. Years before, a very young, very inexperienced Spider-Man had looked the other way while a gunman had made his escape. Later that same evening, Peter Parker had returned home to find that the same petty criminal had killed his uncle. Ben Parker had been the closest thing to a father that Peter had ever known. Losing him had been a brutal shock, and Peter's guilt over his peripheral role in the tragedy had reshaped his life.

"He wasn't your uncle, Peter," she said. "Remember, I met Haberman, I heard your stories about him. He wasn't your uncle, he was your boss, and he wasn't a very nice man."

Peter glared at her. "That doesn't mean he deserved what he got!" His lips had gone white with sudden fury. "That doesn't mean he deserved to be shot!"

"Of course it doesn't," Mary Jane said. She shook her head again. "That's not what I meant, and you know it."

"What do you mean, then?"

"I mean that you're human, Peter. I mean that you're allowed to get angry at someone who treats you badly, and you're allowed to leave a bad situation and blow off some steam. The day you don't react the way you did is the day you should start worrying.'' She took a deep breath, and finally said the words. ''*It isn't your fault, Peter.*''

He stared at her for a long moment. Slowly, color returned to his lips, and the storm in his troubled brown eyes calmed and faded. He nodded.

Mary Jane stood and stepped close to him. She wrapped her arms around him, pulling him close to her, until she could feel his heart beating against hers. After another long moment, his arms closed around her.

''You're right,'' he said. He made a soft sound, a whispering noise in the back of his throat that sounded like a muffled sob. ''You're so good to me, MJ.''

She held him like that for a minute, perhaps two. Bit by bit, she felt the tension flow out of him, felt the steel muscles of his back soften and relax. The worst was over, she knew. She had been down this road with him before. There would be sorrow and there would be guilt and there would be misgivings in the days and weeks to come, but the worst of it was over.

She wished she could stay like this forever, her arms around him, keeping him safe from the world, shielding him from sorrow and pain—but she knew that would never happen. The things that made her love him were part and parcel with the things that made him what he was—compassion and duty and honor. The qualities that made her want him by her side forever were the same ones that made him leave her so often to do the things he needed to do. Another man, bitten by the same ra-dioactive spider, might have become super-powered, but she wondered if he would have become the same kind of hero her husband was.

She doubted it.

Finally, Peter spoke again. "I have to do something," he said. "I have to track down the guys who did this."

"I know." Reluctantly, she let him pull him pull away from her. She looked at him, but said nothing more.

"They let me know who they worked for," Peter said. He sounded deliberately analytical. "I know who they worked for. Hydra."

"That doesn't narrow it down very much," Mary Jane said. She meant it. She knew something about her husband's line of business, and knew that Hydra was one of the larger criminal organizations on earth. "There's thousands of those guys."

"Yes," Peter said. He had reached into one of the compartments on his belt, and pulled forth a small vinyl case that held business cards. Methodically, he sorted through them. "I ran into a gaggle of them last month, remember?"

Mary Jane nodded. She remembered, all right. A bargain-basement mad scientist had kidnapped more than a dozen young men and converted them into fair approximations of the Hulk—and then turned them loose on the city. One of them had been Flash Thompson, a friend of hers and Peter's. The ensuing property damage had run well into the millions before Spider-Man and the real Hulk had put an end to things. The scientist, whose name she did not remember, had been a Hydra section leader.

"I ran into someone else, too," Peter said. He had found the card he wanted. It bore an ornate seal with metallic ink that glinted in the afternoon light. "Sean Morgan. I should get in touch with him."

The doorbell rang, startling them both. Mary Jane looked at Peter, still mostly dressed as Spider-Man. "I'll see who it is," she said. "You're not dressed to receive visitors." A peek through the peephole showed her two men. One wore civilian clothes. *Probably a detective*, she thought. *He has the look.*

The other man wore a quasi-military uniform. Mary Jane did not recognize it, but she recognized his face. It was the man she had met at the Stark function, the too-friendly man who had claimed his name was Duncan Huxtable, but whom Peter had identified later that night as Joshua Ballard.

He didn't look friendly now.

The bell rang again.

"Who is it?" she asked, through the door. "Who's there?"

"Police, Mrs. Parker. Homicide. We need to speak with your husband."

"Oh!" MJ made a surprised sound. "Just a moment."

Peter had heard. By the time she turned to look, he had already donned his mask and was inserting extra web fluid cartridges into their belt compartments. "I heard," he said. "They must be investigating Haberman's death." He spoke in brisk, clipped tones. "I can't hang around for that. Not right now, anyway."

"You're probably right," Mary Jane agreed. "That SAFE goon from the party is out there, too."

"Ballard?"

"Or Huxtable. Where are you going?"

"Long Island to start with, I think. There's Haberman's obvious connection with Stark Enterprises, and one of the Hydra agents mentioned the *Infinity Engine*."

Mary Jane nodded. "What about Morgan?" Behind her, the doorbell rang again, followed by a brisk knocking sound.

"I'll try to call him on the way out there. I don't think its a good idea for Spider-Man to make telephone calls from Peter Parker's apartment, especially to an intelligence service.''

"Good point," MJ said. The previous months had taught her the hard way how vulnerable telephone communicatons could be.

The doorbell rang yet again.

"Just a moment," she called out. "I have to get decent.''

She stepped close to Peter and pulled up his mask. He kissed her, quickly, and smiled, before pulling it down again. ''Take care of yourself,'' she whispered.

"Oh, I will. You take care of those guys," Peter said. "I'll call when I get a chance." He smiled. "Don't worry. Things will work out. They always do.''

Then he was gone, bounding through the window and away.

The doorbell rang a third time. Mary Jane opened the door. "Sorry, guys," she said to the men. "A girl has to get pretty, you know. Now, what's all this about— why, *Mr. Huxtable*, I hardly recognized you!"

"The name is Ballard, Mrs. Parker. I'm a government security agent." The uniformed man presented a leather folder. Besides a badge, it held an identity card with an ornate seal that matched the one on Sean Morgan's card. The other man offered a wallet too, but MJ barely noticed the NYPD credentials he proffered. She was too busy watching Ballard carefully.

The big man was obviously the lead in the investigation. Without moving from the doorway, he looked carefully around the brownstone's living area. Mary Jane suspected that his gaze would miss nothing—but she was sure that there was nothing for him to miss. Years of keeping house with a super hero had taught her the twin values of tidiness and discretion. Spider-Man left no traces of himself in the relatively public parts of their home; he was restricted to his private workshop.

"Ballard?" She made herself sound confused. "I don't understand."

The uniformed man returned his credentials to his pocket. The homicide detective did the same with his. "I'm sorry about the confusion," Ballard said. "When we met, I was on an undercover security assignment. I'm working as a liaison with the local authorities now, on part of the same case."

"And we're delighted to have him," the detective said. He didn't sound as if he meant it. He was a short East Indian man with absolutely no hair in evidence—not even eyebrows—and he was clearly annoyed at his current companion. "Tell me, Mrs. Parker—is Mr. Parker here today?"

"N-no, he's not," Mary Jane said.

"Do you expect him in soon?" That was Ballard again, reasserting control.

"I don't know. He has a very fluid schedule. The life of a freelancer, you know. Have you tried the *Daily Bugle*?" MJ made a strained laugh. "What's this all about, officers?"

"We're investigating the death of Cosmo Emile Haberman, and we'd like to ask your husband a few questions."

"Dr. Haberman is dead?"

The hairless man nodded. "Killed," he said briefly. "About three hours ago."

"And Peter—?"

"Mr. Parker was one of the last to see him alive," Ballard said. "We're hoping he can tell us something we can use."

"May we come in, Mrs. Parker?" The detective asked the question in a very businesslike tone of voice, and stepped forward without waiting for a reply. He obviously expected her to step aside.

Mary Jane didn't. "I don't see why, officer. Peter's not here."

"Are you sure about that, Mrs. Parker?" Ballard looked at her levelly. "We heard some voices a moment ago."

"Voices?" Mary Jane managed to look puzzled. "Oh, that. I was rehearsing some lines. I'm an actress. I told you that last week, Mr. Huxtable."

Ballard grimaced at the use of his cover name. "Yes," he said. "Well, even so, may we come in? I have a few questions for you, too."

"About Peter?"

"About Peter," Ballard confirmed. The other man nodded.

Mary Jane thought for a moment. She could refuse, of course—but that could mean more problems, and maybe even a search warrant. She certainly didn't want anyone poking around in Peter's workroom. That could cause no end of trouble.

She shrugged, and stepped aside. "Come on in, guys," she said. "But wipe your feet."

The homicide detective obeyed, but Ballard did not, she noticed. *About par for the course*, she thought, then gestured them towards the living room.

It promised to be a long afternoon.

Rank had its privileges, and no one at Stark Enterprises outranked Tony Stark. An express elevator connected the underground armory with the penthouse suite that included his private office and a secure conference space. It took him ten seconds to make the trip, and slightly less than that amount of time to pull his thoughts together.

The facts he had to consider were few, but their implications were undeniable, and undeniably unpleasant. Haberman was dead, and Stark had lost the older man's unique insights and knowledge. Worse, he had lost a respected coworker, one who had remained faithful to Stark Enterprises for many years, leaving only when a hostile takeover had made his position untenable—and returning to service when Stark himself had done the same. That kind of loyalty was a valuable asset, at least as much of a treasure as Haberman's undeniable genius—and now Tony had lost both.

Nearly as bad was the news that someone had hijacked the *Infinity Engine*. It was hard to believe that the two incidents weren't related; in fact, there was no way that Stark could see that they weren't. Anna Marie Sanchez said that the two gunmen had demanded the *Engine*'s access codes and operational software. They had probably gotten both, judging from the damage to Odyssey's mainframe. With the codes and software, someone who knew what he was doing could override the onboard systems, at least temporarily, and take control of the specialized shuttlecraft. That capacity had originally been a safety measure, in case the crew became incapacitated. Tony recognized the irony of its present use, but he was not amused by it.

Though he knew why Haberman had died, he still had no idea who had done the job. Tony considered the possibilities, and was appalled to realize how many of them there were. Even setting aside the world's current volatile political situation, and the many belligerent nations that would like to have the *Engine* for their own, the field of suspects was almost impossibly broad. His own career as Iron Man had familiarized him with far too many criminal and terrorist cabals, not to mention an almost endless parade of mad people with personal imperialist agendas and the genius to put them in action. In its present configuration, the *Infinity Engine* was no weapon, but it drew upon theoretically infinite energies, power that could fuel the tools of conquest. Tony didn't want to think about what an A.I.M. or a Hydra or a Mandarin could do with the *Infinity Engine*—but he had to consider the potential for disaster.

The elevator doors slid apart. Before they were fully open, Tony strode through them into his private reception area. Mrs. Arbogast, his indefatigable personal secretary, was already there. She was a heavyset woman in her fifties, and had been with him for many years. He often wondered what he would do if she ever chose to retire.

"They're waiting for you in the main conference room," she said. "I've already set out a full coffee service."

Tony nodded. "Good," he said. "Anything else?"

"Not much. The media people would like to talk to you, of course."

He looked at her, but said nothing. She got the hint.

"Yes, well, Ms. Sanchez arrived a minute or two ago."

"That was fast."

"We sent a helicopter, and the police were very eager to escort her to it."

"Good." That would be the work of Bethany Cabe. She was good with details and logistics, and there wasn't a police department in the region that didn't owe her a favor. "Where is Bethany? Has she already joined the meeting?"

Mrs. Arbogast shook her head, making her horn-rimmed glasses flash as they caught the indirect lighting. "No. She'll be in later. She's out with some of the federal boys, making sure they keep their minds on business. They'll see whatever they need to see—but they won't see anything else.''

Despite the situation, Tony smiled. He considered the diligent, intrusive attention that his operations had received from various intelligence and security agencies over the long years. Some of that attention had been welcome, but most of it had not. *Leave it to Bethany to look out for me*, he thought.

''Okay. Anything else?''

''Two things.'' Mrs. Arbogast sounded hesitant. ''The police called. They're looking into that Peter Parker person you hired.''

''Why on earth would they do that?'' Tony asked, startled.

''They weren't very specific, but I think he's a suspect,'' she said.

''In Haberman's murder? That's ridiculous. They should set their sights higher.''

''I know, sir. I told them that I had run his reference checks myself.''

Tony shrugged. ''I'd rather they not waste their time and effort,'' he said, ''but I guess it's their call.'' For a moment, he wondered if the police might not be right. It was tempting to direct Security to do some more investigation, just in case, but he decided against it. If Mrs. Arbogast had decided the kid was clean, he was. ''Tell Legal to do whatever they can to help him if he asks. What else?''

''The police report that Spider-Man was sighted near Odyssey, at about the same time as the murder. He was chasing some kind of flying delivery truck, but didn't catch it. They were about fifteen stories above street level.''

Flying delivery truck? Tony considered the possibilities, but decided he didn't have enough information to make a judgment. "Somehow I doubt that's a coincidence," he said.

Mrs. Arbogast nodded. "That's why I thought you'd want to know about it."

"Thank you, then," Tony said. "Keep track of things, and I'll speak with you later." He gazed at the pair of closed oak doors ahead of him and sighed. It was time to enter the lion's den.

The conference room could seat twenty comfortably, but it held only about half that many now. Tony had to wonder if more would join them later. Probably; space travel cut across a lot of jurisdictions, and the *Infinity Engine* promised to cut across even more. It had been impossible to keep the government entirely out of his operation when things were going well; it would be completely out of the question now that they were not.

Ten men and women sat at various points along the conference table's perimeter, reading reports and making small talk. Tony recognized some of them, most notably Anna Marie Sanchez, Haberman's administrative assistant, conferring in low, urgent tones with a few members of his own staff. At one end of the table—the head, Tony realized with irritation—Sean Morgan looked up from a whispered conversation with one of his own people. "Hello, Stark. Take a seat," the federal agent said. "Glad you could make it."

"Sorry. Urgent matters demanded my attention." Tony seated himself at the other end of the table. One of Bethany Cabe's security assistants passed him some papers and photographs, but Tony scarcely noticed.

"I hardly think there's anything more urgent than this just now," Morgan said dryly. He was a lean man, tall and well built, with intense gray eyes and a steady gaze. Tony had met him once or twice before at official meetings and functions, and didn't particularly like the man.

He would much preferred to deal with a more familiar face. Some new government regulation had granted SAFE security jurisdiction over the *Infinity Engine* project, however, and Morgan was clearly ready to see the job through.

"True enough, I suppose. But there's a lot going on, and I had to get my people working on their end of it."

"What about Iron Man?" Morgan spoke directly, though not discrespectfully. He did not seem to be a man who valued niceties. "Have you recovered anything from his remains?"

"Iron Man's fine," Tony said. "He'll check in later."

"He's—'fine'?" That was Hayes, a pudgy SAFE officer who wore a science officer insignia on his uniform. "Excuse me, but I monitored that little encounter myself—and the only way I would use that word is to describe the size of the shrapnel."

"Looks can be deceiving, Mr. Hayes," Stark said. "He's survived worse." The armor's remote-control capabilities were a closely guarded secret; the intelligence community and the general public both knew that several men had worn Iron Man's armor over the years, but almost no one knew that sometimes no one wore it. That was one secret Tony Stark intended to keep. "The armory's doing some work on his suit, and I've got him overseeing some other preparations." Stark smiled. "I think I can fill in for him on this one, though."

For a moment, Morgan didn't say anything, apparently considering Tony's words. Then he shrugged, and pulled a small remote control from the stack of papers before him. "About twenty minutes ago, SAFE HQ received a scrambled transmission. I was already here, so my people couriered me a tape. The Secret Service, the FBI, the NSA, and most other intelligence offices received the same message. The folks who sent it made unauthorized use of frequencies and encryption systems that are reserved for official use. We think they did that to prove who they were.'' He paused, then pressed a button. ''I haven't seen it myself yet, but I know what's on it. Watch.''

Several video monitors punctuated the room's oak paneling. One by one, they came to life and filled with static that coalesced into familiar features. Tony flinched as a face filled the screens. It was the face of a bald man, a sneering man who wore a monocle and bore a jagged dueling scar along one cheek. They were the familiar, hated features of a man who was wanted by the authorities in every nation in the world.

It was the German war criminal, Baron Wolfgang Von Strucker. He was the founder and head of Hydra, the world's largest, oldest, and most feared terrorist organization.

That's one mystery solved, Tony thought—but it was a solution he could have lived without. It wasn't a surprise, either; the flying Dreadnought he had enountered suggested Hydra's involvement. He had contended with Strucker and Hydra many times over many years, both as Iron Man and as Tony Stark. He had worked with the U.S. government to establish S.H.I.E.L.D. specifically to counter Hydra and similar threats. His own most recent major encounter with Strucker had involved his own abduction and an experimental energy source that Hydra had managed to commandeer from an offshoot organization, Advanced Idea Mechanics, or A.I.M. The ensuing battle had turned an ancient English castle into nothing more than a smoldering pit of ash, and Tony had doubted the subsequently received reports of Strucker's survival. Part of him had hoped they were not true.

''So he's still alive after all, then. He lived through

that business in England,'' Tony said softly. ''I trust you've notified S.H.I.E.L.D.'' He didn't like to think what such a man could do with the *Infinity Engine*.

''We did, but they already knew,'' Morgan said. ''They were on the address list, for that matter.'' He paused the recording, so that the image froze as he spoke. ''We've all been trying to run Strucker to ground for months. Interpol thought they had him a few weeks ago, in Calcutta, but it turned out to be a case of mistaken identity. The suspect proved to be one Christopher 'Scar' Tobin, an American gangster out on parole and vacationing without a passport.'' Morgan smiled mirthlessly and released the pause. ''There's a man who has a lot of explaining to do.'' The tape resumed playing.

The last time that Tony—as Iron Man—had encountered Wolfgang Von Strucker, the German baron had shrieked epithets and challenges from the windswept parapet of an abandoned castle somewhere in England. Now, in his recorded image, Strucker spoke with a measured calm that seemed more unsettling than the fury Tony remembered, perhaps because it so barely masked the mania lurking beneath it. Tony listened silently to the words of the man who sought to steal the Earth's future—and who, by taking the *Infinity Engine*, might well have succeeded in that goal.

''Good day,'' Strucker said. His monocle glinted in the camera's light. ''I will not trouble to introduce myself. Anyone who receives this message should know who I am and who I represent—and if you do not, I suggest that you are in the wrong line of business.''

''That's for sure.'' The words came from one of the SAFE agents whom Tony had not met. The man fell silent as Sean Morgan glared at him.

''Earlier today,'' Strucker continued, ''agents of my organization confiscated the *Infinity Engine* from the unworthy custody of the decadent American industrialist, Mr. Anthony Stark. Should any of you be unfamiliar with that device, or with its capabilities, I suggest you contact its inventor and former owner for the specifics. Suffice it to say that my personnel are even now modifying the *Infinity Engine* to serve my agenda—with which you should also already be familiar.''

The SAFE agent didn't say anything this time, Tony noticed. No one did. They knew Strucker's goals all too well.

''The craft's crew members are alive and unharmed, for now. They are in a secure area of Mr. Stark's much-vaunted *Ad Astra* space station—which we have also liberated, and given a new name, befitting its new role: *Kriegrad*.'' Strucker smiled, bloodless lips parting in a vaguely reptilian grimace.

Kriegrad, Tony thought. In English, *War-Wheel.*

''Any attempt to reclaim either of our new possessions will result in the slow, exceedingly unpleasant deaths of our hostages,'' Strucker said. ''Just as any refusal of my future demands will result in swift, merciless reprisal. Again, I refer you to Mr. Stark for the details of the power with which he has so kindly provided us.''

Morgan shot a glance at Tony, but didn't say anything.

''You will receive the first of those demands precisely twenty-four hours after this message,'' Strucker said. ''Before then I will provide the world with a demonstration of our new assets.'' He smiled again, more broadly this time, and Tony could see the man's barely controlled madness struggle towards the fore. ''Keep watching the skies,'' Strucker said. He raised his right arm in a rigid salute. ''Hail Hydra!''

The screen went blank as Morgan thumbed the remote again. ''That's it,'' he said. ''No real surprises.

Global blackmail, backed up by your gadget. Strucker's done this sort of thing before, a couple of times.''

"Not on quite this scale," Tony responded.

"Why don't you give us some idea of that scale, Mr. Stark?''

Tony chose his words carefully. "In its original configuration,'' he said, "the *Infinity Engine* is not a weapon. You could do some damage with it, I suppose, but we deliberately designed the beam transducers to make energy transmissions as safe as possible.''

Morgan said a single syllable, in a flat tone that would brook no denial. "But.''

"Energy is energy, Mr. Morgan. You can put it to a lot of uses.'' Tony shrugged. He thought about his own recent encounter with the mad baron, and considered some of the weaponry that Strucker and his agents had used, nearly winning the conflict. "I don't know who Hydra has on its science staff these days, but I've seen some things lately that suggest they're good at what they do. Not quite A.I.M. caliber, but close.''

"How much energy are we talking about?''

"How much do you want?'' Tony said the words grimly. "I named that thing the '*Infinity Engine*' for a reason.''

"It must have some limits.'' The comment came from Hayes. "The hardware itself, if nothing else.''

Tony shrugged. "Everything has limits,'' he said. "But we don't know the *Engine*'s. That was one point of this exercise. We don't know how much power the apparatus can draw and process; just that the numbers are big ones.'' He paused, thinking about one of Haberman's last reports. "Very big.''

"Which means we have to get it back,'' Morgan said grimly. "I've got full jurisdiction on this, and I've been promised all the muscle I need to back me up.''

Tony didn't like the sound of that. "What's your plan?" he asked.

"*My* plan is to put a crew of heavily armed antiterrorism combat specialists in a NASA shuttle, shoot them up there, and storm the place," Morgan said.

"You can't do that," Tony said angrily. "You do, and Ramos and the rest are as good as dead."

"That's what the President said, too. He's not wild about that option, either." Morgan's lips were set in a hard, straight line. "The problem is, you're both fooling yourselves. Hydra has your people. They're as good as dead already." He paused, then continued in a milder tone of voice. "And just because the President doesn't agree with my views doesn't mean he won't let me implement them. It's my call to make. Two members of my personal staff are at NASA right now, working out the logistics of armoring and launching a conventional shuttle. I also have fifty of my best men on standby, armed to the teeth and ready to move at a moment's notice."

Tony stared at the other man, suddenly filled with something very much like horror. During their brief acquaintance, Morgan had never impressed him as being especially compassionate, but this. . . . "Why don't you just shoot it down, then?"

"We considered that option, and rejected it."

"There's the problem of debris," Hayes chimed in. "I analyzed the orbital track. If we use anything smaller than a pocket nuke to blow it apart, we'll leave pieces of *Ad Astra* across most of the Temperate Zone—or as I like to call it, the home of human civilization. Hydra's shifted the thing's orbit slightly, just enought to make it a menace. And if we do use the nuke, we have other problems to consider."

Tony nodded. SAFE was right about that much, at

least. The *Ad Astra* was one of the largest artifacts ever placed in space, big enough that some sections were certain to survive reentry. A nuclear blast would break it up enough to do the job, of course, but that option carried its own drawbacks.

"Any other ideas?" Morgan gazed at him steadily. "I'm open to suggestions."

"Just one—Iron Man."

"He couldn't do the job last time."

"Those were special circumstances."

"In this kind of business, the circumstances are always special," Morgan said. "Tell me what you can do to change them."

Tony glanced at a wiry-looking young man seated near him. It was Luther Hotchkiss, from SE's aerospace division. "Luther," he said, "What's the status on the *Skylark*? How long would you need to mount it on a booster and get it out to the main launch silo?"

"About six hours," the other man said. "But it wouldn't do much good. The navigational control software still isn't out of R&D, and the previous release is full of bugs."

"You've got two hours. Do it. Priority One."

"But—the software—"

"Not your problem. I'll deal with it. Now get going. The clock's running."

Hotchkiss left. He was moving fast when he got out of his chair, and moving faster as he passed through the conference room's heavy oak doors.

"*Skylark*?" Morgan made the word a question. He looked puzzled. Tony liked seeing the expression. *Nice to see I can still surprise the feds*, he thought.

"It's a prototype space rescue vehicle, with heavy shielding and a quick-response steering system," Tony replied. "I'm surprised that SAFE doesn't know about it."

"We do now," Morgan said calmly. "How big is this *Skylark*, and how many can it carry?"

"It only needs one to operate, but it can seat six. Iron Man won't be taking any passengers, though."

"Yes, he will," Morgan said. "He'll have space for five, and the most he'll need on the way back is four. That leaves a seat for one of my men riding shotgun. I want a SAFE presence on this mission, and your armored pal can use the assist."

Tony shook his head. "No. You've seen what these people can do. I can't even guarantee that Iron Man will make it. I don't want responsibility for your agent."

"Maybe not, but you'll want this." Morgan gestured at one of his men, who responded by handing him what looked like an ordinary briefcase. He set it on the table, opened it, and then turned it so that Tony could see the contents. Nestled in a bed of plastic foam were several electronic components of a design that that Tony had not seen before. A web of cables held them together. "Early last month, a Hydra stealth jet crashed in the Arctic," Morgan said. "My men were able to salvage some interesting stuff from the wreckage, including this. It's an IFF beacon, programmed with Hydra's current ID protocols. Interested?"

He's right, Tony thought. *I do want it.* He knew that Strucker's organization had remarkably sophisticated communications and security systems, at least as good as his own. With the Identification, Friend or Foe beacon on board, the *Skylark* would be able to glide past any Hydra automated defense systems—and probably even be invisible to their hands-on targeting systems.

"Does Hydra know you have this?" he asked. "If they do, it's useless. They can update their codes in minutes.'' Despite his skepticism, he was seriously tempted by the gleaming piece of apparatus. He would have loved to take it apart, analyze every chip and circuit and find out what made it tick—but there wasn't time for that. Worse, once they used it, Hydra would know about the security breach, and take steps to offset it.

''They don't know.'' Morgan snapped the case shut. ''Until now, the only people who knew about it were on SAFE's payroll.''

Tony brought up his gaze up from the closed case, until his eyes found and locked with Morgan's wintry gray ones. He didn't say anything.

Morgan spoke. ''Here's the deal. I give you this, you let a SAFE heavy-weapons specialist tag along for the ride. I do everything I can to cut red tape and provide backup—and believe me, I can do a lot. I can get you the launch clearances, the resources you need, the telemetry, and the navigational data. You don't play along, then you don't get squat. I'll find some way to stop your tin-plated pal and I'll do the job myself.''

You just might, too, Tony thought. There was more to Morgan than he had thought. The other man's apparent competence and confident attitude surprised him. As Iron Man, he commanded certain government priorities and clearances of his own, and usually they were enough to do the job—but they might not be this time, especially if SAFE actively tried to block him. After a moment's thought, however, he shook his head. ''I can't do it. I want the beacon, but it's too dangerous. I don't care how heavily you arm your men, they aren't in Iron Man's league.''

Morgan snorted and came close to laughing. ''The SAFE agent I want to send with you shot his way into Castle Doom last month and lived to tell the tale. I think that's tough enough for government work.'' He slid the case across the table's polished surface. It came to a halt, halfway to Tony. "Go ahead, take it. You know you need it."

For a long minute, the others in the room remained silent as the two men stared at one another. Tony studied Morgan's impassive features carefully, wondering what thoughts they hid. How serious was the other man? Would he actually refuse to release the beacon, even knowing that Iron Man was the best chance the mission had for success? He barely knew Morgan and didn't much like him. Moreover, Tony knew from hard experience the risks that accompanied deals with espionage agencies, no matter how benign they seemed.

There were other factors to consider, as well. He thought of a weathered stone battlement in England. He thought of Strucker, wreathed in red energy and wielding a supercharged steel blade that had somehow, impossibly, nearly made him a challenge for Iron Man. With that kind of weaponry, a Hydra agent would be more than a match for any SAFE agent, no matter how well armed. It was bad enough that Ramos and the rest were in Hydra's clutches. Did he really want to add another name to the tally?

A sudden noise interrupted his thoughts. It was the bright electronic chirp that a cellular telephone made. He watched as Morgan pulled a small folding unit from his briefcase and spoke into it.

"This better be important," the SAFE commander answered by way of greeting. Tony could not hear the caller's words, but he could hear Morgan's response. "You're serious? Good, good. Bring him here." He paused. "Yes, now! Do you think I meant next week? Morgan out!"

Morgan folded the phone and set it down on the cluttered conference table. He smiled, but this time the smile seemed honest and open—or as open as Sean Morgan ever got. "Okay, Mr. Stark," he said, "I think I've got the solution to our little standoff."

"What do you mean?"

As if in answer, the conference room door swung open again, framing three figures. The one on the left was Bethany Cabe; the one on the right was someone Tony had never seen before, wearing a SAFE uniform. Between the two, and obviously escorted by them, stood a somewhat more famous figure.

"We found him nosing around the north perimeter, boss," Bethany said. The SAFE agent nodded in agreement.

Spider-Man walked into the room. He glanced around briefly, paused as his masked eyes met Tony's, then looked toward the lean man at the conference table's head.

"Hello, Morgan," he said. "We've got to stop meeting like this."

"You've got my number," Morgan replied.

His words suprised Tony, and so did the friendly tone of his voice. What was going on here?

"I tried. The line was busy," Spider-Man said flatly. "I ran into some Hydra goons downtown. They got away. I figure you can give me a second chance at them."

Fifteen minutes later, they had a deal. It wasn't a deal that Tony liked, but it was one he found livable: Iron Man and the *Skylark* got full cooperation from SAFE and the government, and Spider-Man came along for the ride, representing Morgan's interests. As Iron Man, Tony had worked with the other super hero on numerous occasions and had to admit that the web-spinner could pull his own weight on the proposed mission. As Tony Stark, however, he was a little more skeptical of the proposed arrangements. Spider-Man was one of the more mysterious members of the super hero community, with relatively few official connections and a public persona that alternated between outlaw and hero. What were his interests in the case? How had he gotten involved? How had he known to look for Morgan at Stark Enterprises—or had he come looking for something else?

Most importantly, what was his connection with SAFE?

Watching Spider-Man exchange pleasantries with Morgan, Tony had to wonder.

CHAPTER 8

Even with four empty seats, the *Skylark* was surprisingly crowded and uncomfortable. Spider-Man, in the copilot's seat and wearing a pressure suit that Tony Stark had provided, looked sideways at Iron Man as the countdown progressed.

"This isn't exactly my cup of tea," he said. "I like the wide open spaces." He meant it; years of acrobatic adventure had accustomed him to great freedom of movement. Now, in a pressure suit, tied to the *Skylark*'s systems with wires and hoses, he felt uncomfortably like a prisoner.

"I can't do much about that," Iron Man said. Even run through his helmet's filters and then through Spider-Man's headset, his voice still had a cadence that Peter Parker found familiar. There was something about the way the armored super hero pronounced his words, some odd element of his speech that reminded Spider-Man of someone he had met before. The name danced along the edges of his conscious mind, adroitly dodging any efforts to retrieve and verify it.

"You need the suit," Iron Man continued, interrupting Spider-Man's thoughts. "You won't need it once we get up there, but you need it until we do. If you want to be of any use on this mission, you need to be conscious, and you won't be without the suit, even though the cabin is pressurized."

Spidey nodded in silent acknowledgment. That much was true, he knew. The pressure suit functioned much like a high-altitude pilot's pneumatic outfit. Lined with bladders that inflated automatically in response to acceleration, the suit would keep the blood from pooling in his extremities, at the expense of his brain—and consciousness. According to Tony Stark, more than a few high-altitude pioneers had sacrificed their lives verifying the need for such measures. Stark had also noted that Iron Man's outfit contained a similar lining.

That didn't mean Spider-Man had to like it, though.

He wasn't sure he liked his companion and partner, either. He had worked with the armored super hero on various occasions in the past, but there was something about Iron Man's impassive, expressionless mask that he found unsettling. Plus, there was another consideration. He knew that more than one person had worn the Iron Man armor over the years. There was no way to be certain that he had ever met the steel-clad figure to his left before. The unfamiliarity of Iron Man's current configuration—including massive, tree-trunk-like leggings that Spider-Man suspected held fuel reserves—didn't help much either.

Guess this is how the other half lives, he thought. He felt a sudden surge of vague, slight sympathy for the Eel and Doctor Octopus and the Hobgoblin and all the rest. Spidey's own mask hid his face and features; that was why he wore it. For all the public—or his enemies—knew, there had been more than one Spider-Man. All that they ever saw was his webbed mask and mirrored eyepieces—and anyone could wear them, Peter supposed, though very few could duplicate his feats. Several super-powered criminals had done precisely that, however, in years gone by.

His companion's words interrupted his reverie. "Minus twenty seconds and counting," Iron Man said. "I need to concentrate now, so keep a lid on it, if you can."

Spider-Man nodded, but didn't say anything. Upon entering the shuttle and seating himself in the pilot's chair, Iron Man had unreeled a thick umbilicus of electrical cable from the *Skylark*'s control panel and plugged one end of it into a receptor in his chest plate. In clipped, business-like tones, he had explained that his armor included cybernetic pickups that translated his thoughts into operating system commands. Connecting himself to the *Skylark*'s steering computer made the shuttle function as an extension of his steel suit, and obviated the need for most of the craft's navigational software. The arrangement had its drawbacks, of course; much of whatever the *Skylark* gained from enhanced response time, Iron Man lost to the need for absolute concentration.

Wouldn't want to disturb the big guy, Spidey thought. *Especially not once we're a few thousand feet above some very hard concrete.*

In some secluded corner of his mind, he was still wondering at his role in the mission. There were good reasons for him to tag along, of course, and plenty of them. Hydra was nothing but trouble, certified as Bad News by every government in the civilized world, and by a few in the uncivilized world to boot. He still owed the criminal organization for its recent part in blacking out New York and turning his childhood chum, Flash Thompson, into a quasi-duplicate of the Hulk, temporary though both of those events had been. Moreover, there was the simple lesson he had learned so many times over the years, and with such bitter cost: with great power, comes great responsibility. A good person who didn't act wasn't any better than an evil person who did.

Those were all good reasons, but he knew that none of them was the real one. He wasn't going into outer space for justice, or because of Flash, or even because of a sense of duty. The real reason for this mission was an old man, choking to death on his own blood, and muttering something in German, while Peter Parker stood by in shock, unable to save him.

Hydra had killed Cosmo Haberman. Now, it was up

to Spider-Man to do something about it. He didn't know which of the organization's faceless legions had done the job, but he could make them pay by scuttling their current operation.

Seated in the *Skylark*, listening to the craft's enunciator tick off the countdown, Spider-Man thought about something that Anna Marie Sanchez had commented on over a tranquil lunch break, a lifetime ago. "He just wants *something* to be right," she had said, speaking of Haberman. Peter had promised to do his best to make that happen.

He had failed. He liked to think of himself as a good man, but he had stood by and done nothing while Hydra had acted.

Maybe now, by reclaiming the *Infinity Engine* from the jackals who had slain Haberman to steal his dreams, Peter could make amends. He was still considering that thought as the *Skylark* threw itself upwards, into the beckoning sky.

Baron Strucker reviewed the list that Garcia had handed him. It was a single page, short and to the point, detailing some twenty optimal targets within easy range of the *Ad Astra*, with supporting data detailing their coordinates and specific strategic importance. Most of the entries were obvious candidates for destruction—national capitals, military bases, and the key population centers in a dozen nations. A few were slightly more exotic or specialized; as Strucker ran his gaze down the page's length, he noted other, less obvious options, considered and rejected them, and then read on. Four Freedom's Plaza? Avengers Mansion? No. Each held many technological treasures he would like very much to own, and there was no point in destroying them. Besides, the Fantastic Four and the Avengers were worthy foes, and they deserved to live long enough to see Hydra's triumph. Doomstadt, in Latveria? He considered that one for a long moment, then shook his head. Crushing Doctor Doom would be a joy and a delight, and the *Infinity Engine* would no doubt do the job—but "almost" was not good enough. In many ways, Doom was among the most threatening obstacles to Hydra's triumph, a more imposing challenge than many of the forces of so-called "law and order." Doom would die, of course, but Strucker needed to see it happen. Latveria's ruler had evaded death too many times in the past for Strucker to risk another such evasion now.

A pen-and-ink addendum to the report caught his eye. "A.I.M. HQ," it read, followed by a string of numbers that listed a longitude and latitude. No annotation provided the site's strategic importance, but no such note was needed.

"When did we get this data on A.I.M.?" Strucker purred the words, pleased by his discovery. "Who provided it?" A.I.M. was a perfect candidate for demolition. The rival cartel was a longtime enemy. It had often interfered with his campaigns in the years since its core membership rebelled against Hydra—but had avoided the reach of his vengeance, time and again. Destroying the renegades would serve two purposes. He could rid himself of an enemy and establish the threat of Hydra's newest asset in terms that the world would understand.

Garcia, still standing at what he thought was attention, spoke. "Less than fifteen minutes ago, Baron," he said. For once, he spoke concisely; typically, the paunchy man had a tendency to ramble, a trait that Strucker found infuriating. "Operations received a report from Field Agent Abner Sinclair, the first in more than a month. He provided the information."

Sinclair? The name was familiar. Strucker paused a moment, trying to identify it.

Anticipating his master's question, Garcia continued. "Agent Sinclair was one of Hildebrandt's people, Baron. He was sent on a mission to Latveria and apparently captured there by his A.I.M. confederates. He is in A.I.M. custody now, but managed to send us this data."

"Why?" Even as he asked the question, Strucker thought he knew the answer—and his own response.

"He's requesting rescue, sir. He wants someone to come and get him."

Strucker nodded. "Good," he said. "Give the coordinates to Horst, and tell the orbiting crew that A.I.M. Island is their target." He glanced at his watch. "I want the demonstration to commence within one hour."

"Hail Hydra!" Garcia saluted, then turned on his heel and left his master's office. He did not ask for clarification, or inquire as to the hapless Sinclair's fate.

He knew better than that.

Kellye Nakahara watched the blond Hydra section leader as he went about his work. His name was Horst, she had learned, and he seemed very competent—too competent to make Kellye happy. He moved among the control boards and consoles with absolute confidence, pausing now and then to take a note or make an adjustment, or to bark an order at one of his subordinates. Occasionally one of the oversized, hooded Hydra agents lumbered into the control area, carrying new equipment or components. Horst would tell them where to place their burdens and they would silently comply, then leave the room again for other duties. There were two of the behemoths, she had learned, and fifteen relatively normal operatives including their leader.

Horst seemed to know what he was doing. The section leader displayed a ready awareness of the *Infinity Engine*'s complex workings, a casual familiarity that Kellye found disturbing. Since Powell had integrated most of the *Engine*'s control modules into the *Ad Astra*'s primary computer center, even she had sometimes found herself lost in the vast array of equipment. Horst didn't appear to have that problem and seemed to enjoy his work as he incorporated new components into the sprawling network. She wondered how someone with such skills could have gone so wrong in life.

Horst saw her watching him. He grinned. "Pretty, isn't it?" he asked. "The beauty of nature is greatly overrated, I think. Give me technology any day."

Without meaning to, Kellye found herself agreeing. She was primarily a theoretician, but even she recognized the charm and allure of a well-built instrument. "It was prettier before you got to it, though," she said dryly.

The Hydra section leader smiled more broadly. "Well, eye of the beholder, and all that," he said. He gestured at a new bank of equipment that the two giants had muscled into place and at the thick cables running from it to the *Engine*'s beam formers. "This is my baby," he said. "So I'll always like it best."

"What is it?" She asked the question without expecting an answer and was surprised when she got one.

"Transducer module," Horst said crisply. "Variable flux, with inboard proton fractionators. I designed it myself, though it's based on some work by a man named Burton Hildebrandt."

Kellye nodded. She knew that name, a German physicist who had specialized in wavelength conversions and who had dropped out of sight some years before. She had wondered what had happened to him. "What's it do?"

"It transduces, of course." Horst laughed at his own witticism. "You and your friends have done much to make the *Infinity Engine* harmless. I am merely doing my part to reverse the process. The new module will shift the output frequencies to ones that will have a more—shall we say—*corrosive* effect on stable matter."

"So you're turning the *Infinity Engine* into a weapon."

Horst nodded cheerfully. "Just so," he said. "A rather deadly one. I am pleased that you apprehend so quickly."

"Why are you telling me this?"

"Because my master wants you to know," the section leader replied. "You are to be a witness to Hydra's greatest triumph, Doctor Nakahara. To fulfill that role, you must understand."

Oh, I understand, all right, she thought. Out loud, she tried a different tack. "Where's Johnny?" she asked.

Still agreeable, Horst shrugged. "Flight Commander Ramos? Somewhere on the lower decks, I would imagine," he said. "My men are making some adjustments to the focusing fields, and he is to watch them do it." He paused, clicked his heels, and raised one hand in a mock salute. "Now, if you will excuse me, Doctor, I have work to do." He smiled. "Baron Strucker is a harsh taskmaster, after all."

Once again, Kellye recognized truth in his words.

A.I.M.'s current headquarters was on an island somewhere in the South Atlantic. Volcanic islands are less common in that ocean than they are in the Pacific; the world's second largest sea has no equivalent to the famous Ring of Fire, the band of tectonic hot spots that surrounds the Pacific. Still, Atlantic volcanoes are not rare, and A.I.M. had found one well suited to its pur-

poses. Dormant, nearly extinct, with no eruptions in the
last hundred-odd years, A.I.M. Island nonetheless provided relatively easy access to geothermal energy. Number One's people had drilled shafts deep into the
mountain's interior. Their probes had searched for,
found, and then drawn upon what was left of the extru-
sion of magma that had, centuries before, worked its
way up through the Earth's crust in some misguided
quest to find the surface. The fire that had belched from
beneath the sea centuries before and created the island
now served A.I.M.'s needs, and the volcano's throat now
served to shelter A.I.M.'s headquarters and laboratory.
The lonely, sea-swept island had served the clandestine
organization well.

At some point during the evening, local time, the *Ad
Astra*'s orbit carried it above A.I.M. Island's horizon.
Seven minutes later, the *Infinity Engine* roared to life.

Created by the *Engine*, shaped and focused by force-
field lenses, a pillar of fire nearly eighty meters across
lanced through airless space and into the upper boundaries of Earth's atmosphere. Instantly, the ionosphere
erupted in a fireworks display as the exotic energies tore
ozone molecules apart, first into their component atoms,
and then into more basic particles, as subatomic bonds
weakened and failed before the onslaught. Protons, electrons, neutrons—all were torn from one another and sent
dancing through the upper reaches, colliding with other
particles and then collapsing into basic photons. Chaotic
ribbons of fire, resembling a spasmodically convulsing
version of the *aurora borealis*, stretched across twenty
percent of the world's sky.

Moving at precisely the speed of light, the beam
seared its path downwards, finding and burning into
the denser air below. As the strata thickened, much of
the disruptive energy translated itself into heat, searing

the air like a million lighting bolts might, making it explode in a futile attempt to escape the quantum force. Superheated vapors rushed outward from the beam's perimeter, and smashed into cooler, as-yet-undisturbed air that recoiled from the impact. A roaring thunder filled the air and echoed along the sea's surface. Thousands of miles away, vacationing tourists on cruise ships heard the concussion's echoes, and wondered what they were.

Number One did not need to wonder. She knew.

The lance of subnuclear fire stabbed into A.I.M. Island. Instantly, the weathered stone of the volcano's cone liquefied and boiled, then erupted into flame as its component atoms crumbled before the wave of exotic energies. Gasses trapped within the ancient rocks heated into plasma and exploded, blasting accreted ash into dust. Igneous rock became lava once more, and then less than lava, boiling into thick sulfurous vapors that eagerly sought escape from their hellish birthplace. Around the island, the air continued to burn, as superheated vapors found one another and tried to combine into more stable forms, only to be torn back apart by the withering beam of energy from outer space.

Two minutes into the barrage, the volcano's north face crumbled and collapsed, tumbling down in fragments, to fill and choke the shafts that A.I.M.'s technicians had so painstakingly bored into the island's structure. More explosions followed as the fire found the organization's main underground lab complex and caressed it, but the new blasts were scarcely distinguishable from the greater holocaust that surrounded them. More and more of the concealed facility convulsed and burned as shock waves and energy swept through its confines, destroying in seconds the work of many, many months. After less than two minutes of direct assault, all traces of human occupation were gone, and A.I.M. Island was submerged in a sea of boiling rock and smothered in a fog of superheated steam.

Three minutes after ignition, the *Infinity Engine* clicked off once more.

Despite all protocols, even knowing the risk she took, the woman known as Number One allowed herself a sigh of relief. Many of her fellows, even in A.I.M.'s innermost circles, joined her.

John Garcia had worked for Hydra for much of his adult life. He had been recruited into the clandestine society from art school, a scant few weeks after realizing that a career in freelance illustration was not in his future, but that one in administration might be. His undeniable organizational skills and his nearly infallible memory had served him well in his ensuing tenure, since they were both attributes that Hydra needed, but that did not seem threatening to his fellow agents or superiors. For the past three years, he had worked directly for Baron Strucker, serving Hydra's founder and head far longer than any other personal assistant had been able to manage.

For nearly half that span, he had served Doctor Doom, as well—though he did not know it.

Eighteen months before, he had taken a vacation from service, visiting relatives in Washington, D.C. He had visited them with the permission of Hydra Internal Affairs, and without revealing the identity of his employer. The trip had been a reward for meritorious service and came at a time when Strucker did not need him, so he had been able to relax and enjoy himself. The days and nights had been filled with sightseeing and parties, with long conversations and good companionship. One evening in particular had stretched into the morning's small hours, and Garcia had awoken on a park bench, with a sour taste in his mouth and a pounding headache that he had identified as the symptoms of a hangover.

He had been wrong.

Behind John Garcia's left ear was a faint line, the last, pale scar of a long-healed incision. In the folds of his brain's parietal lobes, three microchips nestled, connected to the surrounding tissues and to each other with molecule-thin wires. Another silver filament ran from the trio to a hydrogel block implanted in his sternum. The filament contained a sub-etheric transceiver unit that linked the whole system directly to a bank of computers in Latveria.

What John Garcia heard, Doctor Doom heard. What he saw, Doom saw. What he knew, no matter where he was in the world, Doom knew. Now, as Garcia reported to Baron Strucker, he did not know that he also reported to the world's most feared ruler.

"Surveillance reports one hundred percent destruction of the target, Baron," he said. "None of the island remains intact above the shoreline. We should have computer-enhanced satellite photographs within the hour."

"Why did Horst end the barrage?" Strucker sounded irritated. He had commanded total destruction of the site, and A.I.M. Island's present status did not appear to qualify as such.

"The transducer modules showed signs of strain. He did not wish to risk overload."

Strucker looked at Garcia. "The transducers were his project, correct?"

"Yes, Baron."

"And he made the decision to curtail the test sequence, in opposition to my direct orders?"

"Yes, Baron."

Strucker nodded. "Note that," he said. "Alert his line supervisor to punish him upon his return."

"Yes, Baron," Garcia said, making a mental note to contact the commander of Hydra's South America launch facility regarding disciplinary measures. The idea pleased him; Horst had been entirely too arrogant in his dealings with other section leaders and staff. A reprimand would take some of the fire out of the upstart.

Strucker stood, an impressive presence in the indirect lighting of his private quarters. He wore his full uniform as Supreme Hydra now. It was an ensemble of green and yellow regalia that might have seemed garish on another man, but merely appropriate on Strucker's bulky frame. On his chest, Hydra's insignia glistened sullenly, a stylized rendition of human skull surrounded by writhing tentacles. The red steel of his Satan Claw made a odd contrast to the colorful fabric. "Is the studio ready?" he asked. His voice said that it had better be.

Garcia told him that it was, and opened the door for his superior. He followed Strucker as the other man strode through it, taking two steps for each of his master's longer strides. The two men walked though *Barbarosa*'s halls in silence, moments away from telling the world what Doctor Doom already knew.

On Long Island, New York, Sean Morgan took stock of the situation. He had chosen to remain in Stark's facility for several reasons. It kept him closer to the action—or at least, closer to the causes of the action. Futhermore, modern communications made overseeing operations from Stark's place at least as easy and efficient as doing it from his own headquarters. Besides, setting up shop here proved to Stark's people that he meant business, that SAFE wasn't about to turn its back while Iron Man and Spider-Man saved the world.

Or tried to save it.

Across from him, on the other side of the conference-

room table, Bethany Cabe reviewed reports and paperwork silently. Stark had left her in charge while he saw
to "other matters." Morgan wondered what those matters were. He couldn't imagine anything more important
right now than the *Infinity Engine*.

Cabe's lips pursed slightly as she finished one doc-
ument and reached for the next. Several times, she spoke
into a cellular phone in low, urgent tones. After one call,
she looked at Morgan with a puzzled look on her ordinarily impassive features.

"I've got news," she said. "But I'm not sure what
it means."

"What is it?"

"Tony sent a team out to recover what was left of
the flying Dreadnought that Iron Man fought and destroyed. Our in-house system tracked it to a splashdown
in Long Island Sound, but all the team can find are bits
and pieces."

"Maybe it broke up on impact."

Cabe shook her head. "No. It was in one piece when
it hit the water, and still mostly in one piece when it hit
bottom. They found an impact crater, but not enough
matter to justify it."

"That is strange," Morgan had to agree. "Could it
have left under its own power?" Cabe looked at him,
but didn't say anything. He got the point. "Someone
took it, then."

"That's what it looks like," she replied. "No rest for
the weary, I guess." She picked up her phone and started
dialing.

Morgan liked her; she was a professional, and he
liked professionals. A year or so ago, while pulling together the staff and facilities for the agency that would
become SAFE, he had tried to recruit Cabe, based on
her long-term experience and expertise. She had de-

clined, and now more than ever, Morgan wished she had not.

"We've got something." The words came from Hayes, his science officer. "Two somethings, actually." He set down a pair of headphones, and reached to the television monitor's remote controls.

"Talk to me," Morgan said.

"Surveillance satellite picked up something nasty in the South Atlantic." He rattled off a series of coordinates. "At first, we thought it was a volcanic eruption, but most volcanic eruptions don't sport a beam of energy connecting them to orbiting space stations, specifically the *Ad Astra*. Hydra has made its move." Hayes thumbed a button on the control.

"And?" That was Cabe. She had set down her telephone.

"Baron Strucker's on the air."

The television monitors placed around the conference room came to life again. Each showed the same image, a skull and serpentine tentacles. It was the masthead of Hydra. Morgan had seen the logo many times before and wished sadly that he could count on never seeing it again—but he knew that he would never be so lucky.

Hayes thumbed the remote, again and again. The image jumped and flickered as he changed channels. Stark's satellite dish allowed Hayes access to more than three hundred broadcast channels throughout the world, and all of them showed the same image.

"He's cut into commercial frequencies this time," Cabe observed. "So much for limiting his remarks to the intelligence community. He's talking to the general public now."

Morgan nodded. "A lot of Hydra is terror and image," he said. "Strucker's got the muscle to back it up, but likes to be sure about things before he publicizes them.''

Strucker's face appeared on the screen. "Good day," he said. "Some of you may recognize me. I am Baron Wolfgang Von Strucker, Supreme Commander of Hydra." He paused. "As of today, I am also master of the world.''

Like hell you are, Morgan thought grimly. He wondered what Strucker's real agenda was. The German madman's plans had changed many times over many years, from amassing a technological power base to seeking outright global domination. In recent years, however, his bent had altered, as he embraced what he called "glorious chaos," and sought to end human civilization itself. That last part didn't make much sense to Morgan, but little about Strucker did. According to reports that Morgan was not sure he believed, Strucker had actually died a few years before, reduced to raw, empty bones by a mishap involving an experimental nuclear reactor. Incredibly, a biological weapon of Hydra's own creation had later restored him, bringing Strucker back from the dead, apparently little worse for the experience.

Physically, that is, Morgan thought.

Whatever had happened to Strucker, whatever the alpha reactor cube and the Death-Spore Virus had done to him, one thing was certain. The man was insane. The remnants of a great military mind, already devoted to power and conquest, had lately been brought to bear on more terroristic activities. Like never before, Hydra had focused its energies on disrupting society, rather than on controlling it. No matter what Strucker said now, Morgan knew that he was after something worse than mere conquest.

Much worse.

Strucker continued: "—orbiting redoubt, I can rain death and destruction on any point of the world's surface. The power that created the universe now serves me. I have proven this, through the elimination of an island in the southern Atlantic Ocean. I chose this uninhabited site to demonstrate my mercy and my goodwill."

"Uh huh," Cabe said, softly. She didn't sound like she believed him. "I wonder who benefitted most from that mercy."

"Here are the first of my demands," Strucker said. "First, I require that all world governments free any and all Hydra agents they hold in captivity. Secondly, I require that the world leaders recognize me as—"

He went on like that for a minute or two, reciting a list of specific demands in rolling, dramatic tones. Most of what he wanted was obvious—promises of fealty, cash payments, gold bullion, and so on. A few demands were more surprising—the surrender of personal enemies for example, a roll call that included both Tony Stark and Doctor Doom. Strucker continued his spiel with a deadline and the promise of more demonstrations in the event of attempted reprisals. "My next target," Strucker said, "will be New York City." His image faded from the glass, and a cartoon rabbit took its place as normal broadcasts resumed. Hayes pressed his remote again, and the screen went blank.

"Well," Bethany Cabe said. "Modest individual, isn't he?"

Hayes shrugged, but Morgan shook his head. "There's a method to his madness," he said grimly. "Most of the world heard that little ultimatum, but I don't think they'll realize what he's really angling for. Strucker's asking for things he knows he won't get. He might get the heads of state to go belly up and swear allegiance, but the payment is another thing altogether. I don't think that there's that much money in the world anymore. And as for getting Doctor Doom to surrender personally—'' Morgan laughed, derisively and dismissively.

''What's his game then?''

''Chaos. Death and destruction. The end of human civilization as we know it, starting with public failures by the world's governments to protect their citizenry—and the panic that will result. Believe me, if he somehow manages to get what's on this shopping list, he'll be back with another, even more absurd.'' Morgan stared at the screen, unhappy to realize how easily he had guessed Strucker's plan. ''He wants to destroy cities, to destroy nuclear stockpiles—simply to destroy, period. But he'll get the most mileage out of it if he can maximize the chaos he causes, by making people think the leaders had a chance to prevent the destruction, but chose not to.''

''So I guess its up to Iron Man and Spidey now,'' Cabe said, a questioning tone in her voice.

Not hardly, Morgan thought. He reached for his own cellular phone, and clicked the switch that put it on scramble mode. ''It's not as simple as that, Ms. Cabe,'' he said. He dialed a telephone number.

Its area code belonged to Florida.

Some three miles below the smoldering ruins of A.I.M. island, beneath thick strata of rock reinforced by sub-nuclear force, Number One sat again at her desk. Ringed once more around her, like shells of electrons orbiting a nucleus, were the faceless men and women of A.I.M.'s inner circles. Now, however, they sat in utter silence at complete attention. All other work had been set aside since Number One had placed the installation in War

Mode and relocated operations to the subterranean bunker.

"Status report," Number One said. "Capabilities, assets, damage."

"We are at less than ten percent of optimal power levels," one operative said. "The force field holds, but barely. If the barrage had continued another fifty seconds, the field would have failed, and the damage would have continued to affect our current location—and beyond. As it is, the stored power reserves from the geothermal tap are almost completely exhausted."

That news did not surprise Number One. A.I.M.'s preferred strategy for dealing with attacks was to defend itself only as long as it took to run and relocate. The force field was a last-ditch protective measure, invoked only if all else failed. By generating the field within the dense matter of the island's lower strata, her scientists had been able to strengthen and reinforce the rock enough that it could withstand Strucker's onslaught.

At least temporarily.

Another agent spoke. "We saved ninety percent of the personnel," he said. "Only the nonessentials were left behind to perish."

That didn't surprise Number One, either. Insofar as A.I.M.'s philosophy recognized the value of any individual human's life, the inner circle personnel were the organization's least expendable in the entire cartel. Scientists, specialists, management leaders—all were vital to A.I.M.'s anticipated success, and all had been relocated to the subterranean redoubt that lay beneath A.I.M. Island proper.

ZYX-319 answered the third part of her question. After some thought, she had moved him to a new desk and assigned him new duties, the better to keep an eye on him. Now she watched him carefully as he spoke.

"The original installation is a total loss, Number One," he said. "There is no hope of salvage, even if the site's location had not been compromised."

He had raised a point worth considering, Number One realized. How had Hydra found them? The location of the current A.I.M. Island had been a very carefully kept secret, and security on the island itself was very, very efficient. Who had leaked the information to Strucker's people? She considered the question for a long moment, then set it aside. There were more pressing matters at hand.

The *Infinity Engine*, for example. It had proven to be even more powerful than she had anticipated. It was entirely too powerful to allow Hydra to have it. Despite the long odds, A.I.M. had to try and take it; at the very least, she had to see it destroyed.

"Communications status? Can we reach the orbital team?"

"Subetheric units on line and fully functional, Number One."

"Raise them, then." Months before, Modok and his pawns had destroyed A.I.M.'s orbiting space station, another in the series of blows that had rocked her organization during the last year. In the weeks since that debacle, she had dispatched a heavily armed team of salvage and clean-up specialists to the station's wreckage. Their brief had been simple—salvage what they could, and kill any stragglers from Modok's forces.

Now, they could serve another purpose. Strucker would be watching for any approach from below. There was no way for Hydra to know that she already had pawns in orbit.

"Change their assignment," she said. "I want them on the *Ad Astra*, and I want the *Infinity Engine*."

"Yes, Number One!"

"If they cannot capture Strucker's new plaything," she continued, "they are to destroy it." She thought for a moment, considering her next words. "Monitor the situation carefully, ZYX-319," she said. "I am making it your personal responsibility."

The prominent assignment would confuse the others, she knew. Her apparent faith in a minor figure like ZYX-319 would confuse her rivals within A.I.M., and make them unsure of their own status in her eyes. It was a dangerous game to play, but an essential one. Now, more than ever, she had to secure her own position. In times of stress and battle, the turnover rate of Scientists Supreme tended to be alarmingly high. The rank had been a prize more worth striving for than worth having, but she was not ready to surrender it just yet.

Besides, some research had suggested that she could trust ZYX-319, at least for now. He had worked for A.I.M. for more than five years, which was a very long tenure by A.I.M. standards.

And in all that time, he had taken only a single vacation.

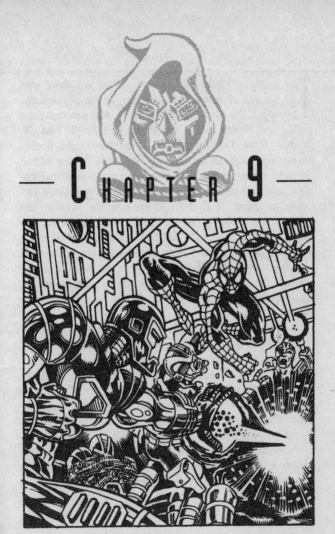

CHAPTER 9

The captured Hydra IFF beacon did its job; there was no sign of resistance or response as the *Skylark* approached the *Ad Astra*. Apparently, Morgan had been right, and Hydra had not realized that SAFE had the device. Tony Stark, inside his Iron Man armor, barely supressed a sigh of relief. This had been the leg of the mission when he and his companion were most vulnerable, and he had been very worried about it. If push had come to shove, if Hydra had fired on the *Skylark*, his own armor probably would have saved him—but the same could not be said for Spider-Man. The pressure suit that the other super hero wore would have protected him from explosive decompression in the event of a major hull breach—but it would not have lasted an instant against the offensive fire that would surely have followed.

"Are we there yet?" Spider-Man asked the question in a childish, singsong voice that he apparently meant to be amusing. "I wanna buy some souvenirs!"

"Our ETA is seven minutes," Iron Man replied. "Did you review those materials I gave you?"

"Sure did, Jeeves," came the reply. "Not quite as much fun as the proverbial barrel of monkeys, but close. Good thing for you I don't get carsick."

Immediately after liftoff, Iron Man had given his passenger a sheaf of blueprints and diagrams, detailing the general layout of the *Ad Astra* and how the *Infinity Engine* docked to it.

"Any idea what kind of trouble we're going to run into up there?"

"I don't know," Iron Man replied. "But we're going to run into something. Lately, Hydra's been fielding everything from street punks to armored demigods."

"You sound like you found that out the hard way."

"I did." Iron Man's voice took on a wry note, and his shoulder twitched in a spasm of phantom pain. "And it was no fun, I can promise you."

Iron Man unplugged the umbilicus that attached his armor to the *Skylark*'s inboard processors. Now that he had downloaded the new short-range navigational software into the console, it would be more efficient to operate manually. He flipped a switch, activating the *Skylark*'s forward-view monitor. It showed about what he had expected.

The *Ad Astra* had been designed, first and foremost, as a scientific research facility. Its docking bay held spaces for three visiting craft, three openings spaced equally around one end of the central spindle. Future space stations might have more such receiving areas, so that the satellites could serve as commerce and transportation hubs, but the *Ad Astra* had only three. Just now, two of them were occupied. One held the *Infinity Engine*; the other held an unmarked shuttle of suspiciously familiar design.

"Wow," Spider-Man said, peering at the screen. "A three-car garage. Must be nice to be rich."

Iron Man ignored the crack. "That's the *Engine*," he said, pointing at the first craft. "The other one must be Hydra's. Look at the collateral damage. It must have been a forced entry. Good thing the *Ad Astra* has automated re-seal systems, or they would all be breathing vacuum."

"Looks that way to me, too. What now?"

Iron Man tapped a series of keys. "They probably don't know we're here yet," he said. "We're invisible to their surveillance systems, and I'm not getting any signals from the *Ad Astra*'s radar. I figure we can go in the front door." He kept tapping keys. "Docking's largely automated and computer controlled. Unless they've wrecked things completely, I should be able to . . ." His voice trailed into silence.

"What's wrong? Incoming?" Spider-Man sounded faintly nervous, and Iron Man didn't blame him; they were terribly vulnerable just now. The *Skylark* had moved well beyond the *Infinity Engine*'s angle of fire, but there was no telling what weaponry Hydra's forces had brought with them.

"No," Iron Man said. "Nothing like that. There's something wrong with the automated docking program. I can't get the protocols to engage." He entered a few more command sequences, but to no avail. In front of him and to his left, a systems monitor filled with screen after screen of apparently random numbers.

"Looks like a pocket calculator threw up," Spider-Man observed. "Any other options? There must be a back door to the program." Behind Iron Man's mask, Tony Stark realized with surprise that his traveling companion knew something about computer programming. The web-spinner was referring to lines of code that would allow someone to sidestep passwords and security measures, giving them direct access to the program's main functions.

It was a good question; unfortunately he only had a bad answer for it. Iron Man pointed at the cascading digits. "That's the back door," he said grimly. "Or was. Someone's patched it."

"More trouble from our friends in the green pajamas?"

"No. I don't think so. I don't think Hydra is that smart, or subtle. They probably would have just welded the doors shut. This looks like someone else's work, but I can't tell whose." He thought for a moment, considering possible suspects and their reasons for acting; then he pushed his own questions aside. They would have to wait. Ramos and the others were the immediate problem.

"So we ram it, too?"

"No, I don't think so. That would mean more damage, maybe to the *Skylark* this time."

"What now, then?"

"We do it the hard way."

A vibration swept through the *Skylark* as Iron Man fired the rescue craft's steering jets and brought it alongside the inner surface of the *Ad Astra*'s outer ring. "Get ready for a bump," he said.

With a hollow ringing sound, the *Skylark*'s lower hull plates found the *Ad Astra*'s outer surface, and slid along them. Metal scraping against metal filled the shuttle's interior with a grinding noise. Iron Man reached out with one steel finger and stabbed another switch. The *Skylark* lurched and locked in place, and the grinding noise stopped.

"Well, I guess they know we're on the scene now," Spider-Man said dryly.

"Unplug yourself and get out of the suit," Iron Man said. "You won't need it anymore."

"Excuse me? I assumed we were going EVA, since we're nowhere near a hatch."

"No." Iron Man clambered into the shuttle's rear and flipped another switch. The four unoccupied passenger seats swung up and away, revealing a square panel set in floor plates. "No extravehicular activity this trip, at least not for you," he continued. "We're making our own hatch." As the panel slid back, the steel plates of the *Ad Astra*'s were revealed. They turned white with hoarfrost instantly, as moisture in the shuttle's atmosphere found the cold metal and froze against it.

"I'm not sure I follow you," Spider-Man said, already shrugging out of his pressure suit. "What's keeping us against the *Ad Astra* now that you've opened the door? The *Skylark*'s atmospheric pressure alone should blow us free. Do you have some big magnets mounted on this baby?''

''No.'' Iron Man pointed at the opening's lower lip. It was hard to see where the gray steel of the *Skylark*'s plates gave way to the *Ad Astra*'s outer hull; the two metals seemed to have merged. ''Magnetism wouldn't give a good enough seal. This one's tight, down to the molecular level. This ship has a flexible steel mounting frame, so that it can configure itself to the station's curved surface. An annealing field that my boss, Tony Stark, came up with did the rest.'' Very few people knew that Stark was Iron Man, and the millionaire inventor saw no reason to add Spider-Man to their number. ''The *Skylark* is a contiguous piece of metal with the space station now,'' he continued. ''Submarine rescue craft do something similar, with rubber fittings and electromagnets. The *Skylark* is a prototype rescue craft, designed for emergency and forced boarding. Stark designed it with just this kind of mission in mind.''

''So we've got a nice view of some deck plates now. Great. What good does that do us?''

''Cover your ears.''

''I beg your pardon—*ow!*''

Spider-Man's good-natured griping turned into a yelp of genuine discomfort the instant that Iron Man fired his repulsor rays in a tight, focused pair of beams. Metal shrieked in protest as the concentrated energy plasma tore through the *Ad Astra*'s newly revealed deck plates, and the sound of destruction echoed loudly inside the *Skylark*. Iron Man guided the beams carefully, defining an arc about one inch shorter on each side than the gap revealed by the rescue craft's floor panel. After long seconds, the two cuts he made met, forming a closed rectangle defined by a perimeter of seared metal.

Spider-Man didn't say anything, but took his hands from his ears.

Iron Man raised one booted foot and then brought it down again, hard, at the precise center of the frost-covered steel rectangle. The flat-armature motors that drove his armored exoskeleton did their work. With a booming noise, the slab of metal tore loose and free, to fly into the *Ad Astra* and leave an opening behind. Fluids squirted from torn conduits, and sparks flew from broken wires within the multilayer wall, severed by the repulsor rays or by the impact. There was a slight rush of air as two atmospheres met and equalized their pressures.

"Does that answer your question?" Iron Man spoke the words as he dropped through the impromptu entrance.

"More or less," Spider-Man said. "It raises a new one, though. What happens when it's time to go?"

"We can worry about that later." Iron Man looked from side to side. The curved corridor, given shape by the *Ad Astra*'s outer ring, seemed empty to the naked eye. A quick proximity scan confirmed the first impression. He looked back at Spider-Man. "Coming?" He let himself sound impatient as he asked the question. "I thought you wanted to buy some souvenirs."

"I wouldn't miss it for the world," Spider-Man said, following him.

That might be the price, too, Iron Man thought.

Space is quiet to the point of silence, because a vacuum cannot carry sounds. Spacecraft are noisy, for much the same reason. Surrounded only by airless space, they keep sound trapped within them. Kellye Nakahara's time on the *Ad Astra* had taught her that much. The space station was a veritable noise factory, with a thousand joints and junctures to creak faintly as metal ground against metal, and countless electrical motors and devices to hum and click and whir as they went about their work. She had gotten used to the constant background chatter, the ambient symphony that the *Ad Astra* played to accompany its course through the void. It had become part of her daily life, like the too-clean air she breathed, or the textures of the food she ate. Even the Hydra craft's forced docking had been only a slight and brief break in the constant muttering din, thanks to the complex damping systems between the receiving bay and the station's main work areas.

The sudden thunder she heard now was a different matter altogether. It seemed to come from everywhere and nowhere, to roll through her tiny world. It resonated through the deck plates beneath her, rumbled and crested and then rumbled again, only slightly more faintly. The effect was somewhat like being trapped inside a struck bell, but the sound was too bass for that, too close to thunder and too far from ringing. It went on for what seemed like long minutes, but it could only have lasted seconds before fading enough for her to hear the angry keen of system alerts, and the even angrier sound of Horst's barked demands.

"What was that? What has happened?" The Hydra section leader said the words harshly and angrily, sounding both annoyed and frightened. He had been working on the transducer module, muttering to himself and cursing as he swapped out one component after another. From where she sat now, shackled to a padded seat, Kellye had been able to hear most of his words and watch most of his work. Now, as he stood and approached one of his men, she had to crane her neck to follow him with her eyes. Several Hydra agents did the same, but the giants did not.

"What has happened?" Horst repeated his question. He glared angrily at his lieutenant. "Explain!"

"I—I don't know, Section Leader. An explosion, perhaps?"

Horst shook his head. "No," he said. "That was an impact, not a concussion. Something has struck us. What do the proximity sensors say?"

"N-nothing, Section Leader! The intruder alert would have activated automatically!"

"What about the *Ad Astra*'s own sensors? Do they confirm the readings?"

There was a long pause as Horst's underling tried not to answer, then gave up and replied. "They aren't working, Section Leader. We can't make them work for some reason."

Horst turned his head to look balefully at his captive. "Doctor Nakahara," he said. "The damage to this station done by A.I.M.—did it extend to the surveillance equipment?"

She couldn't see any reason not to answer him. "It did," she said. "But the Damage Control crew replaced everything. They had to, for the docking systems to work."

"Some other reason, then," Horst said. He looked back at his lieutenant. "Sabotage?"

"P-possibly," came the halting reply. "The fourth crew member, Deeley, is still loose. He may have done something. I can investigate."

"No; there is no time for that now." Horst stepped briskly to what Kellye knew was a diagnostics console and punched in some commands. "Hull breach," he said. "Outer ring, third quadrant. Atmosphere is holding, but hydraulics and electrical connectivity are both gone. We've been boarded."

"Section Leader! That is not possible! We would have known—"

Horst silenced his lieutenant with a single, steely glare. "We can talk later of what is possible and of what is not," he said. "If there is a later. Now, take four men, and investigate the third quadrant." He paused, apparently thinking. "No, take all of the men, and D-1 and D-2, also. We can't afford to take risks."

D-1 and D-2 were evidently the oversized super-agents that Horst's people had been using as stoop labor. Kellye was impressed at how swiftly the massed Hydra forces streamed from the main lab area, eager to fulfill their commander's orders—or fearful of the consequences if they did not. Less than five seconds after Horst's last words, she was alone with the section leader again.

"What about you?" she asked. "Or is your own life one of the risks you can't afford to take?"

"Hardly." Horst lifted a padded case to a convenient work table and opened it. "You do me an injustice. I surrendered all concerns for my personal safety when I enlisted in Hydra, Doctor Nakahara."

For some reason, she believed him. Horst seemed to have an odd measure of integrity. Ideology could make people do some strange things, and Hydra was nothing if not a physical manifestation of a very specific ideology. She had heard too many stories of men doing remarkable, even courageous things in the service of evil masters to discount them entirely.

From the case, Horst pulled a half-dozen small devices. They were turtle-shaped, flattish semispheroids, each with four stubby little outcroppings on its outer edge, and each with a smaller projection on its top. Kellye didn't like the looks of them. She tried to watch Horst as he moved from one bank of equipment to another, stopping at each to do something with the little gadgets. It was only when he reached the transducer module that she could see him clearly again and watch as he positioned one of the turtles inside the still-open unit's workings. Metal met metal with a clicking sound, and Horst nodded with satisfaction.

"What are you doing?"

He looked back at her. "Do not concern yourself with this just now," Horst said. "I see no need to distress you."

She repeated her question. "What are you doing?"

"I am preparing for visitors," Horst said. He did something to the turtle; on its back, a small red light flashed to life.

"Look, if you surrender, the authorities will—"

Horst looked at her in genuine surprise. "The only authority I recognize is that of Baron Wolfgang Von Strucker," he said. "However, I know what you mean. Tell me, Doctor Nakahara, what makes you think that the new visitors to the *Ad Astra* represent your government?"

Kellye didn't say anything, not sure of what he meant.

"Think about it," Horst continued, seating himself in from of the main control panel. "The *Infinity Engine* is a great prize, and a weapon without peer. My own experiment, however sadly truncated, proved that much. It is a prize many would want."

Kellye made no response.

The Hydra section leader tapped keys on the complex panel before him. He continued speaking, but in a distant, almost idle tone. His attention seemed focused elsewhere. "Every government in every nation would like to have the *Engine*," he said. "Even the so-called 'pacifist' states would no doubt kill to take it, despite their alleged principles. A.I.M. would take it in an instant, given the opportunity. I know of a dozen revolutionary armies and clandestine societies that would do the same. Each would no doubt put it to many interesting uses that you would find most unpleasant.''

He spoke the truth, Kellye realized with a sick feeling. Names echoed in her mind. A.I.M., Hydra, the Secret Empire, the Maggia—slightly different peas, but all of them in the same pod, all with similar goals. Until Horst had unleashed his improvised weapon on the "demonstration site," she had never considered the *Infinity Engine*'s lethal potential. Now it was only too obvious that she had helped create and roadtest the world's deadliest weapon. In the hands of an outlaw state, or a terrorist army, or any of the super-powered criminals who were so common in today's headlines—

She shuddered. The potential for devastation was limitless.

Horst was still talking. "They will not have it, however," he said. "Hydra will. Hydra—or no one." He continued his work.

Over the clicking of the keys, Kellye heard new sounds, faint in the distance—impacts and rumbles and electrical crackling noises, unlike any she had heard before, but recognizable nonetheless. They were the sounds of battle. "It sounds like your boys found the visitors," she said.

"Yes." Horst settled back in his seat and gazed steadily at her. In his left hand, he held something that looked like a television remote control. "Yes," he repeated, gazing steadily at her. "It would seem that is the case." His right hand reached out, and pressed one last button on his control console.

Kellye heard something else then. It was a low sound, at the lowest limits of human hearing, a low kind of noise that she could feel more than she could hear. It was distant, rumbling thunder, at once the stuff of dreams and nightmares. She had heard it before.

It was the sound the *Infinity Engine* made as it came to life.

Horst looked at her. He smiled. "No one but Hydra," he said.

Shaped somewhat like a child's toy top, or like a gyroscope without its frame, the *Ad Astra* was a ring surrounding a spindle. The whole assembly spun endlessly on its central axis, so that centrifugal force provided at least part of the artificial gravity in the outer ring. That meant that the direction away from the spindle was "down," and heading inward was going "up." Four shafts containing elevators, stairwells, and other conduits connected the outer structure to the inner. The outer ring held most of the technology, life sciences, manufacturing and research laboratories—but not all of them. In the center of the space station, near the environmental systems, was the main physics lab, and the current home of the *Infinity Engine*'s main control modules.

Walking along the outer rings made Spider-Man slightly dizzy, an unfamiliar feeling that he did not like. There was something about the way the floor curved upwards ahead of him; it seemed to reach for but never quite meet the "ceiling." It was an effect that Peter Parker had seen a few times in movies, and read about many more times in books and magazines, but the reality was somewhat more unsettling. The alternative was worse, though; floating at zero gravity was something he had done before and hadn't liked at all. It played hob with his highly developed reflexes and acrobatic skills.

"Got your bearings yet?" Iron Man, walking beside him at a brisk clip, asked the question. His metal boots made a loud, ringing noise as they struck the deck plates.

"Oh, sure, I could spend the rest of my life like this," Spider-Man lied easily. "Why? Want to pick up the pace?"

"I think we'd better. They know we're here. I want to get to the elevators and the central core."

"They would have to know," Spider-Man said grimly. He just hoped that nothing had happened to the hostages—yet. He leaped forward, bounding to the curved ceiling, clinging for an instant to the cool metal plates, then dropping down again. He hit the floor in an easy cartwheel motion that he turned into a somersault and then a flip, each gyration taking him forward. "I'm ready," he said, bouncing from one corridor wall to another and picking up momentum. "Let's go!"

He had wondered how Iron Man would navigate the *Ad Astra*'s relatively cramped confines; it hardly seemed the place for boot jets, let alone for the oversized versions that his armored companion wore now. He glanced back to see what came next.

To his surprise and delight, Iron Man did something that Spider-Man had never seen him do before. He lifted one foot about six inches above the floor and paused a moment. There was a clicking noise as a pair of steel rollers popped out from the boot's sole, already spinning as he brought the foot back down again. A second later, another step, and Iron Man was roller-skating along the floor's gentle curves.

"I didn't know you could do that," Spider-Man said. "Is that something new?"

"An old trick," the other super hero said. "It comes in handy."

"I'll bet it does. You must be a real terror at the Roller Derby."

Iron Man didn't say anything. In a low crouch now,

he rocketed ahead, moving so swiftly that even Spider-Man was hard-pressed to keep up. He managed to do the job, though, bounding and bouncing in a fluid trajectory that gave him an easy view of what lay ahead. Web-swinging was impossible in these spaces; his web-shooters weren't much more use than Iron Man's boot jets.

Even allowing for the relatively constricted dimensions of its interior, the *Ad Astra* was enormous—much bigger than he had realized. Several times, they passed side corridors that led to other laboratories and facilities. He knew from his hasty review of the schematics that Iron Man had given him that some passages also led to living quarters and recreational areas. He wondered what it would be like to work and live on the *Ad Astra*, thousands of miles from the world that had shaped him—but still almost unimaginably far from any of the other planets. For nearly a week, he knew, the crew of the *Infinity Engine* had done precisely that, four brave souls alone in the huge installation.

Lots of empty rooms here, he thought. *Lots of places a guy could get lost.*

Or hide.

They were making a big assumption, taking it for granted that Hydra's boarding party would headquarter themselves in the central core. Remote controls and closed-link communicators had done a lot to eliminate distance; there was no reason why they couldn't do the same here. *A few transceiver units*, he thought, *and remote monitors, and they could migrate most of the control functions to anywhere they wanted.*

Iron Man had stopped in his tracks, balancing on his skate wheels' edges. Spider-Man wondered how he did that.

"What's going on, ShellHead? Hear something?"

Iron Man raised his hand for silence. Spider-Man complied, even holding his breath for the moment. It was a safe bet that his companion's armor included a sonar system in addition to its more exotic scanners, and there was no reason to make things more complicated than they had to be. His own spider-sense was limited in range, and good only for threats that were immediate both in time and in space. If Iron Man could provide earlier warnings, Spider-Man wanted them.

Then he heard them too: heavy footfalls, much too heavy to be made by a normal human's feet. They had a metallic quality to them, like steel slamming against steel, and at first, he thought Iron Man had started walking again. He looked to one side and realized that he was wrong.

The metronome-like thunder continued, but it was hard to tell where it was coming from, or if it was getting closer. There was something about the *Ad Astra* that played tricks with his hearing, some acoustic quality that made sounds hard to isolate and track. He wondered if his companion was having the same difficulty.

"Trouble," Iron Man said, spinning on one wheel. His hands came up in a gesture that Spider-Man found familiar. "Move it—now!"

Spider-Man moved. He ducked down and out of the path of Iron Man's repulsors, then bounced up to the ceiling again. Even as he moved, streams of energy erupted from his companion's armored gauntlets, blasting through the wall that had been Spider-Man's most recent perch.

Through it—and into what lay beyond.

"Hail Hydra!" The cry came from many lips simultaneously, as a dozen or more green garbed figures surged through the breach that the repulsor blasts had created. They moved fast and with the casual ease of well-trained shock troops, crowding into the corridor and falling into position instantly. Bolts of energy split the *Ad Astra*'s air as agent after agent fired his sidearm, the same kind of energy pistol that Spider-Man had encountered in the city, an apparent lifetime ago.

"Hail Hydra!" A burly man, masked like the others, raised his pistol and fired it at Spider-Man, who dodged it easily enough—and then dodged another in midleap.

They're good, Spidey thought, *but not that good*.

He bounced and bobbed again, spinning in midleap to spray a blob of web-fluid at the burly man. It caught and clung, gluing the guy's sidearm to his side.

"Better luck next time, chuckles," Spidey said, not meaning it. Even as he spoke, he dodged another shot and sprayed more web, snaring two Hydra agents this time. He wondered why Iron Man had struck first, against such relatively conventional threats. This certainly wasn't nearly as much trouble as dodging shots twenty stories above street level. As goons went, the Hydra squad members were more skilled than most— but hardly worth ShellHead's brutal preemptive strike.

Then he saw the real reason.

Behind the torn metal of the wall, another figure stirred. Human in shape but not in size, it lifted itself from the floor and lumbered out into the corridor. Seared fragments of green fabric clung to its seven-foot frame, the tattered remnants of a Hydra uniform that must have served partially to conceal its inhuman nature. The ragged scraps parted and fell, revealing not flesh, but gray steel behind them.

Uh oh, we're in trouble, Spider-Man thought. His spider-sense flared. This was why Iron Man had blasted the wall, and this was what had made the footfalls. *Some kind of killer robot*, he thought.

Another giant figure stepped from the shadows and

joined the first. Still cloaked in Hydra's green, it was unmistakably a twin of its partner.

Make that killer robots, Spider-Man amended silently.

Then the time for thought was gone, as a spike-studded steel fist came rushing towards his face.

Kellye Nakahara stared at the man who held her hostage. There was something nearly hypnotic about the blue eyes that gazed back at her, showing no emotion or even concern.

"You'd be better off giving up," she said. In the distance, she could hear the sound of battle, but she could not tell how far away that battle was. The *Ad Astra*'s trick acoustics made judging distance difficult, if not impossible.

"To whom? If the invaders are my master's enemies, I will die at their hands. If they are your precious authorities, the master will see to it that I die for failing him." Horst held an energy pistol in his right hand now, aimed in Kellye's general direction. "No, Doctor, I am afraid that my fate is certain. It is yours that is in question."

"What do you mean?"

"I have no instructions to execute you, but I cannot allow your genius to fall into certain hands," Horst said. "If my people fight off the newcomers, you will live. If the newcomers are triumphant, and if they prove to be representatives of certain organizations whose interests rival Hydra's, I will liquidate you myself. If, however, the invaders are your 'authorities,' you might just live to bear witness to Hydra's greatness."

It made a certain kind of screwy sense. Even if the attempt was ultimately a failure, Horst and Hydra had demonstrated a certain genius in the last few hours. Having someone left behind to tell about it might appeal to Strucker and his disciples.

Something about Horst's phrasing struck her as odd, however. She thought about it, and considered his last sentence. "Wait a minute," she said. " 'Might'? "

Horst nodded. "A final experiment, if you will. Or a backup plan; call it what you like. I have deliberately misaligned the *Engine*'s primary and secondary siphon circuit banks, and overridden the quark enumerator safety interlocks."

Kellye's blood ran cold, nearly as cold as the sweat that suddenly beaded her brow. "It'll overload," she said. "It'll overload and blow up."

"Just so." He smiled and indicated the remote control he held. "The process is reversible at any point before completion, of course—unless I use this, and render the control panels inoperable."

"An explosion in the *Engine* will reduce the entire space station to kindling."

"Perhaps. It depends on the power accumulation gradient, of course. I believe you are correct, however."

Kellye stared at him in horror, trying to think through the terrible implications of his words. She would die, of course, and so would anyone unlucky enough to be on board duing the blast, but that hardly seemed important. There were other, more widespread effects that such an explosion would have. This high in orbit, the blast wouldn't have much effect on the surface. There was no medium to carry the concussion, and any debris would be small enough to disintegrate on reentry. But off-planet—

She tried to think of it as a complex problem in orbital physics, which is what it was. Reduce the *Ad Astra* to bite-sized pieces. Depending on blast orientation and other factors, maybe sixty percent of the fragments would shoot into space or into the atmosphere, to burn and disintegrate. The remaining forty percent would still be beyond counting, however—and would remain in orbit for centuries to come. She thought of a million or so bits of steel, each moving at bullet speed in its own path around the world—each unmindful of what might be in its path, and each uncaring.

"It'll be the end of space travel," she said slowly. That much was obvious. A cloud of steel fragments that could take centuries for nature to clear would be an effective barrier to any spacecraft humanity could muster.

Horst nodded, and she thought some more. It would be the end of satellites, too, both new ones and the ones already in orbit, for the same reasons. Space was mostly emptiness, but that much debris would find its targets, sooner or later. By destroying the halo of satellites that ringed the Earth, Hydra would effectively destroy all telecommunications, and information exchange, and surveillance, and anything else that had to be in outer space to work. All of the advances of the Information Age, and a few more besides, would be wiped out in an instant.

Her captor smiled. "I believe the phrase you are looking for," he said, "is 'the end of civilization as we know it.' "

The *Infinity Engine*'s rumble, mere background noise a moment before, suddenly seemed like thunder in Kellye's ears.

Iron Man saw the Dreadnoughts before Spider-Man did—or rather, he saw their distinctive signature indicated on his armor's proximity detection system. According to SAFE, the things operated on some kind of internal, cold-fusion reactors. It sounded like an interesting engineering proposition, and Tony wondered how Hydra's engineers had managed it. Magnetic pinch-bottle fields, probably, so that the fusing gasses would expand and cool in the event of failure, instead of erupting in fire and death.

The Dreadnoughts had other ways of providing such goods, of course.

A brief, medium-intensity blast of his repulsor rays was enough to open the wall that hid the Dreadnoughts without killing their human companions. As an added bonus, it knocked one of the armored behemoths off its feet, buying Iron Man a second or two to assess the situation.

They weren't the same as the one he had encountered in the stratosphere. This version was smaller and lighter, more like the original model than the oversized flying Dreadnought that had destroyed his remote unit earlier. A quick systems scan confirmed his visual impression; this pair was less armed and less armored even than the original model.

Tony wondered why. Specialized labor units? A lighter payload and less fuel expenditure for Hydra's spacecraft? Greater speed and maneuverability? Or simple economy? It didn't really matter; even trimmed down, these two seemed quite capable of dealing death.

"Spider-Man! Look out!" The words were moot before they finished leaving Tony's lips. Only a moment before, Spider-Man had been wading into the Hydra shock troops with merry abandon; now, moving with what Tony Stark could only regard as inhuman speed and reflexes, the web-spinner dropped down and under the Dreadnought's fist. As Iron Man watched, the other super hero gripped the robot's arm and dragged it behind his back, apparently trying to capture the robot in a wrestling hold.

"Its hands are weapons," Iron Man said, thinking of

the hydrazine jets. "Don't let the fingers point at you."

"Now you tell me," Spider-Man said. He had caught the robot's other arm in one hand, and was doing his best to keep its fingertips aimed in some other direction. With a fluid motion that defied all laws of human anatomy, he twisted his own body up and around, so that his feet were pressed against the robot's back, one between what would have been its shoulder blades, one just above the thing's waist. Spider-Man's legs were bent almost double at their knees. The robot thrashed and struggled, trying to shake Spider-Man off—or scrape him off, against a convenient steel wall. "Can you can give me a hand here, ShellHead?" There was a note of urgency in Spider-Man's voice. "I can't hold this thing forever."

Iron Man was amazed he could hold it that way at all. *No one can move like that. He must be all joints and rubber bones*, Tony thought.

Unmindful of the other Hydra operatives, uncaring of the ineffectual small-arms plasma burst that splashed against his armor, Iron Man went to his companion's aid. Still riding his skate wheels, he shot across the narrow stretch of deck plates that separated them. Even as he moved, a cybernetic signal from Tony Stark's brain activated circuits in Iron Man's armor. By the time he reached his partner, a diamond-edged rotary saw had already emerged from his left glove's wrist module. It screamed as it bit into the robot's midsection.

"This could be messy," he said. The saw dug through one layer of metal and into another.

"That's okay; tomorrow is laundry day," Spider-Man said. Still gripping the robot's arms, he pulled harder and began to straighten his legs.

The Dreadnought's body bent. At first, it bent where it should bend, at the points in its artificial anatomy that mimicked the human form: at its shoulders, at its waist. Then it bent like metal would bend, the long axis of its body twisting and deforming under the continuous pressure.

Iron Man kept cutting. The first two layers of the thing's armored midsection parted and split to reveal wires and cables beneath. Iron Man drew his blade across the Dreadnought's belly, letting its teeth cut a wider and wider gap. Sparks flew and hot chips of metal bounced off of the golden mask that hid Tony Stark's handsome features.

One of the human Hydra agents fired a plasma burst at Iron Man's head. He barely noticed. Another agent shot at Spider-Man, but the web-spinner managed to dodge the burst without relaxing his grip, twisting his body even as he rode the bucking Dreadnought. Two seconds passed, then three.

Another second, Tony thought. He knew from experience that the thing's main processor was almost certainly in its torso. *If I can just keep this up another few seconds—*

He couldn't. He was concentrating so thoroughly on the task at hand that he didn't notice the proximity scan's flashed warning, or see the oversized humanoid form approach him from his left. He didn't see the two green-gloved fists intertwine their fingers and come swinging towards him in a short, tight arc.

Iron Man felt them hit, though.

Steel rang against steel as Iron Man's head rocked back. He fell as the double-punch slammed into his armored form, knocking him away from the first robot and leaving Spider-Man to fight his own battles. His extended saw retracted automatically into its home in his wrist module.

Forgot about the other one for a moment, Tony

thought. He blinked his eyes rapidly and shook his helmeted head, trying to clear the haze that suddenly filled his brain. That had been a bad mistake; he hoped it wasn't a fatal one.

The second robot smashed into him again. Iron Man brought his own fist up in an uppercut that moved at speed only slightly less than that of sound. He caught the Dreadnought on the point of its jaw and sent it slamming back into the opposite corridor wall. A second later, it had pulled itself together and was coming at him again.

Definitely a lightweight model, Tony thought. *Not lightweight enough, though*.

As the robot leaped on him, he considered his options. For some reason, the thing wasn't using its flame jets or freezing bursts; it was possible that this version of the Dreadnought simply didn't have those accessories. That might make sense, if its main function had been stoop labor for Hydra. It might also mean that its armor plate was lighter. He thought back to his encounter with the first Dreadnought earlier in the day, and his lack of success with the repulsor rays.

Things might work differently this time.

As the Dreadnought landed on top of him, he brought both hands up and pressed them flat against its chest. Another mental signal, and magnetic fields sealed the steel of his gloves to the steel of the Dreadnought's chest. The robot's impact and forward momentum sent shock waves through his arms, but he rode with it, bringing the Dreadnought up and over him. As the behemoth's steel body reached its apogee, he fired both repulsors at maximum power—but only for a split second.

There was a flash, nearly contained by the tight seal between Iron Man's hands and the Dreadnought's armored chest. There was a grinding noise, as metal tore and split and tore some more. There was a muffled concussion as the twin blasts found something inside the Dreadnought that was vulnerable. Then there was sudden thunder, as Iron Man released the robot's inert form and let it drop to the corridor floor. Smoke drifted from the two holes blasted through its body.

Or maybe just lightweight enough, Tony thought.

The entire conflict had taken perhaps a dozen seconds.

Iron Man turned to see what had happened with Spider-Man and his adversary. He had a split-second glimpse of the gash in the first Dreadnought's abdomen widening into a gaping hole as Spider-Man finally managed to extend his own body to its full length. *Spidey's stronger than I realized,* Tony thought. Then there was a sudden, sun-bright flash as the Dreadnought's internal fusion reactor ruptured and died. The Dreadnought made a tearing sound as its metal bones ripped apart. Then the thing fell to join its comrade on the floor.

A telltale light inside Iron Man's helmet flashed, reporting a surge in ambient magnetism. Tony smiled at the confirmation of his own theory. It had been a pinch-bottle system, after all.

"Wow!" Spider-Man stepped away from his fallen foe. He looked disoriented and actually stumbled as he moved. Iron Man realized that the strange conflict had been more of a strain than it had seemed. Spider-Man said, "I ache in places I didn't even know I had!" He massaged his legs. "I don't want to have to do that again!"

"You won't have to." Iron Man spoke in a thoughtful tone, his mind only half on the conversation. Something else in his helmet's displays had caught his eye, an energy signature that was both familiar and disturbing.

Spider-Man glanced around himself. He had managed to web up four or five Hydra agents, but the rest were missing, apparently having fled the scene of battle. "We're short a few playmates," he said. He gestured at the webbed-up Hydra agents. "Looks like your buddies took a powder during the commotion. Like rats on a ship, right, pals?"

Iron Man ignored him. There was something about the energy signature that was almost hypnotic. He had seen it somewhere before, but it wasn't in any of his suit's data banks. He searched his memory, frantically.

"Excuse me," Spider-Man said. "Earth to Iron Man, come in please. Do we go after the half-dozen finks who took off, or do we move on to the big enchilada?" He paused. "And what's that sound?"

As he spoke, Tony Stark finally noticed the new sound filtering through his audio receptors. It was familiar, too, a dull roaring sound, nearly subsonic, that he felt more than heard. He recognized it instantly. With a sick feeling, he recognized the distinctive bundle of energy wavelengths, as well.

They both belonged to the *Infinity Engine*. Worse, the signature was breaking up and becoming more chaotic, as if the *Engine*'s processes were becoming unstable. Lighting-fast, a thousand possibilities raced through his mind, none of them good.

Iron Man turned to face the webbed-up prisoners. "The *Engine* is running," he said. "Why? What are your people up to?"

He got no answer, just hostile, defiant glares. At another time, he might have admired the Hydra agents' twisted loyalty to their demented cause, but not now. The possible consequences were too dreadful. Reluctantly, he raised one hand, and let the captives see the flat lens of his repulsor. "You saw what this did to your mechanical assassin,'' he said grimly. ''Now, talk.''

''Um, ShellHead—'' That was Spider-Man, a tense, concerned note it his voice.

''Not you,'' Iron Man snapped. ''Them.''

He was conscious of Spider-Man staring silently at him, every muscle in the other man's body tensed, as if to spring. *He thinks I'll do it*, Tony thought, with a degree of surprise. *He's willing to try and stop me.* Instead of attacking, however, Spider-Man simply stared at him, as if wondering if he would go through with it. For a moment, Iron Man wondered too—then fear and his implicit threat did the rest.

''We had our orders,'' one of the Hydra operatives finally said. ''The *Infinity Engine* belongs to Hydra, or it belongs to no one.''

Spider-Man looked at Iron Man. ''Not good?'' he asked.

Iron Man didn't bother to answer. Instead, he began moving towards the elevators again, faster than before. He didn't bother to check if Spider-Man was keeping up.

There wasn't time.

— CHAPTER 10 —

"**D**rop them, Mister! Put the gun down, and the other gadget, too!" The words were spoken in an unfamiliar tone, but in a voice that Kellye Nakahara knew well. She took her eyes off of Horst and his gun, spinning her head to see a familiar form framed in the lab door.

Horst did the same. His eyes widened as the saw the husky black man there. "Ah," he said. "The elusive fourth crew member joins us at last."

Douglas Deeley nodded. He held an energy pistol in one hand, and Kellye wondered where he had gotten it. Had he taken it from one of the invaders, or had he brought it along on the trip, for reasons of his own? She had long since begun to think that there was more to Deeley than met the eye. His success in evading the captors had confirmed certain impressions he had made on her earlier in the mission. She realized now that he had earned his medals and decorations.

"That's right," Deeley said. He stepped into the room. "Drop the gun and the control, now."

"I think not." Horst's eyes stared calmly at Deeley as the other man approached. He kept his gun trained unwaveringly on Kellye, however. "That would be to surrender my primary advantage." He smiled. "I suggest, instead, that you drop your weapon, and I will refrain from executing the lovely Doctor Nakahara."

Deeley continued to approach the still-seated Hydra section leader. Without taking his eyes from Horst's, he spoke. "Sorry I couldn't make it earlier, Kellye. I've been trying to make things harder for these goons, and easier for anyone who tries to rescue us."

The radar, Kelley thought. *He's the one who sabotaged the* Ad Astra's *radar systems.*

"Plus, there were too many of them here for me to handle by myself," Deeley said. "This one shouldn't be any trouble, though."

"I would disagree with that assessment," Horst said calmly. The index finger of his right hand tightened around the pistol's trigger. "I would also suggest that you stop where you are." He still stared at Deeley, now paying no attention to his captive.

That was his mistake.

For long minutes, keeping Horst's unsettling blue eyes locked with hers, Kellye had been working her feet against one another, loosening the low-cut shoes she wore. Now she brought her left foot up in a short, sharp kick, like a dancer might. The blow didn't connect, of course; she was seated too far from Horst for her kick to reach him.

Her left shoe, did, though.

It came loose from her foot and flew across the four yards or so that separated her from the Hydra section leader. It smashed into his left hand just below the wrist and sent the remote control device spinning up and away. Kellye tracked the thing carefully with her eyes, allowing it to draw her complete attention. She certainly didn't want to be shot, but Horst's gun was the lesser threat right now. She was only too well aware of what those turtle-like devices on the various lab consoles were, and what they could do.

Horst cursed, a short expletive that split his veneer of courtesy and restraint, and revealed the killer beneath.

The remote shot upwards, spinning lazily in the *Ad Astra*'s simulated gravity.

Deeley leaped at Horst. He dodged a plasma burst from the other man's pistol and slammed into him.

The remote came down and bounced off of a counter top, then rebounded upward again.

Horst punched Deeley in the face as the other man landed on him. Struggling, the two fell to the floor. The Hydra agent tried to shoot again, but lost his grip on the gun as Deeley's left fist slammed into his gut. An instant later, Deeley's gun spun free, too, the victim of a well-placed kick.

The remote clattered to the steel deck plates of the floor and slid to near where Kellye sat.

Horst brought his knee up in a savage kick, knocking the wind from his attacker. He glanced around the room, looking for his gun but finding something else. Without bothering to stand, he threw himself at the remote, reaching for it frantically with green gloved hands. His course took him near the still-shackled Kellye.

Too near, but not near enough.

Kellye brought her right foot down, hard, on Horst's left hand. There was a satisfying sound as bones cracked, and Horst gave a yelp of pain.

He won't be pushing any buttons with those fingers for a while, she thought with grim pleasure.

She was right; it was Horst's right hand that reached for and found the remote.

Deeley threw himself on the Hydra agent again. He had found his own pistol, and pressed it now against Horst's skull. "Last warning," he said grimly, and Kellye was surprised at how right his voice sounded making the implied threat. "Don't do it."

Horst did it. His right index finger pressed down, hard.

Kellye moaned as six explosive charges erupted simultaneously. They exploded at various points about the room, from the homes that Horst had given them, none of them doing much damage—but all of them together doing quite enough. In less than a second, the *Infinity Engine*'s main control banks were smoking ruins.

There was no way to turn the thing off, now, Kellye realized. She wondered how long she had to live.

Deeley cursed, but Horst laughed. It was a ragged, unpleasant sound, nearly a cackle of glee, and almost completely out of keeping with his earlier, polished persona. It was not a good sound, and certainly not the one she would have chosen as modern civilization's death knell.

"Hail Hydra!" Horst said. "Cut off a limb and two more shall take its place! Immortal—"

"Aw, put a sock in it." A new voice interrupted, and a gray blob of what looked like webbing splashed against the Hydra agent's face. It sealed his lips and turned his words to inarticulate, muffled grunts. Horst's eyes bulged from their sockets above the impromptu gag. Deeley and Kellye both looked away from him and at the still-open door, to stare in shock and wonder at the two forms standing there.

"Hello, Doctor Nakahara, Mister Deeley," Iron Man said. "I hope you can tell us what's going on here."

"One of them better," Spider-Man said. "It'll take Laughing Boy here at least an hour to pry his mouth open." He put one fist in the other, and popped his knuckles. "That is, unless he wants some help doing it."

Despite herself, Kellye began to hope again.

It took nearly ten minutes for Doug Deeley and Kellye Nakahara to explain just what had happened during the preceding hours, while Iron Man hastily inspected the damaged control banks. Deeley told about playing a cat-and-mouse game with the occupying Hydra forces, about ducking and dodging the agents until he could make it back to the main lab to free Nakahara. Kellye told about being taken captive and about what Horst had done to

the *Infinity Engine*—and about the potential consequences of his act.

"He knew what he was doing," Iron Man said
grimly, looking up from his work. "These systems are
scrap, and, according to my own monitors, the *Engine*
will reach threshold levels in a matter of minutes."

"So, what do we do?" Spider-Man asked the question in a tense tone of voice. "Aren't there any backup
systems in the *Engine* itself?"

Kellye shook her head. "No," she said. "Not in the
sense you mean. When we docked, we migrated its main
control modules to this deck. All that's left in the mobile
platform is the *Engine* itself—the accumulators, the
beam formers, the taps. Hydra monkeyed around some
with that stuff, too, but just to customize it."

"How about the central processor?"

The physicist looked at him quizzically, as if surprised at his familiarity with the project. "It's still
there," she said. "We didn't need to move it."

Spider-Man looked at Iron Man. "We might be able
to do something with that," he said. "What's the fastest
route there?"

"That's delicate equipment, harnessing enormous potentials," Kellye said. "You could make things worse."

"I'm sorry, Doctor Nakahara," Iron Man said. "I
don't think that's true. Things can't get much worse than
they are now." He had obviously realized the implications of such an explosion in orbit.

As if on cue, Douglas Deeley looked up from a corner console. As the other three were speaking, he had
been working on the *Ad Astra*'s central radar banks. "I
hate to interrupt, folks, but it's necessary." he said.
"I've got this thing working again. We've got company
at three o'clock."

"Friend or foe?" Iron Man asked the question in an urgent tone of voice.

"Oh, come on, ShellHead," Spider-Man said. "At a time like *this*, do you really think friends are gonna come calling?"

Deeley ignored the quip. "I'm not sure," he said. "The silhouette's all wrong for any American-made craft, but it doesn't look like Hydra's buggy, either."

Iron Man looked at the screen. "A.I.M.," he said.

"Aim what?" Spider-Man asked. "And at whom?"

Iron Man's electronically filtered voice didn't hide his annoyance. "It's an A.I.M. shuttle. Heaven knows what they're doing up here."

The deck plates beneath their feet shook and rocked as something slammed into the *Ad Astra*. A low rumble swept through the space station, mingling with and then being drowned out by the *Infinity Engine*'s roar. Sirens wailed in the distance.

Spider-Man pointed at one monitor screen where remote video cameras displayed one section of the outer ring—or what was left of it. Now twisted fragments of torn metal danced through the void. "Heaven knows," Spider-Man said, "But I can guess. If we were planetside, that would have been an air-to-air missile. They're firing on us."

"You'll have to take care of the *Infinity Engine*," Iron Man said. "Doctor Nakahara can help you."

"But—"

"I'm going EVA, to deal with A.I.M. If they make a lucky hit, they'll accelerate the process and cause an explosion that much sooner. If they aren't lucky, all they'll manage to do is kill us."

"That's all, huh?"

"I think it's quite enough," Deeley said dryly.

*   *   *

Behind the controls of the A.I.M. space shuttle, moments before the *Ad Astra* was to come into view, HMV-667 considered his assignment and his options. Even though it was fully armed, the A.I.M. shuttle was not an assault vehicle; it lacked the heavy armor that would have suited it for such a role. Intended for salvage work, it was the wrong tool for this job—but Number One's orders had been very specific.

"Take the Infinity Engine—or destroy it."

HMV-667 and his people had been on the other side of Earth when the orders came; the agents were doing their best to recover what they could from the remains of A.I.M.'s space station. Some weeks before, the civil war waged within A.I.M. by Modok and his artificial lieutenants had spread to encompass the space platform—and the station's occupants had not been the winners. None had survived the battle, but some of the equipment that they used had. That had been HMV-667's original assignment, to salvage certain specific items, and to assess the possibility of reclaiming the station as a whole.

He wished that were his assignment still. He had little taste for battle, and less for facing off with Hydra. A.I.M., in its own way, stood for order and control; Hydra's agenda these days seemed to be chaos, pure and simple. It was hard to believe that the two organizations had long ago been one.

RKG-891's voice sounded in his headphones. *"Ad Astra* in view, sir." She sounded like she was enjoying herself, as if she were eager for battle. "Coming in range—now."

HMV-667 sighed, precisely the kind of human gesture that had limited his advance within A.I.M.'s ranks. "Ready the concussion torpedoes," he said. "Fire on my command."

"Target?"

"The outer ring, I think. That first, and then the central structure. Show them that we mean business before we board."

"Yes, sir. Ready on command."

HMV-667 watched the *Ad Astra* come closer, growing in the monitor before his seat. It looked very much like the ruined space station in orbit on the other side of the world, which wasn't surprising. Stark's construct had been the model for A.I.M.'s. Now, hanging against the black sky, it was an impressive sight, precisely the kind of achievement that he had strove towards since joining A.I.M.. Unfortunately, his career track had taken him away from pure science and engineering, to other, less impressive endeavors. He thought for a long moment, considering choices he had made, and challenges he had failed to meet.

"In optimum firing range, sir." RKG-891's voice held a different note now, as if daring him to hesitate longer.

HMV-667 sighed again, more softly this time. The moment for regrets was past. "Target the living quarters area," he said. "No sense in damaging anything essential." He paused. "And fire—now!"

The shuttle craft shook as the first concussion torpedo leaped into space. A moment later, another one followed it.

Spider-Man repeated his earlier question. "What's the fastest way to the central processor?"

"The elevators in the main core, I guess, then cut across the hydroponics lab," Kellye said. She reached for a tool kit. "I'll go with you."

The *Ad Astra* shook again, as something more slammed into it. Douglas Deeley, monitoring events from a nearby control panel, cursed softly at what he saw displayed there. "Forget that," he said. "We just took a major hit in the main core. The conveyors are junk."

"But—but that means the only way to reach the *Engine* is by going EVA," Kellye said. The idea didn't please her, but she accepted it. "We'll have to go outside, then access it through the docking area airlock."

Spider-Man shook his head. "There's no time for that," he said. "Besides, we'd be sitting ducks for whoever's out there. What about the system umbilicus? That's pressurized, right?"

She looked at him, surprised again by his easy familiarity with the station's esoteric equipment. After docking with the *Ad Astra* and moving the control systems to the main lab area, the crew of the *Infinity Engine* had connected the two systems with a series of cables and fiberoptic connectors, snaked though a flexible conduit that ran along the *Ad Astra*'s central axis. That was the system umbilicus. "It is," she said. "It has to be— but you can't make it that way! It twists and turns like a snake, and you'd—"

Her words trailed off. Spider-Man had already stepped to a section of deck plate behind the main control panel, which still smoldered from Horst's sabotage. He sank his fingers into the floor's metal, got a grip, and pulled. The plate came back with a tearing noise, and he dropped into the narrow gap beneath it. Nearby, a dozen heavy-duty cables led to a large, plastic conduit, generous accommodation for the control linkages, but much too cramped for a human being.

Any normal human being, at least.

Spider-Man gestured at Kellye. "I'll need the tools," he said.

She handed them to him. "You'll need this, too,"

she said, handing him her personal communicator.

"Cell phone, huh?" He took it. "I hate these things. You wouldn't believe how much trouble they can cause." He examined it carefully before tucking it under his belt.

"It's easy to use," she said. "I can talk you through what you have to do."

"Okay. This doesn't lead anywhere else, does it?" He was referring to the conduit.

She shook her head. "Just to the *Engine*, down in the docking segment."

"Good," Spider-Man said. "I can't get lost, then." Then he started moving. Half crawling, half slithering, he forced himself into the plastic conduit. In seconds, he was lost to sight.

Iron Man erupted from the airlock before it had completed its cycle. Traces of water vapor and air followed him into space, to freeze and crystallize and dance like diamonds in the harsh sunlight. He ignored them and stared instead at his helmet's proximity alert monitor. He saw readings for shrapnel and debris, for the *Ad Astra*'s mammoth mass—and for the A.I.M. shuttle's smaller one.

He spun, using his boot jets to tumble and yaw, and his armor's strength to train his repulsor rays on the shuttle. He fired a single burst, trying for what looked to be its fuel tanks, but missing by a few inches as the ship rushed forwards. The repulsors dug into the craft's hull, splitting metal but doing no major damage.

That'll teach me to rely on line of sight, he thought, and activated his targeting system. Instantly, neon-colored crosshairs imposed themselves over his field of vision. It was very much like looking through a bomb sight.

The A.I.M. craft fired another missile. This one slammed into the *Ad Astra*'s central spindle, just above the docking segment. Tony winced. He knew that the space station's automated sealing systems would limit the damage, but the sight was still painful. He had spent many millions of dollars constructing the *Ad Astra*, and nearly as many repairing the damage that A.I.M.'s technovirus had done to it. He wasn't about to let the organization of renegade scientists destroy his dream again.

He trained both repulsors on the A.I.M. shuttle, smiling tightly with satisfaction as the targeting system found and locked onto the ship's main thruster. Eliminating that would cripple the craft and render its occupants relatively easy pickings. He fired.

As he did, the shuttle craft's pilot did the same.

The blast came from a laser cannon located just above the cockpit window. It smashed into Iron Man and splashed across him, blinding him as his mask automatically polarized its eye slit lenses to protect him. Inside his suit, alarms rang and indicators flashed, though he could not see them clearly. Enough glare had gotten through before the lenses darkened to dazzle him, and Tony Stark blinked frantically to clear his vision.

He had missed his target; he knew that much. His armor's refractory coating had taken the brunt of the blast and could probably manage another one, but he didn't want to find out. It was time for evasive action. He fired his own steering jets, cartwheeling in an erratic pattern as he waited for his eyesight to return. Plasma beams cut through airless space surrounding him, but he did not see them, relying instead on his armor's computerized autopilot to guide him through the fiery maze. More concussion torpedoes zoomed past him, and radar alarms rang in his ears. His last tumble brought him to within a dozen yards or so of the A.I.M. craft. As it came into focus again, Tony acted.

A quick burst of repulsors took care of the laser cannon; another blast sealed the missile launchers. Tony examined the ship's contours carefully, looking for other weapons ports and finding none. With a single mental command, he activated his armor's boot magnets and boosted their output to maximum level. That, along with a brief burst from his steering jets, was enough to bring him somersaulting to a perch on the shuttle's upper surface. His boots slammed into place, letting him cling to the ship in much the same way that he had seen Spider-Man cling to buildings. Using the annealing circuits in his boot soles would have made the bond more permanent, but he decided against doing that. This would be a temporary visit.

A voice crackled in his helmet. It was the craft's pilot. He had found Iron Man's frequency. "Surrender or be destroyed." The A.I.M. operative sounded like he meant business.

"I don't see how," Iron Man replied, using the same wavelength. "I'm inside your arc of fire and your main weapons are junk, anyhow. You're helpless." He activated his suit's subsurface scanning and imaging systems. Instantly, a hazy network of lines and symbols imposed itself onto his view of the ship's hull, a detailed schematic of the circuitry beneath. At such close range, he could detect the induction currents created by the shuttle's control lines, and his armor's image enhancement system could convert them into a visual display. In effect, he was peeking beneath its skin to see how it worked. It wasn't quite x-ray vision, but it came close.

"A.I.M. is never helpless," came the reply. The shuttle's main thrusters flared to life again, and the craft began moving in a line that would intersect with the *Ad*

Astra's main core. "Surrender, or we will ram the facility and destroy it."

Like they won't if I do, Tony thought grimly. It was obvious why A.I.M. had taken a hand in the conflict; the organization had a long-established rivalry with Hydra and would never let Strucker's people obtain a prize as valuable as the *Infinity Engine* without a fight. It was entirely possible that A.I.M. would destroy it first. *Take it or break it*, Tony thought. *I can't let them do either*.

He considered the craft's wiring system carefully. He had to act fast; Spider-Man and the others were depending on him. Unfortunately, there wasn't much he could do at this point with just muscle power. He could crack the cockpit open, of course, and maybe reach the controls. That would kill the occupants, however, and he did not want to do that. Most measures he could take would have similar consequences.

Not that A.I.M.'s operatives would have similar qualms, were the situation reversed, he knew.

The imaging system's display became more and more detailed as his suit's sensors accumulated additional data, refined it, and translated it into something that Tony Stark could see. One specific indicated cable seemed especially interesting. It ran along the center of the shuttle's upper surface, from the cockpit to the engine area, like a spinal cord might run along an animal's back. According to his displays, the line was alive with complex signals, the back-and-forth flow of data that characterized a primary command conduit.

"Surrender," came the demand again.

"I don't think so," Tony said grimly. He extended his diamond-edged rotary saw and activated it with a single command, then drew its whirling edge across the ship's hull. Metal chips flew as it bit, and bit deep. He suspected that the A.I.M. craft was not an assault vehicle; its armor was far lighter and less durable than the Dreadnought's had been, and it parted easily. He pulled the revealed cable free from its moorings and tugged gently. Immediately, the line came free as it unplugged from its next connection. He pulled the detached line free carefully, smiling with pleasure as the connector came into view. It was a standard-issue fifty-pin jack, and it would match easily with one of several inside his armor. On his chest, a metal panel slid open, revealing a bank of connector ports.

"What are you doing?" The A.I.M. pilot was beginning to sound concerned. He was probably getting system failure reports on his control display. He knew something was going on, even if he didn't know precisely what. "Surrender now! I demand it!"

Tony snapped the cable into place, as he had earlier with the *Skylark* using the same port. He smiled again, as his suit's BIOS found, assessed, and integrated the new command sequences. Software programs examined each other, then merged—with the resulting amalgam in Iron Man's control. A moment later, A.I.M.'s ship was functionally an extension of his armor, his to do with as he would.

That's that, he thought. *They're done.* He reached out with his mind, sending signals to the cybernetic pickups that lined his helmet, and from there, into his armor's computer system.

Behind him, the A.I.M. craft's main thruster flickered and failed, extinguishing itself in immediate response to his mental command. Up ahead, retro-rockets flared, obeying another order and stopping the craft before it could ram the space station. Iron Man looked at the schematic display lining his helmet, and took the next step. One by one, a dozen or so indicators dimmed and extinguished themselves, as his mental commands rewrote the A.I.M. craft's operating system. Surveillance, controls, guidance, targeting, ordnance—one by one, the ship's subsystems clicked off and stayed dead as he imposed password overrides on them, locking them down and off. It took less than a minute to complete the process. Another few seconds, and he had confirmed that that there were no backups or program backdoors that would enable the A.I.M. operatives to undo what he had done.

"You're dead in space, guys," he said into his helmet mike. "You sit here and don't make trouble, and I'll come back for you later. I've got some nice SAFE agents planetside who would love to chew the fat with you."

There was no answer, but he hadn't expected one. Along with all of the other non-life support systems, he had shut down the invader craft's radio transmitter. The A.I.M. agents could hear him now, but not answer, which was just the way he wanted it. Their own vehicle was their prison now. He disengaged the cable from his chest plate and released it, then launched himself once more towards the *Ad Astra*, leaving the A.I.M. agents helpless in their now-dead craft.

He was halfway back to the space station when it opened fire on him.

Long years before, when Peter Parker was living with his Aunt May and Uncle Ben in Forest Hills, he had been a quiet, studious child—but not without the moments of mischief common to all little boys. One of those moments, coupled with the first stirrings of a scientist's curiosity, had led him to explore his neighborhood's storm sewer system. Armed with a flashlight, he had wriggled his way through a drain grating and into the catch basin, then made his way though a series of cool concrete culverts and tunnels. It had been an exciting afternoon, made even more exciting when his flashlight had failed and left him to wonder, in the dark, if he would ever find his way back.

This situation reminded him of that, but he knew he was playing for higher stakes this time.

At least there was no darkness this time. Nakahara's tool kit had included a headband flashlight, like a miner might wear. Its beam stabbed into the distance, cutting through the shadows and gloom. There was no darkness, but there wasn't much to see, either—just wires and cables, and the gray curving walls of his cylindrical passage.

The plastic conduit was barely big enough to contain him. It was flexible but confining as it wound its way around the *Ad Astra*'s main structural members. It didn't help much that here, in the central core, the station's simulated gravity was nearly zero. Spider-Man's stomach did flip-flops as he slithered toward his destination. His clinging abilities made up for the lack of gravity in some ways and certainly made the trip easier than it would have been for a normal person. They didn't do much for his sense of balance, however, and provided no remedy at all for the nausea that welled up inside him.

Space sickness, he thought. *Well, there's a first time for everything. But not now, please.*

He didn't particularly mind enclosed spaces, but he wasn't wild about them, either. As Spider-Man, his agility and acrobatic skill were at least as important as his enhanced strength—but to use those attributes, he needed room for maneuvering. There was no room here. More than once, the conduit constricted and nearly blocked him as it rounded a corner, and it took every iota of flexibility and strength to make his way along the winding path. Time became an elastic thing; he had no idea how much of it passed as he inched towards his destination. He sweated and he itched, but there was nothing to do about either problem. There was nothing to do but keep moving.

As he traveled, more shock waves swept through the *Ad Astra*'s structure to reach him. He wondered if they were the result of additional bombardments by the A.I.M. newcomers, or something else. He didn't know, and he couldn't know; there was no time to waste on curious phone calls back to the others, even if he had enough space to use the phone. All he could do was ride out the shock waves and keep moving. The two crew members would have to fend for themselves.

Nakahara and Deeley. He hoped they were okay. Both of them seemed competent, and surprisingly good at getting out of sticky situations, but Spidey knew that there were half a dozen Hydra agents still running around loose on the station, and he knew also that they were nothing but trouble. Nakahara had told him about Powell, and Ramos was still among the missing. Spidey had warned the two remaining crew members to be on their guard; now he hoped they heeded his advice, because there was no way he could turn back at this point. All he could do was drag himself along by his fingertips, making his way to the central processor core.

Alone, except for the throbbing wail of the *Infinity Engine*.

— CHAPTER 11 —

The system umbilicus twisted and turned like a convulsing snake as it wound its way through the *Ad Astra*'s guts, marking a tortuous path from the main control room to the space station's docking area, where the *Infinity Engine* waited. Since the umbilicus was a retrofit—a change to existing hardware—it couldn't take the most efficient route, but was limited instead to the only available one. Spider-Man wondered how long the thing had taken to install; certainly longer than he was taking to make his way through it.

According to Haberman—a world away, a lifetime ago—the umbilicus was an automated extension of the *Infinity Engine*. Installing and implementing it had been a matter of powering up some simple minature servo-mechanisms and running a low-grade utility program. It could retract the same way for stowage somewhere inside the spacecraft. "The process," the old man had told him, "is somewhat like a self-threading motion picture projector." Peter Parker, in turn, had looked at the ship's schematics, and been silently grateful that putting the umbilicus in its serpentine place hadn't been his task.

Now Spider-Man wished he had thought to knock wood.

The twisted trail took a final hairpin turn as it emerged from the *Ad Astra*'s central shaft and entered the *Infinity Engine*. Spider-Man had to negotiate the same turn to finish his journey, and it wasn't easy to do. Even his limber body had its limits, extreme though they were, and it was all he could do make himself bend where he had to bend, to twist and writhe and struggle through the constricting conduit, then straighten out again without breaking something that wouldn't bend. It wasn't easy, and it wasn't just hard; it was very nearly

impossible, as draining a task as any he had ever set
himself. His every joint ached and his muscles throbbed
in protest as he twisted and pushed one last time, then
dropped from the conduit's open end into the main hold
of the *Infinity Engine*.

"Whew," he said. "I must have taken a wrong turn
somewhere near Albuquerque."

There was no one to hear him.

The *Infinity Engine*'s main hold was bigger than he
had expected. Even half-filled with banks of humming
equipment, it had more open spaces than some apart-
ments Peter Parker had rented over the years. Electro-
luminescent fixtures set in the curving hull lit the place,
and in their bluish glow, Spider-Man could see empty
fittings and spaces where other banks of equipment had
once rested. Bright metal glinted from cut edges, and
empty connectors looked back at him. At first, he
thought the missing components reflected Hydra's involvement, then he remembered what Kellye Nakahara
had told him earlier—they had moved the *Engine*'s operating consoles to the *Ad Astra*'s main control room
when integrating the two spacecraft.

That must be what the boy genius blew up, Spider-
Man thought grimly.

The space, though large, was still enclosed and insulated to some degree from the surrounding station
structure. The craft's hull caught the wailing throb of the
Engine's processors and amplified it. Struggling though
the conduit with that noise in his ears had been bad
enough; listening to it at point-blank range was awful.
He knew that it resulted from some secondary harmonic
between the *Engine*'s transducers and the supporting
structural members, and he knew that the only way to
silence it was to shut down its source. Despite that

knowledge, the sound was maddening, and made it difficult to concentrate on the job at hand.

His spider-sense wasn't helping things either. Its warning was strictly flight-or-fight stuff; usually, it spoke to the more instinctive areas of his brain, demanding that Spider-Man jump or hide or punch or run or just *do something*, beseeching him to take some simple measure of evasion or defense.

Neither would do him much good here. There was nowhere to hide from the coming cataclysm, and no simple, single foe to smash. This was a more complex challenge, and he had to force himself to ignore the extrasensory warning that shrieked through every fiber of his nervous system.

It wasn't easy.

He raised the communicator that Nakahara had given him to his lips and pressed the microphone key. "Goldilocks to Mama Bear," he said. "Come in, please."

"Spider-Man?" Kellye Nakahara's voice crackled back at him. "Is that you?"

"No, Spider-Man couldn't make it. This is the Easter Bunny," he said.

To her credit, Nakahara didn't dignify that with a reply, but simply asked, "You've reached the *Engine*?"

"Yes, ma'am. Now tell me what I need to do first."

"Okay. There should be a large, gray housing with three readout displays near its bottom, at the far end of the hold. That's the quark enumerator. Find it, and remove the cover."

"Okay if I force it?"

"Sure. I don't think Mr. Stark will mind, under the circumstances," Kellye said, and proceeded to give him his instructions.

She was good, Spider-Man realized, without any trace of surprise or hesitation. He knew of Nakahara primarily as a theoretical scientist, but she apparently knew her way around hardware, too—or at least, around this particular piece of hardware. She spoke in measured tones that carried well, even in the *Engine*'s wailing din, and that betrayed none of the stress she must have felt, mere moments away from unimaginable destruction. Step by step, she guided him though the quark enumerator's inner workings. One minute passed, then two, and a third, as Spider-Man's gloved fingers applied unfamiliar tools to the device's components, making minute adjustments in response to Kellye Nakahara's exceeding precise instructions.

"Okay," he said. "The left potentiometer says 'zero.'" He paused. "What does that mean?"

"It means you've restored the safety interlocks," Kellye's relayed voice said. She sounded relieved.

"That's good?"

"That's very good. We're halfway there."

"Halfway?"

"You've got to realign the primary and secondary siphon circuit banks. That way, with the interlocks back online, the process will restabilize itself and the *Engine*'s operating system should shut it down automatically."

"'Should,' huh?"

"Right now, I'm not taking anything for granted."

Spider-Man blew out a breath. "Probably a good idea. What's next?"

"To your left, you'll find the siphon circuit banks. Open them up, but don't force things. They're much more delicate than the enumerator."

Spider-Man found an access panel on the low, squat console to his left. He selected the appropriate screwdriver from his miniature tool kit and put its blade in place, then spun it with fingers that could twist solid steel bars into knots. The first screw backed out from its home with gratifying speed, and was followed almost immediately by the second. In less than a minute, he had detached the access cover and lifted it away, to reveal a bank of metal and glass components that glistened in the *Infinity Engine*'s artificial light. They looked like nothing he had ever seen before.

"We're in," he said. "What's next?"

There was no answer, so he tried again. "Hello?"

For a split second, he thought he had pressed the wrong switch on the communicator, or that the device had picked the most inconvenient moment possible to fail. A quick check showed him that he was wrong on both counts. Everything seemed all right with the communicator, which meant that something had gone wrong at Nakahara's end. Equipment failure? An accident? Or something else?

He thought about the Hydra agents who had managed to evade capture in the earlier skirmish. If any of them had made their way to the command center—

He forced the thought from his mind. There was nothing he could do about that now, and if he didn't do something about the problem at hand, nothing else would matter.

Spider-Man stared glumly at the equipment his labors had revealed, trying to ignore the howling wail of the *Infinity Engine*, and the persistent buzz of his spider-sense. Less than two feet from his masked features, energy potentials sufficient to shatter a small continent raged and struggled against their electronic bonds, looking for release and sure to find it. Right now, only he stood between modern civilization and its sudden, untimely end.

It was too bad that he had no idea what to do next.

*   *   *

Two plasma bolts cut through space where Iron Man had been an instant before. The fringe corona of one of the twin beams caught his left boot's trailing edge and made the red metal glow briefly before Iron Man's trajectory carried him beyond it. Another ray lanced through the void and splashed against his helmet's impassive mask; his polarized lenses cut the worst of the glare, but Tony Stark still grunted in surprise and dismay, then sent more fuel and control signals to his bootjets, commencing evasive actions even as he assessed the situation.

It was the Hydra boarding craft that had fired on him, still locked backwards in the *Ad Astra*'s docking bay. Unlike the A.I.M. craft, this was an assault vehicle, heavily armed and shielded, well equipped for its intended purposes. It was easy to see what had happened—some or all of the leftover Hydra agents had made their way back to their boarding craft and were doing their best to get home—even if doing so meant going through Iron Man.

Tony Stark looked at the remote imaging system that lined his mask's inner surface. It gave him a high-resolution, virtual-reality schematic of the Hydra craft armament, based on computer-enhanced remote visuals. He didn't like what he saw. Missile ports studded the Hydra ship's leading surfaces and a pair of high-energy plasma cannons were placed at its nose, angled to have almost 360-degree firing ranges. He wouldn't be able to get beyond their arc of fire the way he had with the A.I.M. ship. All he could do for the moment was dodge their output, and he wouldn't be able to do that forever.

Two bolts found his chest plate and converged, heating the red metal to near incandescence before his thermocouple could absorb the majority of the energy and divert it to other purposes. His diagnostics display claimed that the suit's interior readings were all within acceptable ranges, but he could have sworn he felt the heat against his chest, despite the intervening layers of insulation and coolant. *These guys are good*, he thought. *Too good.* He brought his hands together, trained the palm repulsor units on the Hydra shuttle, and fired. Something sparkled in the darkness, and his beams dissipated into nothingness several meters before finding the ship's steel hull.

No doubt about it, he thought. *Strucker has some skilled people working for him these days.* He knew what had happened, even before his suit's computers assessed the situation. A few of his own experiments had pointed the way to something similar—a low-power force field that wouldn't offer much barrier to physical weapons but that would screen and disperse the frequencies of his repulsors. *They were ready for me*, he thought grimly. His preferred weapons, the repulsors, were close to useless, and the plasma cannons' jockey was good enough to keep him from getting much closer without risking substantial damage.

It was time to try something else. The oversized wrist pods on Iron Man's armored gloves slid open, revealing twin banks of specialized equipment. There were the diamond saws he had used earlier and the similar drill bits. There were magnetic impulse generators and a variety of physical probes. All of them moved aside on hidden tracks as the tools he needed now emerged from their hiding places inside the suit. Silently, a pair of parabolic antenna-like structures unfolded and locked into place.

They were particle beam generators.

Another Hydra plasma bolt caught Iron Man in his midsection, but he barely took notice of it. Alarm signals wailed in his ears as he brought his hands together, but he ignored the warnings. The miniature beam projectors were deadly weapons and demanded his full attention, at least for the few moments it took to deploy them. He brought his fingers and palms together, and smiled tightly as concealed receptors locked into place. Automated subsystems reset, overriding his own motor controls and locking his wrist and hand modules into a single, integrated unit. Precise alignment was essential here; the particle beam projectors could tolerate an error range of approximately zero, and any mistake could carry dreadful consequences—for his target, and for himself.

Two more plasma bursts streaked toward him; he dodged them easily. His suit's computers were better than Hydra's targeting systems, but not so much better that he could dodge the beams at close range and take matters into his own hands.

At least, not in the traditional sense. Tony glanced at his hands and smiled at what he saw there. The two glove systems had merged in precise alignment, and the metal fans of their projection antennae had merged to form a contiguous steel bell with his hands in the middle. He moved the joined hands now, training them in the general direction of the Hydra craft, and was rewarded as a crosshair appeared on his mask's imaging system.

He was ready.

"Ahoy, the ship," Tony said. He spoke into his helmet microphone, set to what he knew was Hydra's hailing frequency. "Do you read me?"

The only reply was another plasma burst.

"Ahoy, the ship," Tony repeated. "This is your last warning. Cease fire and surrender, or risk total destruction."

Along the Hydra craft's length, metal slits opened and steering jets flared. They were making a run for it, and Tony wondered why. The Hydra agents obviously thought they had the strategic advantage; they were wrong, of course, but that didn't explain their behavior. A glance at an internal display answered his question; the *Infinity Engine*'s readings were going off the scale. Whatever Spider-Man and the others were trying to do, they weren't doing it fast enough.

Well, there was no reason to let Hydra leave the party early.

Iron Man trained the particle beam projectors on the Hydra shuttle's nose assembly, focusing them precisely between the two plasma cannons. He fired a half-second burst.

"You had your chance," he said softly.

' The Hydra craft's hull dissolved into gray ash as focused, high-energy particles ripped through it, shattering intermolecular bonds the way a sledgehammer might shatter fine china. The effect was gratifyingly well defined; though the beams had focused on a half-inch circle, the zone of destruction was nearly a meter in diameter, but still precisely circular. Its edges were as clean and keen as a razor's.

The sphere of devastation included the plasma cannons. Like their mountings, like the structure that held the mountings, they collapsed instantly into dust. The microparticle debris dispersed instantly as gasses erupted from the craft's interior, rushing through seals that had similarly dissolved.

Iron Man considered that for a moment. He certainly didn't owe the Hydra agents any favors, but he wasn't much for cold-blooded murder, either. He flew closer to the now-unresisting ship and examined the damage at close range. It wasn't as bad as it could have been; he had chosen his target well and managed to limit the damage primarily to tactical systems. The leaks were little ones, made obvious by the white plumes of escaping, freezing vapor, and there really weren't very many of them—but there were enough. If someone didn't do something about the various pinholes, the Hydra agents would be breathing vacuum soon.

Tony shrugged and disengaged his particle beam projectors. They folded shut and returned to their hiding places. Even as they did, two other units replaced them. The new devices were chemical spray nozzles that spat a viscous plastic sealant into the ship's damaged fuselage. *No rest for the weary*, Tony thought, as the plastic fused and hardened against the ruptured seals. He played the streams carefully along the sundered metal, making sure he caught each of the ruptures. In moments, he had repaired the worst of the damage, and the passenger area was airtight again.

"Third chance, guys, and your last one," he said into his microphone. "Surrender, and we can avoid further unpleasantness. Otherwise, I can do this again, and I won't bother with the tire kit patch next time."

"We surrender, we surrender!" The word crackled in his earpieces. The steering jets, deploying themselves only a moment before, shut down and went dark.

Iron Man considered what to do next. He had to see about helping Spider-Man shut down the *Engine*, but he didn't trust the Hydra agents to sit quietly and wait for further instructions; in his experience, Strucker's snakes weren't prone to keeping promises. The moment he turned his back, they were likely to make a run for it. He could access their control systems and shut them down, the way he had with the A.I.M. ship, but that wouldn't be as effective under these circumstances. The Hydra craft was still docked in the *Ad Astra*, which meant they could escape out the back door, and cause more problems for Nakahara and the others. He didn't really want to board and take them into custody, but it didn't look like he had much choice.

Besides, there was still the matter of the missile ports that stared darkly from the craft's lines.

A new voice sounded in his helmet. "Ahoy, the ship," it said. "Prepare for boarding!" It sounded on several different frequencies—the ones used by Hydra, and by the Avengers, and by government agencies.

Now what? A.I.M.? More Hydra? Or someone else, eager to snare the *Infinity Engine*'s secrets? He looked at his proximity detection display. Dissolving the Hydra craft's nose assembly had created enough chaff in the vicinity to cloud his radar system, but not enough to blind it. He could see that a new craft had entered range, even if its silhouette was sufficiently obscured by ambient debris to be unrecognizable. Warily, Iron Man drifted away from the Hydra craft's damaged nose. In response to another mental command, the plastic spray nozzles retreated back into his glove assemblies, and the particle projectors took their place once more.

"Ahoy, the ship!" The words repeated themselves. "Prepare for boarding!" An unfamiliar vehicle came into view from beyond the *Ad Astra*. It looked very much like a standard issue NASA space shuttle, but that didn't mean anything. At least a dozen other organizations had pirated the design in recent years. This one sported armor plate and some weaponry that looked like after-the-fact additions.

Tony shrugged, even as he bought his hands together again. He needed knowledge before the could act. "Ahoy, yourself," he replied, along the same frequencies that the newcomer had used. "Who are you? What is your authority?"

"Identify yourself," came the response.

"I am Iron Man. I operate on Avengers Priority One,

and I am here with the full authorization of Stark Enterprises, of the United States government, and of the United Nations Security Council.'' That was overstating matters a bit, but there was no reason to take chances that didn't need taking. The receptors on his gloves locked together again, and the crosshair display appeared once more, this time making an apparent halo around the mystery ship. ''Now, identify yourself,'' he said, ''or risk immediate destruction.''

''This is Major Nefertiti Jones, Iron Man.'' The voice suddenly sounded less hostile. A visual display near Tony's right eye flared to life, exhibiting the tiny image of a competent-looking black woman wearing a familiar uniform. ''And my craft is SAFE Shuttle One, fresh out of Cape Canaveral, Florida.'' She smiled, and said a password Tony recognized. ''Sean Morgan thought you folks could use a hand up here.''

I'll just bet he did, Tony thought. He still wasn't sure about SAFE's agenda, even if the new organization was technically on the side of the angels. Aloud, he said, ''The more the merrier, Major. If you're willing to clean up some spilt milk for me, I've got some loose ends that need tying up onboard the space station.''

''Tell me what you want us to do, sir.'' Jones smiled again. ''We live to serve, after all.'' She paused. ''We passed an A.I.M. shuttle a few minutes ago, dead in the water. It looked like your work.''

''It was, and it's not quite dead. That's some of the spilt milk I mentioned.''

''I take it the crisis is over, then?''

''Not hardly,'' Iron Man said wryly. As the SAFE shuttle came closer, he looked back at the *Ad Astra*, taking in with a single glance all of the damage that the various attacks had done to one of his most glorious dreams. Somewhere in that metal wheel, he knew, Spider-Man and the others were doing their best to shut down the out-of-control *Infinity Engine*. "But you'll have to wait until later for the details."

If there is a "later."

The innards of the *Infinity Engine* were like nothing that Spider-Man had ever seen before. They were barely recognizable as electronics components, taking instead the form of metal and glass whorls and disks and jagged shapes that seemed to exhibit colors without precedent in his experience. If they reminded him of anything, it was of certain occult artifacts he had run across during his long and adventurous career, but he knew that they were nothing magic. To tap into the underlying quantum field, Stark's people had managed to create three-dimensional equivalencies to certain seven-dimensional forms. The *Infinity Engine* included things entirely new to the human brain's field of reference.

Looking at them made his head hurt. He closed his eyes for a second to obscure the image—and then realized to his surprise that doing so made no difference. This close, with the *Engine* operating at these levels, his brain perceived its output directly, without using its intervening senses. He could still "see" the components, even with his eyes tightly shut.

I wonder what a camera would show, he thought. *With no mental coding system, it might not even detect this thing's output as light, the way I'm doing. I wonder how much of this noise I'm "hearing" is even sound.* It was an interesting problem, and one he would have loved to consider at his leisure—but right now, he didn't have the time.

"Last chance, Doc." He spoke into the communicator, not really expecting a reply, and not surprised when none came. "Okay, then, we do this the hard way."

The tool kit held a number of specialized gadgets, as unique and unfamiliar as a watchmaker's tool set. Nakahara had told him earlier that he would need to realign two siphon circuit banks. Those were almost certainly the two jagged shapes to his right, one of which looked vaguely like a pineapple from hell, the other of which looked like a porcupine with a glandular problem. A series of flat, ribbon-like leads made of some silvery metal connected them both to a half-dozen smooth, glassy shapes that seemed to quiver and flow beneath his unsteady gaze. At the base of the first of the glass blobs was a series of knurled fittings with calibrated markings; that looked like as good a place as any to start. He reached into the tool kit and pulled out an insulated probe, then went to work.

The fittings were tight. He had the impression that they were factory-original settings, not intended for after-the-fact adjustment. That was the job of the complex consoles back in the main control room; unfortunately, thanks to Hydra's Poster Boy of the Year, they were so much junk. Spider-Man took a deep breath and forced the first fitting a quarter turn to his left, until one of the hairline markings on its surface aligned with a new indicator.

Nothing happened.

Spider-Man shrugged. *In for a penny, in for a pound*, he thought, and forced the knob to spin another quarter turn. In instant response, the *Infinity Engine*'s keening wail dropped a quarter octave. Spider-Man closed his eyes again and was relieved to see that the image, though still present, had faded noticeably.

Now we're getting somewhere, he thought.

He placed the probe against the second fitting. Its tip

found and settled into a recess on the top like it had been made for the job. Gently, he twisted left again. This one spun more easily than the first one had, moving an eighth of a revolution more easily than the other had moved a half turn—and with greater effect.

The *Infinity Engine*'s wail tripled in volume and quadrupled in intensity, but Spider-Man didn't notice. The equipment before him suddenly flared white with heat, searing his fingertips and nearly making him drop the probe, but he didn't care. Those were little problems, compared to the sudden crescendo of agony that filled his skull.

Spider-Man screamed in pain and surprise. His spider-sense, until now a constant throb that was more like background noise than any real warning, roared to new life. It felt exactly as if someone had smacked him in the back of the head with a good-sized club—then struck him again without warning.

And again.

The pain was enough to make him drop to his knees. As he fell, his fingers twisted spasmodically, spinning the knob backward a full quarter turn. Instantly, the pain stopped, and the spider-sense warning subsided again to a dull roar.

Okay, not that way, Spider-Man thought. *Wrong button altogether.* He gathered himself up, fought back waves of nausea and pain, and stared once more at the *Infinity Engine*'s interior. He had been forced to work this way before, fooling his spider-sense into helping him decide which adjustment or alteration was, if not the right one, then the least wrong one. It was never easy, but it was rarely this painful. His spider-sense was invaluable, but it wasn't an especially finely calibrated instrument. Choosing between a fire and a frying pan was not its forté.

He considered the second knob again. Turning it one way had caused trouble. Turning it the other way had made the trouble subside, maybe back past its starting point. He looked at the knob carefully. Now it was at about the halfway point. What would happen if he turned it all the way to the right?

He set the probe in place again. He twisted gently, one quarter turn to his right.

There was no result—at least, none that he could notice. Certainly, there was no new warning from his spider-sense.

He twisted again, an eighth of a turn. The pitch of the machine's wail changed again, dropping, and the hot metal surfaces below his fingers cooled noticeably. He paused a moment, holding his breath, then spun the knob some more. It clicked into place with a satisfying sound.

As that sound faded, he heard something else. For a long moment, he tried to identify the new sound but failed—and with failure, came pleased delight as he realized that what he heard was nothing at all. Rather, it was the absence of sound. The *Infinity Engine* had silenced itself.

He closed his eyes. No phantom images filled his field of vision. He saw only darkness.

He concentrated on his spider-sense, trying again to find the background warning buzz that had been his nearly constant companion since boarding the *Ad Astra*. He could not find it.

The *Engine* was down.

Spider-Man let himself smile, and allowed himself a single, deep sigh of relief. The worst of it was over. The *Engine* was disarmed. He could see to Nakahara and Deeley now, and give them whatever help they needed. Compared to what he had just accomplished, that would be easy.

*   *   *

Douglas Deeley stood near the smoking hulk that had been the diagnostics console, keeping a watchful eye on the bound Horst even as he listened to Kellye's conversation with Spider-Man, somewhere in the bowels of the *Ad Astra*. Before leaving for his repair mission, Spider-Man had webbed the Hydra agent in a convenient seat, gluing his arms to those of the chair. Now the blond man's unsettling blue eyes stared at Deeley from above the band of webbing that still gagged his mouth.

Deeley didn't like Horst, and not just because of the man's employers, or even his actions. Deeley had fought in enough battles to realize that there were good men on both sides of most conflicts. He supposed that even Hydra included some likable types in its ranks, and maybe even some good men who had made bad choices. No, Horst's problem wasn't that he was a Hydra agent; it went deeper than that. There was something about the man that Deeley found disturbing, some vague suggestion of mental imbalance that had colored his perception of the man, even in the brief moments the two had fought. The fanatical tone in his voice as he chanted the Hydra oath after detonating the explosive charges, for example, or his unresisting arrogance as Spider-Man webbed his wrists to the chair arms. There was more to Horst than met the eye, Deeley knew, and he also knew that he didn't care to find out just how much more there was.

''He's there!'' Kellye called out to Deeley from across the room. ''Spider-Man made it to the *Engine*!''

Deeley glanced at her. She sounded excited, and he understood why. The fact that the super hero had completed the first leg of his journey, though, wasn't enough. If they were going to live, Spider-Man had to do more than that. "Good," he said. "Keep me posted."

He looked back at Horst. The bound man's sapphire-blue eyes stared back at him, unblinking and intense. Kellye had mentioned something about them possessing a hypnotic quality, and he hadn't believed her; now he found himself giving some small credence to her words. He wondered if it were due to some special training the Hydra agent had received. Probably. From what little he had heard of the infamous cabal's inner workings, there was much, much more to the organization than the head-lines told.

"He's corrected the enumerator," Kellye said. Again, Deeley looked at her as she spoke. "All that's left now are the siphon banks." Deeley looked back at his captive as Kellye continued her conversation, saying something about the next step. He looked back just in time to see Horst make his move.

The Hydra agent's bound wrists twisted once, then a second time. Deeley was surprised to see that the man could move at all; then surprise faded as he saw the reason. The heavy bands of gray mesh webbing split and tore and fell away as a pair of concealed steel blades cut though them, having first shredded the green fabric of Horst's Hydra uniform.

"What the—" Deeley cried out in surprise as Horst liberated himself. He raised his gun quickly, training it on the suddenly free Hydra agent. "Kellye! He's loose!"

Still silenced by his gag, Horst threw himself at Deeley. His injured left hand came up and slashed down in a karate chop. Instinctively, Deeley raised his own right hand to parry the strike. It was only as white agony cascaded through him that he knew he had fallen into Horst's trap; the Hydra agent's wrist blade cut deep into his fingers and palm, cutting though flesh as easily as it had though Spider-Man's web. Deeley cried out in pain, and realized in a furious panic that the shock had been enough to make him drop his pistol.

The thought flickered through his brain with surprising intensity: *We're a matched set now. Kellye hurt his hand, and he's hurt mine.*

Horst's hand had found Deeley's throat now, and his strong fingers were digging deeply into the unresisting flesh that they had found. Deeley brought both hands—injured and intact—up and slammed them into his assailant's chest, hoping to dislodge the attacker. It didn't do much good; Horst rocked back in his perch on Deeley's chest, but held onto his erstwhile captor's throat for dear life.

Deeley grunted. The pain in his left hand flared, as the nerve endings abruptly realized how great the damage was. The agony helped him now, spurring him to greater, desperate strength. As things went black around him, he planted one leg on the floor's steel deck plates, pushing his prone body upwards and tilting it slightly sideways. This was enough to throw off the Hydra agent's balance. Horst instinctively attempted to break his fall by taking one hand away from his victim's neck. Deeley's world came back into focus as more blood began to reach his brain. A woozy-looking Horst half-sat, half-lay on the floor beside him.

"Kellye!" he yelled. "I could use some help over here!"

Horst had gathered his wits again, and was preparing for another attack. Deeley could see his twin blades clearly now. They were wicked scythes of metal that had evidently lain flat along the other man's forearms until they were needed. Fully extended now, they glistened in the cabin's artificial light as Horst slashed down at him again. Deeley wondered why the Hydra agent hadn't used them in the earlier battle. Overconfidence? Caution? The simple desire to retain a secret weapon for later? It really didn't matter; all that counted was that he had them now.

Suddenly, Kellye Nakahara's slim, tan hands could be seen, wrapping themselves around Horst's neck from behind. She found a good grip in less than a second, then yanked hard, pulling Horst up and back. The Hydra agent, utterly unprepared for the attack from behind, fell back in surprise, pinning Kellye beneath him.

Kellye was wrestling now with the Hydra agent, who seemed to be enjoying the conflict. He had broken her grip on his throat and was doing his best to see to it that she couldn't get another one. The two of them were a whirling mass of arms and legs, pounding and kicking at one another. Horst made unpleasant grunting noises that his gag did little to muffle. Kellye was holding her own for the moment, but Deeley didn't think that would last.

She was good, but Horst had the blades, after all.

Deeley glanced around the room hastily. His energy pistol, knocked free during the struggle, had bounced and slid beneath a nearby counter. He dropped to his hands and knees with a grunt of pain and reached for it. By the time he had the weapon's reassuring butt in his hand again, Horst had somehow managed to pin Kellye's arms and legs to the floor and was bringing one razored wrist back, preparing to slash forward and down.

"Freeze, Mister!" Deeley snarled the words. He raised the pistol. "The next inch you move is the last inch you'll move!"

Horst looked back at him, and so did Kellye. The man's eyes were as opaque and unfathomable as ever; the woman's were filled with fear and concern.

Horst grunted. The muscles in his raised arm relaxed—then they tensed again, as his hand slashed down.

Deeley fired. The energy pistol's bold beam caught the blade's leading edge, reducing it to droplets of molten metal that splashed downwards.

Kellye twisted free from the man who had pinned her, rolling out of the searingly hot metal's trajectory. The droplets struck the deck plates. Immediately afterward, Horst's hand did the same, carried by momentum and unchecked speed, smashing into the metal floor. The deck plates weathered the impact somewhat more easily than Kellye would have.

Horst gave a muffled scream of pain as the force of his own blow made more fingers bend and snap. Instinctively, he drew his newly injured hand close, cradling it against his body.

He was still moaning when Deeley brought the pistol's butt down against the back of his skull, rendering him unconscious.

For a long moment, the black man stood unmoving, catching his breath and gathering his wits. Horst had been good at what he did, all right—too good. If the section leader had been typical of Hydra forces, folks like Spider-Man and Iron Man had their work cut out for them. That was something to consider. He panted a few times, then spoke. "Kellye? You okay?"

She nodded. "He's a persistent one, isn't he?"

Deeley nodded. "I want to find about six miles of steel cable and tie him down again," he said. "You better get back to Spider-Man."

— CHAPTER 12 —

In Latveria, Doctor Doom sat silently before the main control console in his private laboratory. Around him, several robots toiled in similar silence, moving heavy components about and otherwise implementing Doom's will. They were his only companions now; deep within Castle Doom's innermost recesses, this private complex was Doctor Doom's personal domain, and visitors to it were few and far between. Some weeks before, for reasons of his own, he had had a captured trespasser brought here for interrogation. That man, Joshua Ballard, managed to escape the granite chamber, using the bank of teleport equipment that still stood in one corner. What Ballard, apparently a man of some courage, had not realized at the time was that Doom had allowed him to escape. Ballard had been one of a team of marauders whose invasion of his castle had been a prelude to the game that Doom played now, a clandestine competition for a grand prize—specifically, the world. Others had joined the game since then, among them the Hydra overlord Von Strucker, along with Tony Stark, Sean Morgan, and two members of America's vaunted super hero community.

There were many players now, but Doom intended to take the prize.

Doom's hands roamed his computer's controls. Armored fingers that housed weapons sufficient to shatter entire regiments moved with surprising delicacy along switches and keys, prompting test runs and diagnostic displays. Before Doom's hooded eyes, monitors presented complex schematics and energy flow readings. Remote command links and system monitors tied the computer banks to the *Ad Astra* space station that orbited the earth, many thousands of feet above the earth's surface, and to the computers onboard Hydra's insipid *Barbarosa*. On Doom's screens, the *Infinity Engine*'s secrets showed themselves to him, one segment at a time. Doom examined each carefully, fully appreciative of the genius that had shaped them.

Stark was good, that much even Doom had to concede. The American was an accomplished scientist in his own right, but he also had a real genius as a systems engineer. He had been able to combine wildly differing phases of theoretical physics and hardware engineering in a single, integrated unit. Doom was perfectly willing to recognize the special kinds of skills that were required to yoke such disparate oxen together and make them work towards a common goal. He had done so himself more than once, of course, but Doom had managed the deed through the use of skills and options that Stark would not consider. As far as Doom knew, Stark thought himself too scrupulous to use the tools that worked, kidnapping and extortion and mind-control helmets. Stark was a fool, but Doom was willing to grant that the American was an accomplished fool.

He pressed a button that activated an intercom. "This is Doom," he said. "Report."

A voice came back to him; whose it was, he did not care. "All proceeds apace, Excellency," some nameless attendant said. "The Ministry of the Interior has processed the interlopers. They know their new names now, and they are ready to live their new lives."

Doom considered that for a moment. He sometimes wondered at his own mercy, concerned that it might betray some hidden streak of weakness, but he had decided that such was not the case with the captive A.I.M. and Hydra agents. The two men had paid for their crimes against Latveria, and done him a small service besides.

They had earned their lives. "Good," he said. "Release them, then."

"Yes, Excellency."

"But remind them of the consequences of any attempted betrayal. They would do well to avoid my future attentions." He pressed the button again, closing the connection before the speaker had the opportunity to respond, and returned his attention to the monitors.

The two men who had once borne the names Sinclair and Krelm were among the minor loose ends remaining from the previous month's debacle. It pleased Doom to see their fates resolved; he admired order and detested unresolved issues. Others still demanded his attention, of course, and it would take more to resolve them than simply issuing some directives.

But not much more.

He ran his fingers along the control panels again, tapping in long lines of code and command sequences with easy speed. Orbital coordinates, launch vectors, and thrust parameters coursed from his fingertips into the computers like music might flow from a pianist's hands. He typed flawlessly and with blinding speed, without pause for assessment or recalculation. He needed neither; he was Doom. After a long minute or so, he raised his hands from the keys and considered the central monitor screen where the computer had echoed his commands, and where they shone in arcane splendor. He pondered their consequences.

Doom smiled.

He pressed the steel-clad index finger of his right hand against another key and pushed. Instantly, the monitor screen went blank as the commands he had typed vanished from the computer's file buffers and into its main processor. From there, Doom knew, they could rush to the satellite uplink atop Castle Doom, and thence to the orbiting space station above. He was confident that the *Ad Astra*'s occupants would find the consequences of those command files interesting.

The world would too, for that matter.

A buzzing sound caught Spider-Man's attention. At first, he thought it was some kind of sensor or display in the *Infinity Engine*'s equipment banks, but a quick glance showed that not to be the case. It was the personal communicator, hanging almost forgotten at his belt. He smiled, and flipped it open. Nakahara and company were apparently back on line.

"Sorry, wrong number," he answered.

"Spider-Man?" It wasn't Nakahara's voice after all; it was Deeley. "Is that you?"

"Oh, come on—who else is going to be answering this thing?" Spider-Man allowed some of the testiness he felt to enter his voice. "What's going on up there? The phone went dead, and I nearly did too."

"Sorry about that. The guy you webbed up got loose. We tussled."

"Oh? There must have been more to him than met the eye. That stuff's usually good for an hour."

"Not your fault. Mine, I guess. I should have searched him. He had a couple of pop-out wrist blades. Like I said, we tussled, and I couldn't make it to the phone."

Spider-Man considered the other man's laconic words. Even in his brief contract with the captive, something about the Hydra agent had struck him as unsettling. He wouldn't have cared to engage in a knife fight with the guy. There might be more to Deeley than met the eye, too. "Oh," he said. "Everything else okay?"

"Okay enough, I guess. Kellye says the *Engine*'s shut down, so you must have pulled off your end of the gig."

Spider-Man looked at the still-open access panel, and at the exotic components that glistened inside the equipment bank. "More or less," he said. "I wouldn't want to make a living doing this kind of thing, though. What's the status on Iron Man and the rest of the operation?"

"I'm not completely sure, but things seem to be quieting down. A SAFE contingent just showed up, so we're either in for a big fight, or just some mopping up."

"Yeah, well, they can work it out among themselves. I've had enough excitement for this trip."

"I know what you mean. Think you can make it back up here?"

Spider-Man looked at the system umbilicus's open end. It didn't look very inviting. "I guess so," he said. "But I sure don't—hey!"

He paused, startled. Something was happening at the umbilicus. Narrow metal wedges had emerged from the opening's edges, and were sliding together in a rotary motion, closing the gap the way a camera's iris closed its aperture. The metal plates seemed to move slowly, but appearances were misleading; already, less than half of the gap remained.

"What is it?"

"I don't know. Are you guys pushing any buttons up there?"

"What do you mean?"

"The door's closing." The last of the gap closed and vanished. There was a whirring sound as another sheet of metal slid across the closed opening, sealing it behind a featureless slab of steel. It looked airtight, which was to be expected on a spacecraft, but the image said bad things to Spider-Man just now. "What the heck's going on here?"

A new voice took the place of Deeley's. "This is

Kellye, Spider-Man. Doug told me what you told him. Has the inner hatch sealed, too?''

"Oh, yeah," Spidey said. "There's some kind of clattering noise just behind it, too. What are you people doing up there?''

"Nothing. We can't. But it sounds to me like the system umbilicus is retracting.''

"What's that mean?'' Spider-Man asked the question, but already knew the answer.

Kellye's reply carried a hesitant tone with it. "That's the first step in the launch sequence," she said grimly. "It sounds to me like the *Engine*'s getting ready to take off.'' She paused. "Did you do anything to the main controls? Hit any buttons, anything?''

"Nope. I'm not even out of the equipment hold yet. Can't you override things from your end?''

"We can't do anything, Spider-Man. These controls here are a complete loss.'' She paused again. "I don't know what's going on, but you've got to get out of there, before the ship launches.''

Spider-Man stepped over to the hatch that he knew led to the ship's cockpit. It was sealed, and sported a numeric code lock and keypad. "What's the combination to the door lock?''

Kellye rattled off seven digits. Spider-Man punched them in rapid sequence. Nothing happened. He tried again. He got the same lack of results, and shrugged. *If at first you don't succeed, then the heck with it*, he thought. He sank his gloved fingers into the heavy steel, then pulled. The hatch pulled free from its frame with gratifying ease and a loud groaning noise. Metal bolts split and tore, and the sheared hinge pins ricocheted like bullets. Spider-Man set the door aside and sprang through the gap he had created.

"Okay," he said into his communicator. "I'm

through. What now?'' Something caught his eye.

"There's an airlock in the main cockpit. You can use it to get out of the craft and into the docking bay. You won't need a suit if you move fast enough, since that area is still pressurized. It won't be for long, though, if the launch command sequence has started. The airlock controls are on the central panel, to the pilot's left.''

"Okay. What about Ramos? Does he know his way around this stuff?

"Johnny? Well, sure but—'' Her words broke off, and took a muffled tone as she apparently spoke to someone else. ''Doug! He's found Johnny!''

Ramos sat in the pilot's seat, conscious and apparently unharmed, but wrapped in a veritable cocoon of nylon cord. He eyes bulged in their sockets as he saw who had joined him in his cockpit. ''Spider-Man!'' The dark-haired man said the words with a degree of awe and respect that a younger Peter Parker would have savored from the local hero. ''What the—''

"Hush,'' Spider-Man said. ''I'll explain later.'' He began tearing at Ramos's bonds, easily shredding the cords with his fingers. As Ramos's right hand came free, Spidey placed the communicator in it. ''Here,'' he said. ''You've got friends who are worried about you. But make it fast; we're in a hurry.''

Ramos spoke a few words into the communicator, then listened, and spoke again. He clicked the communicator shut as Spider-Man tore through the last of the ropes. ''The Hydra goons caught me when they boarded,'' he said. ''I guess they thought I would be out of the way, stashed in here.''

"Obviously,'' Spider-Man said, a trifle impatiently. ''Why don't you see what you can do with the airlock controls before we all go for a ride?'' He could hear liquids gurgling in concealed pipes and the soft click of hidden switches as the *Infinity Engine*'s rocket motors came on line. There was a clattering noise as equipment components retracted and stowed themselves away. "I don't know how much time we have, but it can't be much."

"I can do better than that," Ramos said. "I can shut this baby down." He tapped a few keys on the control panel, then frowned at one display screen. "That's funny," he said.

"Funny as in 'ha-ha,' or funny as in 'uh-oh'?"

"See for yourself," Ramos said, gesturing.

Spider-Man looked, and didn't like what he saw. The screen was filled with cascading numbers and symbols, flickering briefly into existence before giving way to more like them. Spider-Man had seen that type of display before, only a few hours ago, when Iron Man had pulled it up on the *Skylark*'s control screens. He knew what it meant; whoever had tampered with the *Ad Astra*'s docking protocols had taken control of the *Infinity Engine*'s navigational control software, as well. Was it Strucker? Or A.I.M.? Or someone else entirely, trying to hijack the craft or destroy it?

Did it matter?

"I can't do anything with this," Ramos said. He shook his head in disgust. "We're locked out."

"You mean locked in," Spider-Man said grimly. "But not for long. Cover your ears. I'm busting us out of here." He stepped over to the main airlock hatch, only to stop in his tracks as Ramos grabbed his shoulder.

"You can't do that," the flight commander said urgently. "That hatch opens in the main receiving hold area."

"So?"

"So right now, that main receiving hold isn't pressurized, and we don't have suits. We're three quarters of the way through the launch cycle. You pop that door, and you pop us too. We'll suffocate before we can get to the pressurized areas of the station.''

Spider-Man wanted to curse, but he resisted the temptation. He knew enough about the space station's operations to know that Ramos was right. They had passed the point of no return. "So what do we do now?''

"Strap yourself in,'' Ramos said, settling into his own seat. He began fussing with the belts and fasteners. "I don't know where we're going, but we want to get there in one piece.'' He opened the communicator and stabbed a key. "Kellye? It's Johnny again. We've got a problem.''

I'll say we do, Spider-Man thought.

Iron Man saw the *Infinity Engine* disengage from the *Ad Astra*. He saw it happen in a variety of ways, on his proximity radar screen and on the systems schematic of the *Ad Astra* he had pulled up on his helmet's imaging system. Most importantly, he saw it through the eye-slits of his mask. He watched as thrusters flared and metal clamps opened, as the docked mobile platform disengaged from the space station and become a separate craft once more. He had anchored himself momentarily to the SAFE shuttle's outer surface when he saw it happen, and was in midconversation with Nefertiti Jones.

"What the heck is going on over there? It looks like someone's trying to make a run for it,'' she said.

"I don't think so,'' Iron Man replied. He opened another communications link, this one with the *Ad Astra*. "What's going over there, Doctor Nakahara? I'm registering some activity in the docking area.''

"We don't know,'' came the response. She sounded worried. "Spider-Man shut down the *Engine*, but then the automated launch sequence started. He says he's locked out of the computer and can't stop the process."

"Spider-Man is still on board the *Engine*?" As he spoke, Iron Man launched himself once more into the void, his bootjets flaring as he pushed off from the SAFE shuttle.

"Yes. He found Johnny there, too." Nakahara sounded concerned and very nearly frightened, as if the strain of the preceding hours had finally caught up with her. "I can't do anything at this end, Iron Man. Most of the outboard control systems are junk now. But Doug's put together a vector map, and I don't like the looks of it."

"Give it to me," Iron Man demanded, rattling off a frequency for her to transmit on. Seconds later, the systems schematic display lining his mask gave way to a simplified animated simulation of the *Infinity Engine*'s orbital track. He could see what she meant. It was still early in the launch process, but the projected track looked bad. He glanced at the terminal coordinates, and realized that things were worse than bad; they were terrible. Without major course corrections, the *Infinity Engine*'s path would bring it to Earth somewhere in the midst of Times Square.

Iron Man suspected that those corrections would not be forthcoming. This looked like deliberate sabotage, the product of Hydra, or of A.I.M.—but more likely, of someone else. He thought back a few hours to the *Skylark*'s flight and the moment when he had realized that someone else had overridden the *Ad Astra*'s docking system. This looked like more work by the same unseen hand; the only mystery was whose hand it was. Either of the cabals might have tried to steal the craft; neither had any vested interest in simply destroying it.

Apparently someone else did. Or was willing to do it, anyhow.

He considered what would happen if the *Infinity Engine* followed its present path. There wasn't much danger from the quantum tap itself; now that it had been shut down, its exotic energies damped, the equipment was little more than dead weight. The craft it rode was a different matter, however. Stark's engineers had spent many hours of wind-tunnel simulation to make the things as aerodynamically efficient as possible. If the *Infinity Engine* followed its present path, it would still be reasonably intact when it returned to the Earth's surface, a hundred or so tons of superheated steel crashing into the busiest area in the busiest city in the world.

In a very real sense, Strucker would win.

He couldn't let that happen.

"Doctor Nakahara, please prepare for boarding. There's a shipload of SAFE agents out here, ready to help you and Mr. Deeley."

"We'll be looking for them." That was Deeley, chiming in on the conversation. "What about the *Engine*?"

Iron Man didn't answer. Instead, he shifted channels on his helmet communications system. "Major Jones, I'm going to need your boss's help on this one."

"He says anything you need, you got."

"I hope he's serious." Iron Man recited a series of coordinates. "I need a complete evacuation of that area, and I need it about an hour ago. That's where the *Infinity Engine* is coming down, and I don't want anybody in its way."

"But that's off in the Atlantic somewhere, near Long Island. Our orbital analysis puts the touchdown point in midtown Manhattan."

"Right now, that's where it is," Iron Man said grimly, as his armored feet touched down on the *Infinity*

Engine's hull. "These things have a way of changing, though."

"But—"

"Just do it. And be careful when you board the *Ad Astra*; there are still some mighty unhappy Hydra agents in there, somewhere."

"Yes, sir."

Iron Man watched as the SAFE craft approached and docked with the *Ad Astra*, using the bay recently occupied by the *Infinity Engine*. For whatever reason, the space station's docking system seemed operational again. Maybe the unseen hand had moved on to other matters, or maybe the intelligence behind it simply didn't care about the *Ad Astra* any longer. He didn't know which was the case, and at the moment it didn't matter. There were other, more pressing matters that demanded his attention.

The *Infinity Engine* wasn't moving very fast yet, but that would change. It was picking up speed as it slid down the walls of Earth's gravity well. It was nearing the critical point now, the segment of its trajectory where he could do the most to change its track. He walked along the hull until he reached the point he wanted, back near the main thruster, inside a recess shaped by the craft's heavily reinforced fuselage. There was a hinged panel there, an easy access point to the *Infinity Engine*'s conventional power system. He drew a cable from behind the plate and plugged it into the universal adapter inlet at his left hip, integrating his armor's power systems with those of the spaceship. Then he drew two shielded fuel lines from within the same cavity, and plugged them into his armor's boot assemblies. Ambient feed did the rest; pressure in the *Infinity Engine*'s tanks forced the compressed fuel into his boots' rocket motors. He didn't even attempt to access the *Engine*'s guidance systems; from his own experience, and from what Kellye Nakahara had said, they were shut down completely.

He placed his hands and feet carefully, crouching so that his boot jets aligned perfectly with the spaceship's central axis. A single mental command, and his suit's annealing fused the metal of his armor with the metal of the *Infinity Engine*.

We're in this together now, he thought grimly.

Strucker did not seem to notice Garcia entering the room. He had been reviewing a dozen or so communiqués, the first round of responses to his initial ultimatum. The world's leaders had seen what the *Infinity Engine* had done to A.I.M. Island, even if many of them remained unaware of the site's hidden strategic importance. Now those same leaders were only too eager to accede to Strucker's wishes, or to seek an alliance with him. The latter suggestions made him snort derisively. There was little anyone in all the world could offer him that was not already his, by right of conquest. The world would learn that soon enough; now, after many years of very hard effort, success was at hand. He smiled, and finally deigned to notice Garcia, still standing at attention before him.

"Report," Strucker said. "I presume that all goes according to plan."

"It does," Garcia said, his voice a strained monotone. He seemed to struggle against the words. "But not according to *your* plan."

Strucker looked up, startled at the words that came from Garcia's lips. The other man's features, typically indolent and almost sleepy, were locked in a pale stare as Garcia looked back at him. Sweat trickled from the attendant's brow, and his lips twitched spasmodically.

"Explain yourself," Strucker said angrily. "Explain your words, or die."

Garcia seemed to force the words from his mouth, or perhaps he fought to keep them from emerging; Strucker could not tell which. "I—I do not fear your threats, fool," Garcia said. "I fear no man's threats." The cadence of his words became easier, as if the last vestiges of conflict had begun to fade. Garcia's voice took on a new tone, one that Strucker had never heard from the other man before—the tone of command. Garcia smiled, but it was not his smile. He spoke, but the words were not his. He said, "Doom fears nothing."

"Doom!" Strucker hissed the name. He stood. In response to a mental command, the capacitors in his Satan Claw whined as they charged its blade with deadly force. "Explain yourself, Garcia!"

"Mindless incompetent," Garcia snarled. His lips twisted in a wolfish grin, utterly out of place on his indolent features. "You speak to your flunky, but you hear the words of Doom—and you would do well to heed them!"

Strucker stared at Garcia with something very much like horror. It was hard to believe, but he had to credit the evidence of his own senses. There was something different about Garcia, something beyond the surprising words and their demanding delivery. The pudgy man stood now with a regal bearing, and his body language was that of one accustomed to rule. Strucker had seen that stance before, the exaggerated grandeur that marked many of history's most feared despots.

"Know this, Strucker," Garcia's voice said. "You live at my sufferance, as does the rest of the world. I have allowed you and your rivals to play your little games of conquest and destruction, in part because they amused me and in part because they diverted the world's attention from certain of my own campaigns. In recent weeks, however, you have interfered in my operations. Your agents have invaded my home, and your organization has sought to steal a prize that your doltish brain cannot comprehend. Hydra and A.I.M. are like children playing with matches, and it is time that you learned your lesson.''

"Why are you doing this, Doom?'' Despite himself, Strucker accepted the reality of the situation. In some way he could not understand, Latveria's ruler was speaking through Garcia's lips. "*How* are you doing this?''

"Do not concern yourself with such trivialities,'' Garcia said. He moved with an easy grace now, as if Doom's control of him had become complete. The pudgy Hydra agent stepped over to one of the illuminated map displays that covered one wall of Strucker's command center. Garcia's hand rose and gestured, as Doom continued. "The world is too dear a treasure for one such as you to have dominion over it, Strucker. Your vision is too small to rule,'' he said. "That task must fall to a true ruler, to a king,'' Garcia said, smiling. "To an emperor, if you will—or even if you will not.''

"Bah! Those are strong words,'' Strucker said. "But the only crown you wear is of a postage-stamp kingdom, scarcely a flyspeck on the world's maps.''

Doom laughed. It was an ugly sound "True enough, for now,'' he said. "Mighty oaks from tiny acorns grow, however, and appearances can be deceiving.'' He paused. "And Latveria may be small, but its borders are sacrosanct, and the world's rulers contend for my favor daily. Do not presume to judge me, Strucker. That is my prerogative, and mine alone. Content yourself with whatever small share of the spoils I allow you. There is always a portion for jackals. Do not bring yourself to my notice again, or you will regret it.''

Strucker approached him. The Satan Claw was fully charged now, and the red steel of its blade sparked and crackled with barely contained energies. He wasn't thinking clearly now; all that mattered was that he silence the mocking presence before him. "Your threats are hollow, Doom. I possess the *Infinity Engine*, and that means I rule—"

Doom laughed again. "You rule nothing," he said. "You have nothing, except what I allow you to have. Certainly, you no longer have the *Infinity Engine*."

"What do you mean by that?"

Garcia's lips pulled back as Doom smiled once more. "The prize is lost," he said. "Lost to you, and lost to Stark. Do not seek to reclaim it." Doom's words trailed off as another change swept over Garcia. "I will leave your underling to explain," he said. "Your audience is ended." The other man's features relaxed, and his entire body seemed to slump and settle. The mien of command was abruptly gone, as easily and abruptly as if a switch had been flipped.

"Baron?" Garcia spoke hesitantly. His voice was normal again. "Baron? What has happened? Why am I here? The last I remember, I was in my quarters—"

Strucker cursed. Doom was gone, but his puppet remained. Strucker brought the Satan Claw back and up, then forward and down in a glittering arc that intersected Garcia approximately three inches below his chin. The blade whistled as it cut through the air and found scarcely less resistance in the flesh and bone of Garcia's neck. There was a wet noise, then something meaty spun up and away, and then Garcia's body fell to the floor with a thud.

"Hail Hydra," Strucker said softly, the musing tone in his voice a marked contrast to the sudden, futile fury that surged through him. He gazed at the body sprawled across his office floor. ''Cut off a limb, and two more shall take its place.''

No one heard him speak.

''There is always a portion for jackals.''

The words had barely emerged from ZYX-319's lips before they were cut short by a blast from Number One's energy pistol. Years of command had done little to dull skills earned in her tenure as a field operative; her aim was true, and the rogue agent died instantly. But she had fired too late, Number One realized grimly. ZYX-319 should never have been allowed to deliver Doom's proclamation, especially not in the relatively public venue of the council chamber.

''Dispose of this carrion,'' Number One said. ''Take it to the Biological Section and dissect it. I want a full report on how Doom was able to do this, and I want it in one hour.''

No one moved to obey her. She could feel the eyes of the inner circle staring at her, in silent challenge. This was it; this was the crisis point that would define her rule. She had invested ZYX-319 with some of her own authority by promoting him to new duties; the fact that he had proven to be Doom's puppet threatened her standing within A.I.M. She had been through such moments before, both during her reign and before it. A year ago, she had sat as the members of the inner circle now sat, considering her possibilities and deciding whether or not to act.

Her actions then had given her the rank of Scientist Supreme, and the rule of A.I.M. Her actions now could as easily cost her the rank, and her life.

''Are you deaf?'' She snarled the words, trying desperately to invoke the authority that Doom's proclamation had undermined so badly. ''Dispose of the corpse!

Then give me a complete status report on the project!'' She turned to face the chief security officer. ''And you! I want to know how this happened!'' She raised the pistol again. ''You have failed A.I.M., and that failure carries a high price!''

''No.'' Someone spoke from behind her; she did not know who. ''It is you who have failed A.I.M., Number One.'' She heard the words, but then she heard nothing at all—not even the pistol fire that punctuated them.

Sean Morgan hung up the telephone, and looked across the cluttered conference room table at Bethany Cabe. ''That was the Coast Guard,'' he said. ''They'll clear the area, except for a recovery team. I told them to expect some of your people. I assume you want representation there.''

Bethany Cabe nodded. ''I've got seven specialists and a 'copter already, eager to go. Medics, equipment specialists, the works.''

Morgan nodded. ''Okay. But you and I are going to have a long talk about this when all is said and done. The next time your boss tries an operation this big without federal cooperation, SAFE won't be as easy to get along with.''

''Tony's a little leery of government intervention these days,'' Bethany said. ''He's had some problems in the past.''

Morgan looked at her levelly. ''That might be so,'' he said. ''But those were on someone else's watch. There are some games I don't play, and Stark better learn that, because I'm here to stay. Cutting SAFE out of this situation didn't help things, and you know it. I'm getting tired of cleaning up other people's messes.''

Bethany shrugged. ''That's one way of looking at it,''

she said lightly. ''I don't know that Tony would agree, but I'll talk to him about it.''

''Good.'' Morgan paused, then smiled. ''I told you we'd end up working together, Beth.''

She smiled, too. ''Well, that's not quite the way you put it, and this isn't quite what you had in mind,'' she replied. ''But it's close enough.'' She gathered up her papers, and snapped a briefcase shut. ''We'd better go,'' she said. ''The seven-person headcount on that chopper includes us.''

Morgan nodded and joined her. He wanted to see how things would end.

— CHAPTER 13 —

The communicator, still hanging at Ramos's belt, made a buzzing noise. Ramos did not seem to notice it. Instead, the *Infinity Engine*'s flight commander devoted himself to punching one command sequence after another into the main control panel. None of them seemed to do any good. Since the *Infinity Engine* had disengaged from the *Ad Astra*, its big thrusters had flared once in a long, fifty-second burn, then fallen silent, leaving the space craft to follow the path that the engines had set for it. Nothing Ramos did seemed to make a difference; the main monitor continued to display gibberish, and none of the systems responded to his commands.

The communicator buzzed again. Spider-Man asked, "Are you going to get that, or do you want me to?"

Ramos glanced at him, and passed the device to his companion. "Here you are," he said. "Go wild."

Spider-Man snapped it open. "Joe's Pizza," he said. "Free delivery within a ten-block radius."

"Spider-Man? This is Iron Man."

"I read you, ShellHead. How's life in beautiful outer space?"

"It could be a lot better. I need you to do something for me."

"Um, sure, but right now, we've got our hands full. I don't know if Doctor Nakahara has told you, but this thing's out of control. Can you get back to us after we crash to Earth in a flaming mass of wreckage?"

"That's not going to happen," Iron Man said, clearly annoyed. "At least, not if I have anything to say about it. Open the console to the right of the main systems monitor. There should be an access plate there. Just peel it back."

Spidey complied. The thin sheet of metal offered even less resistance to his super-strong fingers than the door to the cockpit had, and it tore free easily, revealing a series of circuit boards mounted in a common frame. Ramos looked up, startled, as Spider-Man acted, but relaxed when his traveling companion gestured at the communicator. "Got it," Spidey said, as he finished his assignment. "What now?"

"Pull the first three boards out and set them aside. That'll kill the navigation and rocket control systems. Don't break them, though. You might need them later."

"Excuse me? According to Johnny, here, they're already dead as the proverbial doornail."

"For us, they are. Not for whoever took over the controls. This is going to be hard enough as it is, and I don't want to deal with backseat drivers."

"Good point." Spider-Man plucked the circuit boards free, one after another. They came loose from their mountings easily, and as he pulled the last one out, the main systems monitor went dead. Spider-Man passed the electronic panels to Ramos, who stowed them in an insulated overhead compartment. "Done, done, and done," Spider-Man said. "What next?"

"Strap yourselves in, and try to enjoy the ride. I'm going to be too busy to offer commentary."

Spider-Man folded the communicator shut and hung it from his belt. This was the kind of situation he hated most in all the world—to be in great danger, but unable to help himself. He thought of Mary Jane, and of his friends and coworkers in the city. He wondered fleetingly if he would ever see any of them again. For a moment, he considered trying to call MJ on the portable phone, but then decided that it could do more harm than good. She was almost certainly beyond range of the communicator, even if he patched it into the ship's radio, and there would be nothing he could say on an unsecured channel. The words would need to wait until he could speak to her in person.

The last of the Hydra agents made his move as Nefertiti Jones passed through the final stretch of corridors leading to the main control room. She saw him out of the corner of her eye as he leaped at her from a side passage, a garrote's shining length spanning the gap between his outstretched hands. "Death to the enemies of Baron Strucker," the man yelled. "Hail Hydra!"

"Yeah, yeah," she responded. She raised her rifle and squeezed the trigger once. She didn't bother to take aim; the guy was at point blank range, and with this type of weapon, precision wasn't especially important. "Hail this," she said.

A capsule flung itself from the rifle's muzzle. As it flew toward the Hydra agent, it exploded, erupting in a gossamer cloud of polymer strands. The gummy strips wrapped themselves around the assassin, binding his limbs to his body, then tripping him and making him stumble and fall. An instant later, the Hydra agent lay on the steel floor, rendered unconscious by a contact anesthetic in the tangler gun's shell.

"You want to get this one, Gull?" Jones asked the question of the other SAFE agent, about ten paces behind her.

"Sure," the man said. "It's my turn." He knelt, and scooped up the cocoon-wrapped goon, then set him on the motorized cart that he was shepherding through the corridors. Five other Hydra agents filled the rest of the cart's surface, struggling against a variety of bonds. So far, Jones and Gull and the other members of the boarding party had found a total of fifteen Hydra agents, none of them very happy to see the newcomers. Some of them still wore Spider-Man's webs, and the rest sported tangler strands or handcuffs. "I hope this is the last of them," Gull said. "We're running out of room."

Jones shrugged. "There are more carts on the shuttle," she said. "Just be happy we don't have to lug the broken robots around, too."

"They're a tenacious lot, aren't they?" The words came in a semifamiliar voice, one that Jones had heard before, but not for many years. She glanced ahead to see a husky black man framed in the control room entrance, and recognized the speaker instantly.

"Hello, Doug," she said. "It's been a while. How's life in the civilian sector?"

"I'll let you know when I see a difference, Nef," Deeley said, smiling. "I might as well be in the service still, with all the action I've seen this trip."

"You know, it's funny," Jones said, setting aside her rifle. She reached out to shake his hand, then noticed the bandage and thought better of it. She kissed him on the cheek instead. "Most months, all I do is file reports and run practice drills, and wonder when I'll see action. Then I see some, and get all nostalgic for filing reports again." She paused. "It's good to see you, Doug."

"Same here, Nef. We'll have to get together when all of this is over, and talk about old times."

"I know someone else who'd like to be in on that chat."

"Morgan?"

Jones nodded.

"Good. I think I want to talk to him, too. Some of the things I've seen this time around—" Deeley's words broke off. "Well, we can talk about that later."

"I take it you two know each other," a new voice said. Jones recognized the speaker as Kellye Nakahara. The physicist was waiting for them just inside the con-

trol room. She sat in a folding chair, with an energy
pistol trained carefully on a blond man who lay on the
floor, wrapped in what looked like miles of steel cable.

"Let's just say our paths have crossed," Deeley said.

"Who's the guy on the floor?" Jones asked.

"His name's Horst, but I call him trouble," Deeley
said. He gestured with his injured hand. "Keep an eye
on him. He's not much for conversation, but he can do
some amazing magic tricks."

Two factors defined the *Infinity Engine*'s orbital track,
and neither of them were good. The experimental craft,
slightly ungainly in the best of times, was dead in space,
moving too slowly and at the wrong angle of descent.
Simple orbital mechanics defined its path as a long, slow
spiral that would carry it in several cycles through pro-
gressively thicker layers of the atmosphere, before bringing it to rest somewhere in downtown New York. Its
precise touchdown point was hard to tell; Iron Man's
best estimate still put it somewhere in Times Square, but
there was a twenty percent likelihood that the thing
could smash down somewhere in the Garment District.
It didn't really matter which, he knew. The craft's lines
were aerodynamic enough to keep it relatively intact in
its journey, and a hundred tons of superheated steel
wouldn't do the Big Apple much good, no matter where
it came down. The impact would be functionally iden-
tical to that of a meteor, with all of the associated damage—a concussive explosion, shock waves, and
atmospheric debris. Naturally, Spider-Man and Ramos,
the ship's passengers, would be first among the casual-
ties, but there would be more—many, many more.

He couldn't let that happen.

The first, faint wisps of the exosphere were already
tugging at the *Infinity Engine*'s surface when Iron Man's

inboard orbital computer completed running its initial projections. The remote imaging display in his helmet went blank for a second, then presented columns of numbers and an animated display, imposing the *Engine*'s orbital track over an animated schematic of the Earth's surface. He reviewed the values and rejected them; it wouldn't do much good to avoid the city and then hit the water at Mach Three speeds. The resulting shock waves would be catastrophic in their own right. He fed another set of parameters into the computer, and waited for the new results.

These were better. If he could boost the craft's speed by twenty percent, it would cut through the upper reaches at a steeper angle, and reach the denser strata at a lower rate of speed. Once he was there, he could take other measures, ones that wouldn't work in the near-vacuum of the exosphere and ionosphere, or in the turbulent hell of the stratosphere. The problem was that such a boost would exceed this suit's ratings and safety parameters, even augmented with the *Engine*'s systems. Tony considered the new numbers and the new track, and accepted them.

It wasn't like he had much choice.

He fired his boot jets. They flared into hyperactive life, drawing reaction mass from the *Infinity Engine*'s fuel tanks, superheating it and then spitting it out in a high-energy plasma. His armor took the brunt of the thrust and relayed it to the *Infinity Engine*'s structure, but he could still feel it. Even the pneumatic lining of his suit wasn't enough to compensate completely for the hydrodynamic shock to his body. Blood rushed to his legs and feet and sought to pool there, and black spots crept in from the edges of his vision. It was worse here than it would have been inside the ship, he knew; at least the passengers would have some support from the antiacceleration couches. A digital diagnostic readout displayed blood pressure numbers and other values that looked bad, but he ignored them. All that mattered now was the relative speed indicator, and the *Engine*'s animated descent track.

Neither looked right, so he gritted his teeth, locked the suit's joints and increased the acceleration.

This time, he actually blacked out for an instant, and the diagnostic computer screamed a warning in his ear, but the suit's automated systems took over for the three seconds or so it took him to recover from the shock. He could feel the bladders lining the armor distend to their maximum, and hear the cooling system click in as the *Engine* dropped another few thousand feet into the atmosphere. This was going to be the critical point, he knew. This particular suit hadn't been intended for direct re-entry from orbit. It didn't have the insulation tiles or liquid nitrogen heat sink reserve that such efforts demanded. Riding in the *Infinity Engine*'s slipstream would help, but his best estimates suggested that it would be a close thing.

Too close, actually.

On the display lining his helmet, a new line appeared. It presented the *Infinity Engine*'s optimal track, superimposed over the current trajectory. Real and actual were surprisingly close to one another; another three percent increase in cumulative thrust, and the lines would match precisely. A single mental command, and his boot jets gulped more fuel, then spat it out again. The *Infinity Engine* lurched forwards and down, into the upper levels of the stratosphere.

Another alarm rang. The outside temperature was rising as the air became thicker and resistance increased. The outer layers of his suit were durable and tough, but he watched the readouts carefully. He knew that he had to be careful. This suit could take direct, localized assaults from high-temperature weapons easily enough, but a systems-wide, generalized increase in heat would be more problematic. The numbers rose, building on themselves in incremental bursts, then the values dropped as the armor's thermocouple came on line. Just as with the remote drone unit that the Dreadnought had destroyed, this one could convert ambient heat above certain levels to usable energy, a capability that was coming in handy right now. He didn't need the power, but he did need the net cooling effect—and that need would become desperate soon.

He looked at the orbital track indicator, eager to see if his efforts had been successful. They had. The two trajectories were one now; the *Infinity Engine* had found its optimal path, allowing for the fact that ''optimal'' really wasn't a very good word in this case. If he could maintain this speed for another three minutes, the *Engine* would have enough velocity to carry it through the stratosphere in relative safely. After that, the question became one of deceleration.

Iron Man opened a communications link to the ship's interior. He hoped that he acceleration hadn't knocked the passengers out. ''We're halfway home,'' he said. ''How are things going in there?''

''I think I left my stomach about fifty miles back,'' Spider-Man replied. ''Any chance we could go back for it?''

The wisecrack annoyed Iron Man, but he supposed it was how the other super hero dealt with stress. The web-slinger was a man of action, and probably didn't like being helpless in the plummeting ship. ''Not today,'' he replied. ''Maybe next week, if you're good.'' He paused, thinking. ''Let me speak to Ramos, please.''

There was a pause as the communicator passed from

one hand to another. "Ramos here," a new voice said.
"How's it going?"

"Fast and hot," Iron Man said grimly. "Your navigational computer's down, but here's some raw data that should give you some idea of what's going on." He recited a string of numbers and units of measure. He didn't bother to sugarcoat it; as Tony Stark, he was well aware of Ramos's qualifications.

The flight commander whistled in response. "That path's a squeaker," he said. "Anything I should do, other than get my affairs in order?"

"Plenty," Iron Man said. "You know this buggy like the back of your hand. I want you to power up every auxiliary system, everything that still works, and get ready to act. When the time comes, you'll have to move fast."

"What do you mean?"

Iron Man told him.

"I hope you're kidding," Ramos replied.

In Latveria, in his private laboratory, Doom gazed somberly at his computer's main display. There was something wrong with the data it presented to him, some minor mismatch between his will and reality that annoyed him. The *Infinity Engine* was falling, but not at the right angle and not at the right speed. On his computer's display, a long, lazy spiral led from the *Ad Astra* to New York City, home of many of his most hated enemies. Instead of following that looping trail, however, the *Engine* was falling at a sharper angle, dropping into the atmosphere's lower strata without earning the cumulative momentum that would make its impact as deadly as a small atomic bomb. Still more disconcerting, its current path did not lead to the city at all, but ended instead in the Atlantic Ocean, fifty miles or so from shore. Doom wondered what had happened. Could a final safety system override have taken hold? Or had one of Stark's various agents taken extraordinary measures?

He activated the remote control link again and punched in the access codes that he had assigned to the *Infinity Engine*'s navigational computers. This time, there was no response as he entered new system commands. He tried a second time and then a third, still to no avail. A quick diagnostic check revealed nothing wrong at his end, so the problem had to lie somewhere in Stark's toy. Either a component had failed, cutting him off from the control systems, or one of the crew members had managed to sabotage the computer so that it would not work for anyone.

Doom shook his head in disgust, but felt only mild disappointment. There was nothing more he could do now without making his part in this affair obvious even to the world's uncomprehending eyes—and he did not want to take that step just yet. Bringing the *Engine* down in the heart of New York would have been an amusing diversion, but he had not really expected to fell his enemies this way. The Fantastic Four, the Avengers, and all the rest of them had a disturbing tendency to survive "certain" death, time and again. His inevitable victory would be more certain—and more satisfying—when his enemies fell at his own hands.

Fall they would, he knew. Even with this final, minor disappointment, today had been a day of triumphs. Hydra and A.I.M. had both felt his fury; it would be many months before either cabal would dare interfere with his affairs again, or allow their renegade members to do so. The sanctity of Latveria's borders had been avenged. Strucker, especially, had learned that Doom's reach extended far, indeed. The American, Stark, had seen one of his most cherished dreams fail, and had learned that it would not fall to him to remake the world.

That would be Doom's task, and his ultimate triumph.

He pressed another switch, and closed the communications link between his computer and the plummeting shuttle. Another system sprang to life in its place, presenting a digitized readout of complex data and system schematics. Certain of those readings confirmed experiments of his own and pointed the way towards promising new avenues of research.

Doom smiled. It had been a good day, after all—and just perhaps, it was the dawning of his day.

Doom's day.

Iron Man's left boot jet gave out at about three seconds past the troposphere's upper boundary. He couldn't be sure precisely what had happened; the final diagnosis would have to wait until he could make it back to his lab. Right now, his best guess was that a minor impurity in the *Infinity Engine*'s fuel supply had jammed and blown the boot's microturbines, which were machined to far less forgiving tolerances than the spaceship's motors. In the end, however, the cause didn't matter; all that counted were the results.

As the boot motor blew, he unlocked its joints and twisted his foot to one side, hard. The improvised link between the *Engine*'s fuel tanks and his suit split and tore, sending gouts of compressed liquid fuel gushing from the sundered hose. Almost immediately, the squirting propellant bust into flames as it found the right boot's exhaust, proving that that they had reached oxygen-rich layers of the atmosphere. A split second later, the plume of fire extinguished itself as automated valves shut and sealed the fuel line. Iron Man returned his left foot to its original mooring, and ran a quick diagnostic check on his suit.

The numbers didn't look good. The outer temperature was climbing again, and had already exceeded the thermocouple's upper limit, even after he had relayed the excess energy to the *Infinity Engine*'s banks. He didn't need the thermometer to tell him that; he could feel heat building, making him sweat and pant. According to the diagnostic, the armor's outer layers were beginning to melt and boil from the accumulating heat. The refractory coating was the first to go, vaporizing as its long-chain plastic molecules gave way to friction. The outer shielding layers would be the next to go, followed by the strength-augmenting exoskeleton and data processing systems. He wouldn't be around to see that happen, of course; long before Iron Man's metal skin melted, Tony Stark would expire from the heat.

Worse, the remaining boot assembly was close to failure. It struggled to keep functioning, and obviously couldn't handle the added burden of its defunct partner. Tony looked at the orbital track again and at the relative speed indicator. Both looked good, or at least as good as he could reasonably expect them to look. The *Engine* was on track and moving at the best angle and speed that he was likely to be able to coax from it under the circumstances. Better still, its thicker hull and aerodynamic lines had kept it cooler during its fall, so Spider-Man and Ramos should be all right, at least for now.

The right boot jet coughed and stuttered, then continued firing. He was running out of time.

Iron Man opened the communications link. "Ramos?"

"Here." The man didn't sound particularly happy, and Tony didn't blame him.

"Get ready. I've done as much as I can."

"Yes, sir."

"What's up, ShellHead? Getting too hot to handle?" That was Spider-Man's voice. He sounded worried, to a degree that surprised Iron Man, his bravado somewhat hollow.

"Something like that," Tony replied. He looked at the outer skin temperature indicator. It was well into the red zone, and still climbing. The *Infinity Engine*'s heavier insulation could handle it, but this suit couldn't. He released the fields and grips that held him to the craft's fuselage. "Iron Man out," he said. "I'll see you after splashdown."

The *Infinity Engine* fell down and away. Iron Man's remaining boot jet slowed his own descent, but did nothing for the *Engine*, now that he had released it. Tony hung in midair, nearly motionless, as the remaining fuel conduit stretched and snapped, leaving his armor's internal systems to do the job. He watched for a long moment as the *Infinity Engine* fell, plummeting like an outcast from heaven, shrieking as it tore through the air and hurtled towards the sea below.

Then, abruptly, the right boot assembly failed, and he fell, too.

Joshua Ballard stood on the deck of his hovercraft and watched as the half-dozen other members of his SAFE team surveyed the ruins of A.I.M. Island. There wasn't much to survey; Strucker's energy beam had done its work only too well, converting the place into little more than smoldering ash and cooling lava. The air was heavy with the stink of vaporized rock, and Ballard had insisted that the other members of his squad wear filtered masks as they went about their duties. It was hard to believe that, mere hours before, the place had been home to the inner council of one of the world's most feared terrorist organizations that had representatives and minions in every nation. Now the only signs of human habitation were the remains of a few underground bunkers, crumbling and empty. Those—and a few anonymous cadavers.

His satellite uplink communicator buzzed. He opened it. "Ballard here," he said. "Talk to me."

"This is Morgan."

Despite himself, Ballard came to attention. Sean Morgan was one of the few men in the world who commanded his respect, and the air of superiority that Ballard habitually wore fell from him as he replied. "Nothing to report," he said. "This place is deader than my sister's ant farm—and it looks like it was about as comfortable."

"That's about what we expected. A.I.M. moves fast, at least when it comes time to run and hide. How about Strucker?"

"No luck there, either. He was using some kind of scrambler on his transmissions, and we couldn't triangulate it any more precisely than to somewhere in the South Atlantic. Hayes thinks that he's got some kind of mobile base, like a floating island, but I'm not sure I believe that."

"Don't doubt it too much," Morgan said. He sounded glum. "After this little caper, nothing Strucker does is likely to surprise me. What happened with the Parker kid? You left before I had a chance to read your report."

"Nothing there. He's goofy but clean, as far as the NYPD and I can tell. His wife's a looker, though," Ballard said. "I didn't mind questioning her. How are things at your end?"

"Jones says the *Ad Astra*'s clear now. She's got a

couple truckloads of human garbage ready for processing, including a guy named Horst that Interpol has been trying to nail for years.''

"Sounds good. How about the crew?''

"One casualty, Powell. Some kind of robot got him. Nakahara seems okay; she's coming back with Jones and the others.'' Morgan paused. "Oh, and Doug Deeley sends his respects.''

"Doug? There's a name from the past. I haven't seen him in years, not since that business in Iraq.'' Ballard smiled. "That's great. He made it through okay, then. Have you talked to him?''

"Not yet, but he wants to talk to me. I plan to debrief him personally.''

"What's next?''

"You might as well call in the troops and come home. If A.I.M. isn't there anymore, there won't be anything left behind for us to find. I'm on my way to rendezvous with Iron Man and the *Infinity Engine*. Report to HQ, and I'll meet you there.''

"Right. Ballard out.'' He clicked his communicator shut and returned it to his belt. At some point in the conversation, a lieutenant had joined him on the hovercraft deck. "Round up the others,'' Ballard told her. "We're going home.''

Ramos looked at Spider-Man, and Spider-Man looked back at him. There was something about the huge, blank lenses of the super hero's mask that Ramos found disconcerting, but he didn't comment on them. "It's our turn now,'' Ramos said.

"Okay. Are you sure this isn't going to cause more trouble?'' Spider-Man was holding a circuit board in one gloved hand. "I mean, Iron Man wanted this out, and you want it in. One of you better know what he's doing.''

"I know," Ramos said grimly. "That module drives the retrorockets. We've got to slow down at least a little before the parachute can do us any good.''

"You're the boss," Spider-Man said. He didn't sound like he meant it, but he slid the module back in place. It clicked easily. As it did, Ramos rammed a lever home. In instant response, the bank of retrorockets that fringed the *Infinity Engine*'s nose assembly flared. The ship bucked and rocked, and it was all that Ramos could do to keep it moving in a straight line.

"This is good?" Spider-Man asked the question in the skeptical tone that Ramos had come to know and hate, even during their brief time together.

"They weren't built for this," Ramos replied tensely. "Those aren't landing jets, they're steering units, and they're doing the best they can. I've got to keep them at an inverse inclination to our current thrust vector, or we're dead men." He looked at the radar locator and speed indicator, and watched as the numbers fell. "We've got to slow down just enough to—" He broke off. "There! That's it! Brace yourself!"

He released the lever and hit another control. The rockets died, and a shock wave swept through the ship, as if it had hit a solid wall. For a brief instant, Ramos thought they had hit the water, but then the dash indicator lit, and he knew that he was wrong. The *Infinity Engine*'s parachutes had deployed, now that the ship was moving slowly enough and in thick enough air for them to do some good. Wind shrieked along the outer hull and its noise filled the cabin as they fell, slowing more and more.

Another indicator flashed, and the wind's noise died

and gave way to a heavier, more resonant thunder. Even as it had passed from space to air, the *Infinity Engine* crossed to the boundary between air and sea, plummeting deep into the Atlantic Ocean.

Spider-Man looked at Ramos. He asked, "Do you know how to swim? Or should I plan on taking you out piggyback?"

Ramos shook his head. "Thanks for the offer, but it won't be necessary," he said. He flipped another switch. "Flotation devices will take care of us," he continued, as pontoons emerged from the *Engine*'s fuselage and began inflating. The craft rose. "All we need to do is wait for a ride home," he continued. He paused, then added, "I sure hope Iron Man is okay, though."

Tony felt the boot motor stutter and gasp, and twisted in midair the second before it failed. He tumbled and twisted as he fell, doing his best to angle himself away from the still-falling *Infinity Engine*. Even at a reduced speed, the craft was going to displace a lot of water when it hit, and he didn't want to get caught in the undercurrents from its strike.

He tried to restart the boot jet, but couldn't. That wasn't a surprise; the microturbine motor had been overstressed and redlined for most of the trip down, and shouldering the load of its failed companion had been enough to make it fail completely. It wasn't going to be good for anything without a few hours of reconstruction work in the armory.

He twisted again, bringing his body into a straight line. His armor was still hot, but noticeably cooler, now that he was in free fall and didn't have to drive the *Engine* forward. The heat had done its damage, though. The flat-armature motors were at less than eighty percent efficiency, and his joints felt like they had sand in them.

It was a major effort to bring his arms together and up, to lock his legs together in a diver's inclination. He knew that most of the smaller mechanical systems were dead, and he gave a brief moment of thanks that the steel-hard plastic slabs that sealed his eye-slits were already in place.

Wouldn't want to hit the water wearing an iron suit with an open mask, he thought.

Then he did.

The waters of the Atlantic Ocean, though warm by some standards, were far cooler than the still-hot metal of his armor. It boiled as he hit it. As he parted the waves, he could hear his suit's steel skin fracture and break, like heated glass suddenly immersed in cold dishwater. The cracks began small, fanning out and finding one another, merging as they dug though the layers of his armor. Almost immediately, the seal at his left eye ruptured and gave, letting warm, salty water gush inside. The right lens failed a second later. He clenched his lips around the armor's rebreathing mouthpiece and held on. The suit's recycled air filled his lungs even as water filled his helmet.

And still he fell, his momentum only partially checked by the water. He fell in a lazy, slow-motion kind of way, slowed but not halted by the water's drag, surrounded by an eerie near-silence. He felt wetness fill his suit as more and more of the metal seams parted and let the waters flow inside. Electrical systems shorted and died, and the displays lining his helmet went blank as their processors shut down. Darkness gathered as he sank deeper and deeper into the cloudy waters.

There was an emergency release switch behind one belt panel. He reached for it, with steel-gloved fingers made suddenly clumsy by shorted motors and turbulent water. Tony fumbled with the recessed panel briefly, before a spring-loaded catch engaged and the thing popped open. There were three oversized buttons behind it. He sought and found the right one, and pushed it.

Two more panels, these on his back, popped open and away, released by systems that were more mechanical than electric. A pair of plastic bladders ballooned out, and filled immediately with inert gasses created by the chemicals inside them. He felt a shock as the balloons pulled against the dead weight of his armor, slowing his descent and then reversing it. In moments, the concealed flotation system was fully engaged, and he was well on his way back to the surface.

After what seemed like an eternity, gloom gave way to light, and the waves parted again. The air in his mouth suddenly became sweet and fresh as the inlet system activated itself. A miniature mechanical pump clicked on, draining the water from his nearly full helmet and spitting it back into the sea.

Iron Man looked around himself, at the bobbing horizon of the Atlantic Ocean. To his left was the similarly bobbing mass of the *Infinity Engine*, held by its own flotation collar. To his right, and about three feet above the white-tipped waves, a SAFE hovercraft floated. On its open deck, he could see some familiar figures. Bethany Cabe stood beside Spider-Man, who was saying something to Johnny Ramos. Apart from both of them stood Sean Morgan. To Iron Man's surprise, the espionage chief was smiling broadly, and had raised one thumb in a respectful salute. Despite himself, despite the grinding resistance of the ruined armor, Tony managed to return the gesture. A moment later, a retrieval boom reached from the hovercraft and lifted him from the water, then set him down on open deck.

"Good job, ShellHead," Morgan said, his words carrying suprisingly well over the hovercraft's muted rumble.

"I don't believe it," Spider-Man said. "That outfit comes with water wings?"

EPILOGUE

Peter Parker watched sadly as the oak coffin that contained the mortal remains of Cosmo Emile Haberman receded slowly into the earth. A moment later, Anna Marie Sanchez, dressed in black, knelt and scooped up the first handful of loose soil, then cast it into the grave. It seemed only right that she take part in the ceremony; Haberman had died saving her, after all, exhibiting an almost inadvertent courage and compassion that had belied his hostile demeanor. Peter watched Anna Marie carefully as she stepped back from the grave's edge, and away from the man who had been her boss, and partner, and tormentor for so many years. He had spoken to her briefly before the ceremony, but he wanted to say something to her now, to make some gesture at comforting her.

That role fell to someone else. A young man with delicate features and an athletic build took Anna Marie's hand in his, and led her back to a small party of mourners. Peter wondered if the man were her son, or a brother, or just a friend, and then he realized that he would probably never know.

He hadn't particularly wanted to attend the funeral itself, but he had felt the need to pay his respects, and the last few days had been extremely busy ones. As Spider-Man, he had spent more than a few hours conferring with Sean Morgan and his staff, filling them in as best he could on the details of what had happened on the *Ad Astra*. Debriefing sessions and after-the-fact reports were the kind of loose ends he typically left for others, but he had felt he owed Morgan the courtesy of playing by the rules this time, if only because of the faith that the SAFE chief had shown in him. As Peter Parker, he had spent slightly less time talking with an extremely annoying NYPD detective, spinning some sort of lie about his whereabouts in the hours immediately following Haberman's murder. That had been a formality, too; Joshua Ballard's earlier investigation had cleared him of any involvement, but the police liked to do things their own way sometimes. The two interviews, along with his workload at the *Daily Bugle* and registering for classes at ESU, had gotten in the way of any memorial services or viewing, and had left attending the funeral as his only option.

He hated funerals. He always had, and he always would. Death had been a close companion for too many years, beginning with his parents, who had died while Peter was still very young. Uncle Ben had been the next to go, killed by a burglar shortly after the chance spider bite that had given Peter his powers. After that, through all the years he had spent as Spider-Man, he had seen entirely too much of death. Friends and enemies, loved ones and bystanders, he had seen them all cut down by death's cruel scythe. Even as shovel-loads of dirt buried the coffin, Peter knew that Haberman's death was not the last he would see, either. Fate had chosen a hard road for him, and duty made him follow it. Now, this late, there was no leaving that path.

"Peter." Mary Jane's fingers found his and squeezed. She leaned against him and whispered in his ear. "We'd better be getting back. Our ride's waiting."

He turned and looked at her. MJ's green eyes were cloudy with tears. He knew that they were more for him than for Haberman, either in recognition of his own pain, or in tense apprehension of the danger that she knew lay in his future. He wondered again at the compassion and patience she had shown him for so many years, since long before they had married. There were days when it seemed that her love was all that made his life worth living.

"Okay," he said. He turned and offered her his arm. She took it, and the two of them began the walk back to the chapel. Haberman had been laid to rest in a small graveyard in New Jersey. Today, the air was fresh and clean, and the sunlight was a gentle caress, but Peter barely noticed. His mind was on other things. He was thinking about an old man with a dream, and with the dogged determination to make that dream a reality, no matter what obstacles business and health put in his way. Wherever Haberman was now, Peter hoped that he had found happiness—or at least peace.

Happy Hogan was waiting for them in the church parking lot. The big man looked surprisingly at ease in a chauffeur's uniform and standing beside a black Rolls Royce. Earlier, the ex-boxer had explained to Peter and Mary Jane that his original job with Tony Stark had been as the millionaire's personal driver, and that he had taken the assignment today for old time's sake. Now, as he opened and held the door for his passengers, he winked at Peter. "Like riding a bicycle," he rumbled. "Once you learn, you never forget."

Despite himself, Peter smiled, and winked back. "Always good to keep your certifications up to date," he said. "Job security, and all that." He stepped past Happy and into the car. The big man closed the door behind him and took his place behind the wheel.

Tony Stark was waiting inside. The millionaire industrialist looked as elegant and comfortable in the black of mourning as he had in his tuxedo at the Long Island reception, a lifetime ago. As Peter and MJ settled into their seats, Stark broke the connection on a cellular phone and returned it to its cradle. He smiled at them.

"That was Bethany," he said. "She had news I think

you'll want to hear. They caught Lyle Chesney and Eustace K. Winwood.''

Peter looked at him blankly. The two names meant nothing to him.

"Those are the two Hydra agents who broke in at Odyssey Designs and did—this,'' Stark explained. He gestured in the general direction of Haberman's grave.

"Oh?'' Peter was surprised to realize that he had nearly forgotten about the two men who had taken him on such a merry chase through the concrete canyons of Manhattan. The hot fury that he had felt at their callous murder of an old man had somehow transferred itself to the more general goal of rescuing Haberman's dream from Hydra's clutches. He had succeeded in that, but it was good to know that someone else had tied up the loose ends.

Stark nodded. "The NYPD rounded up some stragglers in a Hydra safe house out in Queens. Chesney and Winwood were among them, and it didn't take much to get them talking.''

"The police, huh? Not SAFE?'' Peter was surprised.

Stark shook his head. "It was a cooperative effort,'' he said. "But the police had the lead, and they provided the personnel for the raid, about three hours ago. It should be on the news tonight. They're good at that type of thing.''

Peter thought about that as the car pulled out into traffic. As Spider-Man, he had met many police officers, most of them good. They were all hard workers, and he had wondered more than once what kind of man or woman would face such challenges without super powers or exotic weaponry. Even as Spider-Man, with all his powers and gadgets, he had his hands full. He wondered how he would fare with just a badge and a gun.

"That's good," he said. "I'll sleep a little easier tonight, knowing that they're in custody."

"Me, too."

A second of awkward silence stretched into nearly a minute before Mary Jane broke it. "What about the people on the *Ad Astra*, Mr. Stark? Are they okay?"

Stark smiled. "Please," he said. "If Peter can call me 'Tony,' you really should too."

"Tony, then. What about them?"

"The Hydra operatives are all in custody, awaiting trial. Doctor Nakahara and Flight Commander Ramos are taking well-earned vacations, at my expense." Stark made a sad expression. "It's the least I could do, under the circumstances. And poor Powell is dead, of course." He sighed. "His funeral is Monday; I'll be there."

Peter noticed that one name was conspicuous by its absence. "What about Deeley?"

This time, Stark looked embarrassed. "You know, I pride myself on a low workforce turnover," he said. "I've always tried to make my companies pleasant and challenging places to work. Lately, however, I've lost some good people." He paused. "Doug Deeley is one of them."

"He quit?"

Stark nodded. "Resigned, effective yesterday, to explore opportunities elsewhere. A shame, really, because he's good at what he does, and he had skills that came in handy this time. I'll miss him."

"Where's he going?"

"SAFE."

Stark's single-word reply was completely unexpected, and it stunned Peter. It made sense, though; Deeley was a war hero, and he had seen the man in action onboard the *Ad Astra*. *Sean Morgan's netted himself a prize this time*, he thought. Out loud, he said, "That's a surprise."

"It is and it isn't," Stark said. "Doug's background is in the military, and he knows a lot of the higher-ups in the organization. I think he'll find a good fit there. And if he doesn't, there's always a job waiting for him with me."

"Working on the *Infinity Engine* again?"

Tony shook his head. "No. I'm tabling that project for a while. It's too big, and there are too many men like Strucker in the world."

Words Peter said to Joe Robertson two weeks before came back to him now. "You can't put toothpaste back in the tube," he said. "You can't close Pandora's box, and you can't uninvent fire. You brought the *Infinity Engine* into the world, and you can't turn your back on it."

Stark seemed startled by Peter's vehemence. "I'm not turning my back on it," he said. "I'm putting it on the back burner, until I can figure out a way to make it safe enough, or at least secure enough, for civilized use. There's an island in the South Atlantic that isn't there anymore, and it could just as easily have been New York City. I can't let that happen again, and I certainly can't be party to it."

"I understand, I guess," Peter said. He did, too; but the knowledge was galling. He remembered Tony Stark's prophetic words about a clean, safe future for all the world, with limitless energy and opportunity for everyone. Stark's capitulation on the issue meant that Strucker had won after all, even if it was only a small, muted victory. He didn't like it.

"What about you, Peter?" Tony asked the question in a matter of fact voice. "What's next?"

"Me? Fall classes start soon, so it's back to the books

for me. J. Jonah Jameson may be a pain, but the *Bugle* gig pays my bills, and lets me set my own schedule.'' He turned to face MJ, and smiled. ''And we've got bills, right honey?''

She rolled her eyes. ''They can't take those away from us,'' she said.

Stark nodded. ''I can find you something more to your liking, if you want,'' he said. ''Cosmo and Anna Marie both had good things to say about you, and neither of those two are easy to work for. There's always room in SE for one more, and I'd like to have you on board.''

Peter looked at Stark, literally shocked by the man's words, and by the possibilities they presented. For the millionaire, it was a casual gesture, a little thing, if a sincere one; for him, it was a life-altering opportunity. He could feel MJ's steady gaze on him, and thought about what he could do for her with a steady paycheck. Of course, there was more to it than that; his current schedule, even as busy as it was offered him—offered Spider-Man—a degree of much-needed flexibility. And the events of the past few weeks had proven to him that, as good as he was as a lab assistant, his biggest contribution to the world was as Spider-Man.

He considered the possibilities for a long moment, then shook his head sadly. ''I'm tempted,'' he said. ''More tempted than you'll ever know. But I'm not ready yet. I need to finish my studies, and work out some things on my own first.''

Stark nodded, as if he had expected the reply. ''Fair enough,'' he said. ''But there's no expiration date on the offer. You've got my card. When you've got your degree, when you're ready, give me a call, and I'll find you something.'' He extended his hand. ''Promise,'' Stark said.

Peter took his hand and shook it. "You'll hear from me," he said.

It was a day for surprises.

Kellye Nakahara was seated at her vanity and fixing her hair when she heard the knock at the door. She had enjoyed a relaxing first day on the *Princess Victoria*; after her hellish stay on the *Ad Astra*, a day of laying in the sun on a cruise ship's deck had been just what the doctor—and Tony Stark—had ordered. Now as she ran a brush through her long, dark hair, she looked forward to the remainder of her cruise through the South Pacific. Moreover, she looked forward to dinner that night. This would be her first evening at the captain's table. The seating chart had her next to the handsome redheaded Irish guy who said he was a doctor, but who obviously had something other than surgery on his mind. Kellye smiled. After her wrestling matches with Strucker's goons, a little feint-and-parry over dinner would be fun. And after that, who knew what the evening would bring?

Knuckles rapped on her stateroom door.

Kellye's smile froze, and her hairbrush paused in its track. She hadn't been expecting anyone. "Who is it?" She called the words over her shoulder, reluctant to leave the vanity just yet.

"Room service."

"I didn't order anything."

"Captain's compliments, ma'am."

Kellye shrugged. She took one final pass with the brush, and a last glimpse in the mirror. What she saw pleased her. She was as ready for dinner as she would ever be. "I'll be right there," she said.

Opening the door revealed a tall man with broad features, who wore immaculate whites and pushed a wheeled cart. Atop the cart, Kellye saw covered dishes and gleaming utensils, delicate china and a spray of red roses. She looked at them in confusion tinged with mild dismay. "This is dinner," she said. "I'm eating at the captain's table tonight. He knows that."

"Oh." The attendant looked puzzled. "Are you sure? I've got the cabin right. I know that."

"I'm sure," Kellye said. "Do you want to call, or should I?"

"Perhaps you should, ma'am," the man said. He was already unfolding extensions on the cart, and arranging a service for two. "I'm sure I have the right cabin."

Kellye shrugged, annoyed, and turned towards the telephone. As she did, she caught sight of the attendant in the vanity mirror, and paused. There was something about the image that disturbed her, an odd break in resolution at its boundaries that didn't seem quite right. In fact, it looked almost like a reflected hologram—

She turned just in time to see the attendant's outlines waver and melt. In a second, the man was gone, and in his place stood a seven-foot purple figure, either an armored man or a robot. Kellye was willing to bet it was a machine; its proportions and anatomy were subtly wrong. She realized suddenly that she had seen robots like that before in news reports or magazines, but she wasn't sure where—and right now, she didn't care.

Oh no, not again, she thought.

"End image inducer run, terminate auditory camouflage," the automaton said. It seemed to be speaking to itself, and its words suddenly had an unpleasant synthetic sound. "Initiate abduction sequence."

That was stupid, and a bit of an oversight on the part of whoever had programmed the thing. Kellye couldn't imagine the logic of having a robot announce its every move, but she wasn't going to look a gift horse in the mouth. Knowing what the thing was going to do meant she could act first. The linkage between its jaw and neck looked as if it might conceivably be vulnerable; at any rate, it was the only chance that she could see. No matter how small that chance was, she had to take it. She brought the heel of her left hand up, hard and fast, striking at the exposed joint.

"Resistance is futile," the robot's enunciator crackled. Before Kellye could complete her blow, one of the thing's metal hands lashed out and caught her flesh one between its steel fingers. "Resistance will only cause injury to self."

Kellye took a deep breath, and brought one leg up, hard. A human assailant would have been crippled by the impact, but this was a robot, and the only cry of pain came from Kellye's lips as her knee smashed into reinforced steel.

The robot's free hand came up and paused an inch or so from Kellye's face. She could see a grilled opening on the palm of its hand.

"Commence anesthesia," the robot said, as greenish gas erupted from the opening. "Prepare for return to home base. Abduction run at ninety percent completion point."

There really was something quite annoying about the way that the thing announced its actions, Kellye realized, as the gas filled her lungs. Maybe that was why the machine did it, following some obscure directive of psychological warfare.

Then the thought faded, even as the world around her collapsed into darkness.

She awoke an unknowable length of time later, cleanly and without any lingering drowsiness or other obvious side effects from the gas. She awoke in a chair, in front of a table, to see china plates and silver utensils resting before her on embroidered silk. For perhaps a single second, she thought she was still onboard the *Princess Victoria*, about to enjoy the dinner at the captain's table that she had been promised.

"Ah, you awaken," someone said. "And precisely on schedule. Promptness is an admirable trait, especially in a scientist." The words were spoken in perfect English, and in a tone that was an odd mixture of command and amusement.

She raised her head, to see who had spoken. At the far end of a formal dinner table's cluttered expanse, hooded eyes met her gaze. They looked out from slits in a gray steel mask, and were further framed by a green broadcloth hood. A sick feeling swept though Kellye as she recognized her host.

"I am pleased you could join me this evening," Doctor Doom said. "We have much to discuss, you and I."

Kellye didn't say anything. With a forced calm, she considered her options. Doom was at least twelve feet away, separated from her by dinner service and covered platters, by candlesticks and centerpiece. It would take at least ten seconds to reach him, and she wasn't sure what she could do if she made the attempt and succeeded. She knew about Doom, knew the kinds of things that the man had done, knew the foes that he had faced—faced, and survived. Super heroes had managed to defeat the would-be conqueror in the past, but he had returned, time and again. If the best efforts of the Fantastic Four had amounted to little more than a holding action against Doom, what could she hope to accomplish against him?

"Please do not attempt any unpleasantness," Doom said. "It would be quite futile, and you would only injure yourself. The misadventure with my robot no doubt taught you that lesson."

That was true enough; Kellye's knee still throbbed, and throbbed more as the last, lingering effects of the knockout gas faded. If she hadn't been able to stop the robot, she certainly wouldn't be able to defeat its master. Even if she somehow did, she was obviously in his stronghold, behind national boundaries and stone walls, countless miles from home. She was helpless.

At least for now.

"Why have you brought me here?" She forced the words out through fear-numbed lips. "What do you want from me?" She thought she knew the answer to the questions, even as she spoke them. Obviously, Doom wanted what Strucker had wanted and taken. He wanted the *Infinity Engine*.

"Your expertise," Doom said. "Your skills and your service. You will accomplish a task for me, Doctor Nakahara. After your success, I will reward you."

"And if I refuse to serve you?"

Doom did not respond.

From Kellye's left, a robot attendant served her. A purple steel hand, like the one that had gushed green gas in her face—perhaps the same hand—placed a bowl of steaming consommé on the saucer in front of her. She ignored it. She wasn't hungry.

"Because I won't," she continued. "I won't give you the secrets of the *Infinity Engine*."

Doom lifted a spoonful of his own soup, slid it though the mouthpiece of his mask to his own lips, tasted and swallowed. "I prefer not to speak of business at table," he said. "However, if you insist—I will not require that you provide me with those specifics." He paused and took another spoon of consommé. "I already possess them."

His words, spoken calmly, nonetheless had the sound of death and despair to Kellye Nakahara. She had seen what the *Infinity Engine* could do when harnessed to the dreams of a madman; Sean Morgan had shown her videotapes of the smoldering patch of seared rock that had been A.I.M. Island. Strucker was bad, but Doom was worse, by at least an order of magnitude. He was, quite literally, the deadliest man in the world.

And he had the *Infinity Engine*.

"What do you want from me, then?"

Doom looked at her as he replied. "For the moment, nothing more than the pleasure of your company, and your enjoyment of this most delightful meal."

"And then." Kellye said the words flatly, making them a statement and not a question. "After dinner."

Doom set down his spoon. A robot took his bowl. "After dinner," he said, "and in the days and weeks to come, we will discuss another of your fields of expertise. I have some minor queries regarding subspace and extradimensional geometries, and the technical considerations that attend them."

"You want to know about the Negative Zone." The realization surprised and puzzled her, and made a thousand questions race through her brain. She was something of a subject-matter expert in the pocket universe that Reed Richards had discovered years before. She had cowritten several papers that attempted to define that strange place's obscure laws and properties. With a quick, sharp pang of sorrow, she recalled that her coauthor on one of those papers had been Cosmo Haberman.

Doom smiled. She could see it in his eyes if not on his lips. "Not precisely," he said, an indulgent tone his voice. "I wish to know *more* about the Negative Zone." He paused. "And you will tell me."

Kellye wondered.

Long ago, after the Earth cooled but before the dinosaurs ruled, **PIERCE ASKEGREN** wrote comic book scripts for Warren's *Creepy* and *Vampirella* magazines. He's also contributed to *Asimov's Science Fiction*, *The Ultimate Silver Surfer*, and *The Ultimate Super-Villains*, and will have collaborative stories in the upcoming anthologies *The Ultimate Superhero* and *Untold Tales of Spider-Man*. Pierce lives in Northern Virginia, where he is hard at work on the third Doom's Day volume, which he is coauthoring with Eric Fein.

DANNY FINGEROTH is a graduate of the legendary Cinema Department of the State University of New York at Binghamton. From there he went on to edit and write at Marvel Comics for eighteen years, during which time, when he was Group Editor of the Spider-Man line, sales of the wall-crawler's titles soared to all-time highs. Danny's many writing credits include the *Darkhawk* series, *The Deadly Foes of Spider-Man* limited series, the *Venom* graphic novel *Deathtrap: The Vault*, the previous Doom's Day volume *Spider-Man & The Incredible Hulk: Rampage*, and a forthcoming short story in the *Untold Tales of Spider-Man* anthology. Today, Danny is braving the electronic frontier as the Director and Editor in Chief of Byron Preiss Multimedia Company's Virtual Comics line, for which he also writes *They Call Me . . . The Skul*.

STEVEN BUTLER has worked in comics since 1990, when he was the last person to draw *The Badger* for the now-defunct First Comics. He has been the regular penciller for Marvel's *Web of Spider-Man* and *Silver Sable and the Wild Pack*, Malibu's *UltraForce*, and Virtual Comics's *Stan Lee's Riftworld: The Ex-Wives*. His work in book illustration includes the other two volumes of this trilogy and *The Ultimate Super-Villains*. He has a Bachelor of Arts from the University of Southern Mississippi. He is living comfortably in Mississippi with his wife Samantha and their cat Herself, and vehemently denies the rumors that his mind is controlled by wombats.

NOW AVAILABLE IN HARDCOVER

THE GRIPPING NEW THRILLER

SPIDER-MAN ®

WANTED: DEAD OR ALIVE

BY *NEW YORK TIMES* BEST-SELLING AUTHOR

Craig Shaw Gardner

Putnam

SPIDER-MAN ®

__SPIDER-MAN: CARNAGE IN NEW YORK by David Michelinie & Dean Wesley Smith 0-425-16703-8/$6.50

Spider-Man must go head-to-head with his most dangerous enemy, Carnage, a homicidal lunatic who revels in chaos. Carnage has been returned to New York in chains. But a bizarre accident sets Carnage loose upon the city once again! Now it's up to Spider-Man to stop his deadliest foe.

__THE ULTIMATE SPIDER-MAN 0-425-14610-3/$12.00

Beginning with a novella by Spider-Man cocreator Stan Lee and Peter David, this anthology includes all-new tales from established comics writers and popular authors of the fantastic, such as: Lawrence Watt-Evans, David Michelinie, Tom DeHaven, and Craig Shaw Gardner. An illustration by a well-known Marvel artist accompanies each story. *Trade*

__SPIDER-MAN: THE VENOM FACTOR by Diane Duane
1-57297-038-3/$6.50

In a Manhattan warehouse, the death of an innocent man points to the involvement of Venom—the alien symbiote who is obsessed with Spider-Man's destruction. Yet Venom has always safeguarded innocent lives. Either Venom has gone completely around the bend, or there is another, even more sinister suspect.

Prices slightly higher in Canada

Penguin Putnam Inc.	Bill my: ☐Visa ☐MasterCard ☐Amex_____ (expires)
P.O. Box 12289, Dept. B	Card#_____
Newark, NJ 07101-5289	
Please allow 4-6 weeks for delivery.	Signature_____
Foreign and Canadian delivery 6-8 weeks.	

Bill to:

Name_____

Address_____ City_____

State/ZIP_____

Daytime Phone #_____

Ship to:

Name_____ Book Total $_____

Address_____ Applicable Sales Tax $_____

City_____ Postage & Handling $_____

State/ZIP_____ Total Amount Due $_____

This offer subject to change without notice.